ANY GROOM WILL DO

Also by Charis Michaels

The Bachelor Lords of London
The Earl Next Door
The Virgin and the Viscount
One for the Rogue

Coming Soon
All Dressed in White

ANY GROOM WILL DO

A Brides of Belgravia Novel

CHARIS MICHAELS

AVONIMPULSE
An Imprint of HarperCollinsPublishers

ANY GROOM WILL DO. Copyright © 2018 by Charis Michaels. All rights reserved. Printed in the United States of America. No part of this book may be used or reproduced in any manner whatsoever without written permission except in the case of brief quotations embodied in critical articles and reviews. For information, address HarperCollins Publishers, 195 Broadway, New York, NY 10007.

Digital Edition FEBRUARY 2018 ISBN: 978-0-06-268579-7

Print Edition ISBN: 978-0-06-268580-3

Cover design by Fredericka Ribes

Cover photographs © imranahmedsg/Shutterstock (couple), © HotDamn-Stock (background)

Avon Impulse and the Avon Impulse logo are registered trademarks of HarperCollins Publishers in the United States of America.

Avon and HarperCollins are registered trademarks of HarperCollins Publishers in the United States of America and other countries.

FIRST EDITION

18 19 20 21 22   HDC   10 9 8 7 6 5 4 3 2 1

*This one is dedicated with
love to my sister Shelly and her husband, Tim.
Living proof that a Couple is a Family.*

In the early spring of 1813, eight-year-old Lady Wilhelmina Hunnicut fell ill from a bout of peritonitis that nearly took her life. For ten days she lay contorted in pain and wracked with fever, fighting an infection that simmered and glowed like the hot coals of a low fire.

Her mother and father, not particularly attentive parents even in the best of times, hastened to their daughter's bedside. They pursed their lips and wrung their hands; they cried.

Willow's father, Lord Lytton, was an earl, and their home in Surrey, Leland Park, was a lavish estate with renowned stables. Immediately, the earl sent for the best doctors from London. They arrived posthaste to bleed and swab and minister to the child. All the while her parents implored her, "Be a brave girl, darling. Do *try* to survive."

By some miracle, Lady Willow did survive. She sat up in bed on the eleventh day, requested toast and tea, the lavender coverlet, and a view of the gardens. A cadre of footmen and maids descended, and the chief surgeon took Lord Lytton and his lady wife aside.

"It is a miracle that the child has pulled through," the doctor whispered. "Praise be to God. But I must warn you that an infection of this severity—the abdominal colic, the fever, the ague…" He paused, blotting his temple. "The girl will be barren, I'm afraid. Unable to have children all of her life. Her belly was inflamed for weeks. She will never be a mother, mark my words."

Her father scarcely heard this news, so relieved was he that his daughter would not die.

Her mother heard the prognosis but chose to ignore it. "But how could he possibly know what may or may not happen?" the countess told Willow whenever she ventured onto the topic. "Dr. Whiting is not *God*. He cannot read the future. He said for two weeks that you would not live to see the next morning, and look at you now."

Yes, Willow thought, each time her mother said this, *look at me now*.

She grew into womanhood—tall and lithe, with clear skin and a bright smile—but with no trace of the monthly cycle that would prove the doctor wrong or her mother right.

And so a childhood illness decided Lady Willow would never be a mother, but it was Willow herself, some nine years later, who decided that she would never—not ever—become anyone's wife.

"I will never marry," she vowed to her two dearest friends, Sabine Noble and Tessa St. Croix. "What man would marry a woman who cannot provide him with an heir and a family? And despite what my mother suggests, I cannot lie."

Instead, Willow pursued other interests, cultivated her talents, and never allowed herself to wallow or waste time.

She was a spirited girl, determined but cheerful, with an eye for visual harmony and unexpected beauty. Her life's passion was design. Color and texture, form and light. She commissioned a workshop on the grounds of Leland Park and made over the rooms and corridors of the manor house, one at a time. She sent away for books about the interiors of stately homes and castles from around the world. She learned to weave intricate trim for tapestries and rugs, to paint plaster, to create mosaics with little bits of colored tile. Her parents indulged these pursuits because they kept her occupied, and an occupied daughter required less of their time.

If Willow noticed the young men who noticed her, who complimented her auburn hair or blue-green eyes, she didn't dwell on it. She encouraged nothing, she danced never, and she always refused the rare young man who asked to walk with her in the village. Social diversion was limited to the exclusive company of her two old friends, Sabine and Tessa. Beyond this, she was content to create and seek the beauty in everyday life.

"Spinsterhood?" she would say. "So be it. Why wrestle with the futility of a union that I will never have?"

But futility, Willow soon discovered, did not come in the form of a union (or lack thereof); it came as the absence of nearly all of her rights. Without the protection of marriage, Willow was not permitted to seriously pursue anything she truly enjoyed. Without her father's permission, she could not travel alone outside of Surrey. She could not let a flat in London. She could not submit her sketches for publication. After her father died, she was forced to seek this permission from her brother, Phillip.

In the end, it was not the solitude that troubled Willow; it was the limits.

Through it all, she relied upon Sabine and Tessa. They encouraged and supported her; they served as touchstones when her own parents were dismissive or away; and they understood that loneliness and contentedness could, in fact, exist at the same time.

What they did *not* understand—what even Willow herself did not know—was that a "contented" life, lonely or not, was but one of many paths that young women may take.

And a path that leaps clear of contentment and deals instead in courage and determination and true fulfillment is what this story is about.

Chapter One

October 1830

Surrey

When Lady Wilhelmina Hunnicut decided to advertise for a husband on the docks in London, she knew in advance who would oppose the idea.

Her mother, first and foremost. Lady Lytton would be highly opposed—if she bothered to notice, which she would not.

Her brother, Phillip, second, who would oppose the plan in theory but would be easily convinced in the end. The great value to her and the complete lack of bother to him would be irresistible.

Third, the well-meaning people of Pixham, Surrey. Collectively, they would be opposed, as they were to all imaginative thinking, to anything different or new.

And finally, her father (may God rest him). Earl Lytton would be opposed from a heavenly realm, but considering the dowry he'd left her, he was an unwitting enabler. In essence, he was the sponsor of the plan.

There were others, of course. If pressed, Willow would say that most anyone she cared to ask would oppose her plan, but she'd designed it with both discretion and speed in mind, and the whole sordid business would be over before action or voice could be put to opposition from any side.

Unless, of course, the opposition came from the two young women the plan was meant to save.

As it did now.

Annoyingly.

Inconveniently.

One day before they were meant to launch the plan from conjecture to real life.

"I wish you would look again," Lady Willow said to her friends, swallowing a sigh. She felt the tips of her ears burn red. "I've not changed a word since breakfast." The brightness in her voice was forced. She jabbed her pen in the ink pot. "It's nearly there."

"Nearly *where?*" asked Sabine Noble, squinting down at the large expanse of yellow parchment sprawled across the desk.

"Nearly perfect," said Willow, carefully carrying the parchment to a low table near the window. They'd met in her father's library, a room she'd redesigned two years ago in stately mahogany and masculine blue. It had seemed dignified and scholarly at the time, but now the room felt foreboding. Too dim to properly read the advertisement, too hushed and shrouded to allow for open points of view. Lantern light only revealed so much; for this, they required sunshine.

Willow smoothed the parchment and stepped back, allowing the window to illuminate her carefully scripted words.

"Read the whole of it before you make any remark," she instructed. "Pretend you've stumbled upon it on the docks in London, completely unaware."

"Which docks?" asked Tessa. She had not moved from the desk across the room.

Willow narrowed her eyes. "It makes no difference *which* docks. First we'll compose the advertisement. *Then* we'll determine where to post it. Mr. Fisk is a native of South London. He will help us."

She stepped away and gestured the two women closer. "Come and have a better look. I am prepared for your reactions, good or ill."

"This, I doubt," said Sabine, crossing with marked reluctance to the window. Tessa trailed tentatively behind.

"Go on," prompted Willow.

Sabine sighed and read aloud from the parchment:

WANTED
PROFESSIONAL TRAVELERS
GENTLEMAN SAILORS
ENTREPRENEURS WITH FOREIGN INTERESTS.
INVESTOR SEEKS SUITABLE CANDIDATE FOR DISBURSEMENT OF MODEST FORTUNE.
FUNDS MUST BE APPLIED TO

<u>INTERNATIONAL</u> ENDEAVOR.
CHOSEN MAN MUST PERSONALLY
MANAGE
VENTURE ABROAD.
**SLOW-YIELD INDUSTRIES
PREFERRED.**
PROGRESSIVE-MINDED,
UNMARRIED MEN
WITH <u>NO DEPENDENTS</u> ONLY.
APPLY BY **INTRODUCTORY
LETTER** TO
W. J. HUNNICUT, LELAND PARK,
PIXHAM, SURREY.

For a long moment, no one spoke. Willow held her breath and glanced at Tessa. Of the two friends, she was more likely to be generous. Now, she remained generously silent.

"What is a 'Gentleman Sailor'?" asked Sabine.

"I thought we agreed that it was best to solicit gentlemen," said Willow.

"This assumes that the advertisement will solicit anyone at all," said Sabine. "Now 'tis only to be *gentlemen* who apply?"

"And why shouldn't we ask for exactly what we want?" said Willow. "'Gentleman Sailor' is an inspired phrase."

"It's an imaginary phrase," said Sabine. "If you mean to ask for exactly what you want, why not say 'Will Trade Dowry for Absentee Husband'?"

Now Tessa spoke up. "I think it a very…dashing advertisement, Willow."

"Dashing?" Willow repeated dully. "Dashing? It is brilliant, and you both know it. It will solicit hundreds of applications. We'll interview as many as necessary until we identify the perfect *three*." She took up the pen to thicken the letters of her script.

For a long moment, the two other women watched in silence. Finally, Tessa asked, "What if they're awful, Willow? These men. Will you consider horrible men? Will you consider toads?"

"Toad or not, we're only meant to endure them long enough to marry them and bid them bon voyage," said Willow.

"In other words, yes," Sabine said. "They will be awful. Depend upon it."

Willow gritted her teeth. "We do not, at present, luxuriate in unlimited options, do we? Tessa, you are in a delicate situation and refuse to appeal to your parents. And you, Sabine?" Willow sighed heavily. "I shudder to think what will come of you if you continue to provoke your uncle."

Neither friend contradicted her; how could they when she spoke the truth? Willow went on. "And I have the opportunity to follow my passion to London—to actually *make something* of my life. But as you know, I've no acceptable way to make a home there. Not in my current situation: young, female, and alone.

Willow held out her hands, palms up. "As obstacles go, these are considerable, but our fathers settled dowries on us for a reason. Not *these* reasons, I'll grant you, but we shall seize what we can. If we cannot buy freedom outright, we shall buy three men desperate enough to marry us and let us go."

This speech, which had been rehearsed down to the last "desperate enough," was met with still more silence. Her friends shared a look.

"Might I remind you that I was set to never marry?" Willow added. "For obvious reasons, *painful* reasons, I had reconciled myself to a life alone. I've flipped those intentions to save the two of you—"

"We aren't denying that you do this to help, Willow…" said Sabine, trailing off.

Willow tried again. "I've explained that my aunt's townhouse in Belgravia is large enough for the three of us, and she's welcomed us all. When we conceived the idea, it was that we would go together."

"Yes, but conceiving it," Sabine said, "and actually doing it are…" She held out her hands as if the correct words could be snatched from the air. "It's one thing to discuss the plan in theory, but quite another to post your name and direction in London and invite these men to…apply to you. And that's not the worst of it. It is a gross misrepresentation to refer to *my* dowry or *your* dowry as a 'modest fortune' to 'disburse.' We are not investors, Willow, we are girls who these men—strangers to us—would be forced to *marry* if they wished to receive one farthing."

"Not strangers," corrected Willow.

"Excuse me, these 'gentleman sailors,' which, by the way, is not a known distinction."

"Alright," Willow agreed, "the plan is wholly outrageous—is this what you wish to hear? If so, I'll be the first to admit it. But that doesn't mean it cannot happen. Outrageous is not *impossible*. Remember Gwen Pierpont? Shall I tell the story again? Gwen married a sea captain who spends *years* at sea. *Years*. He is practically never at home in England, and when he is, it is only long enough to provision for his next voyage. Gwen, therefore, has complete freedom to do as she pleases—in London or Surrey or wherever she cares to go. She's a married woman, and no one says a word against her. Can you imagine answering to no one? She is the happiest woman we know."

"But married to a man she never sees?" said Tessa, dropping into a chair. "That sounds wretched."

"You would do well to see *fewer* men, Tessa," sighed Sabine, "not more."

"Sabine, please," said Willow.

"You've said yourself that Tessa does not have the freedom to be selective," Sabine shot back. "None of us does."

"I *can* be selective," Tessa asserted. "I can select my brother's friend Randall and marry him. He would marry me tomorrow if I would but say the word."

In unison, Sabine and Willow said, "You're *not* marrying Randall."

Tessa's daily threat to marry the dull and dim-witted Randall elicited the reliable chorus of "You're not marrying Randall." It was why she had said it. But they could only reassure her for so long. Tessa's situation was distressing, and it grew more urgent with every passing day.

Sabine said, "Willow, you cannot fault us for wanting more assurance than one neighbor who *happened* into an absentee marriage with a particularly diligent sea captain. This hardly guarantees our same luck. Especially as we will 'happen' into nothing. You're endeavoring to *construct* this arrangement. From the start."

"We will have constructed it together, and good for us," said Willow. "What choice do you have, Sabine? Tessa's condition will be obvious to everyone in a matter of months."

Sabine walked to the window. After a moment, she said, "I would do nearly anything to escape my uncle—you know this—but your plan isn't something *to do*, is it?"

"We *are* doing something," insisted Willow. "We are soliciting potential husbands."

"No, you have written this advert, and now we must sit idly by and *wait*," said Sabine, turning back. The light from the window illuminated the healing bruise beneath her right eye. "If a stranger eventually writes us, there is a very great risk that he'll report the scheme to your mother, or Tessa's parents, or, God forbid, my uncle." She made an expression of *what if?* and put a hand to the top of her head. Her hand trailed from her hair and down her face, lingering idly on the healing eye. She looked at Willow. "I cannot."

"But the men will introduce themselves by letter first, and we shall only meet in person with the candidates who portray themselves as the most fitting and safe. And even then, we shall broach the terms carefully, feeling our way. I'll not reveal the full extent of the barter unless an applicant appears amenable to a marriage spent in separate corners of the globe."

"Effective immediately," said Tessa skeptically.

"And extenuating always," added Sabine.

Willow carefully replaced her pen. She walked a small circle in the room. What did they want? To be begged? To agree that the whole scheme was a great risk? To snap her fingers and magically produce ideal husbands who would whisk them away from their hopeless situations in Surrey?

She settled each of them with a hard look. "You are running out of time, each in your own way. I've the least to lose, but hear me now; this advertisement *will go* to London tomorrow by Mr. Fisk. Five copies *will be* posted. The applications will surely follow. After that, I'll convene interviews. You know me well enough to appreciate my determination. I *will* marry when the correct man comes along. You may join me with the other men the advert will surely bring, or you may remain in Surrey to deal with your own fates."

"But Willow," Sabine asked after a pause. Her voice was softer now, careful. "What about your…barrenness? Will you tell him? This *correct man*, when he comes along—will you tell him?"

Willow looked away. "Of course I will tell him. Immediately, in fact. I've always said I would not misrepresent the truth."

The truth, of course, was the childhood illness that left Willow unable to bear children.

"However," Willow continued slowly, "it is my great hope that intimate…obligations will not be part of our arrangement."

Sabine made a scoffing noise.

Willow rubbed at an ink stain on her hand. "There is no guarantee, of course. But these men are meant to be out of the country most of our lives. How much of an issue can it be?"

Conjugal relations and children were variables that Willow was not sure she could stipulate. She had shoved aside the notion of the…er, marital bed until…well, until they were a bit further along in the process.

She looked back to see her friends share a glance, but Sabine leaned down to read the advertisement again. "You sound very determined," said her friend, finally. "Although

I cannot say I am surprised. When you get an idea into your head, you are not one to let it die a natural death, are you?"

"But don't you see?" said Willow. "This is so much more than an idea. An *idea* was to paint the dining room orange. An *idea* was to rebuild the stairs in marble tile. *This* is the admission to the entire Rest of My Life."

Sabine chuckled sadly. "But you aren't being terrorized by a lunatic uncle. Or expecting a child with no father." She and Willow glanced at Tessa. Rarely did they discuss her predicament in as many words. Tessa dropped her head back and slowly closed her eyes.

"No," said Willow. "What I seek is the wildest, most brilliant dream I've ever known."

"You want it that bad, do you?"

"It's only been my passion for as long as I can remember." Willow paused, waiting for some response. Her friends looked away.

She said, "If I am able to get to London, I will have come all the way back around, don't you see? Aunt Mary was the start of everything. She was the one who took me in hand, years ago, and taught me how to look for beauty in all things, to curate it, and to apply it to the rooms in which we sleep and eat and live. It's one thing to be the relation of renowned designers such as Aunt Mary and Uncle Arthur, but to have the two of them invite me to live in their home and be their apprentice? Why, over the next five years, they will design the interiors of the finest, most modern new homes in the city. They could have chosen anyone to assist them, anyone at all, but they chose me. *Me.*"

"But you've not even seen these homes your aunt and uncle will design," said Sabine. "You've not even seen the home in which you are inviting us all to move and start this new life."

"I don't need to see them," said Willow. "If my aunt and uncle say that Belgravia is the height of modish luxury, it will be. The homes of society's elite are their stock-in-trade. And honestly, I don't care. Anything would be better than redesigning the same rooms of Leland Park again and again."

Tessa looked over. "What a great injustice that your mother will not simply allow you to go. Why must you enlist a strange man and marry him, simply to live with your aunt?"

Willow waved the idea away. "Aunt Mary went against the family wishes and married a commoner. She's been shunned for years. My mother won't speak of her. It makes no difference that my uncle is a famed furniture craftsman, sought after by the wealthiest families. The notion of my relocating to London as their apprentice is unconscionable."

Willow drifted to the window and peered out. "As long as I am under my mother's purview, Belgravia, the design work, leaving Surrey—it is a locked door." She turned back. "Unless I become a married woman who makes her own decisions. Unless I can come and go as I please—a bride with a long-lost husband, and happily so, living in Belgravia, making all my dreams come true."

The room was silent again. Sabine walked back to the advert and read it over. Tessa traced a swirly line in the dark-blue velvet of her chair. After a moment, Tessa asked, "What if no one applies, toad or no toad? No one at all?"

Willow shook her head. "This will not happen. We've one circumstance working in our favor, and that is the money."

She walked to the massive desk and leaned against it, crossing her arms over her chest. "Life may have disappointed us, each in our own way, but the money, I'm confident, will not let us down."

Brent Caulder, the Earl of Cassin, wound his way through the slouching sailors of the Gull and Trident, searching for his partners in the smoky gloom.

"Evenin', your lordship," slurred a grime-streaked sailor, swaying in the seat. "Lookin' for the captain, are ye?"

The earl nodded, trying to place the man among their last crew. While his partner Joseph Chance knew each man by name, and his other partner, Jon Stoker, knew them by trade, they all looked the same to Cassin. His mind was already filled to overflowing with the names and faces of men who considered him their leader and employer, but these men lived two hundred miles away, in Yorkshire, and they waited for him to lead them or employee them. It was a struggle to add twenty more.

The sailor at the door didn't seem to mind, and he grinned, happy in his drink. He jerked his chin to a rear table, half obscured by the belching hearth. "Not drunk enough yet, I reckon. They've only just come in." He brought the tankard to his mouth, sloshing his beard with foam.

Cassin nodded again and started for the table, stepping over boots and sleeping dogs. Joseph, he now saw, was blocked from view by a trio of barmaids, while Stoker sprawled across two chairs and a trunk, his hat covering his eyes.

"A word, if you please," Cassin said when he reached them. He scooped up four empty tankards and handed them to the maids. "Ladies, may I trouble you?"

"Bloody hell, Cassin," said Joseph, scooting back his chair, "I was in the midst of a conversation."

"No, you were not."

"The bleeding hell I wasn't."

"Flirtation is not a conversation. It's a transaction."

"Speak for yourself, Cassin. I don't rely on negotiation to get a woman into bed."

"Nor do you rely on *speech*," said Jon Stoker from beneath the brim of his hat. Joseph's blue eyes had always done the talking for him.

The women accepted the empty tankards and sauntered away while Cassin wiped the wet table with his sleeve.

"Read," he said, spreading a rolling expanse of parchment next to the dim candle. He took coins from his pockets to weight the corners.

"What's this?" asked Joseph. "An apothecary cure for your eternal bad mood?"

"Read," repeated Cassin, thumping the parchment with his finger.

Something about his tone pricked their attention, and Joseph leaned in. Stoker slid his boots from the trunk one by one, taking his time, slouching forward.

"Where did you find this?" asked Joseph.

"Posted above the trough in Redmond Street."

"Redmond?" mused Joseph. "I know the spot. Wall is littered with bills and notices."

Stoker shook his head and returned his boots to the trunk. "It's a fabrication."

"We've no idea what it is," said Cassin.

"I'd like to know the motive, if it's a fabrication," said Joseph. "What value would this"—he leaned in and read the name from the bottom line—"W. J. Hunnicut glean by offering money if he doesn't have it? Why bother?"

"To steal ideas," said Stoker, resetting his hat. "Trade secrets."

"Why does any investor contribute to an endeavor?" said Cassin. "To multiply his money when the investment pays off."

"Do you know him, Cassin?" asked Joseph. "W. J. Hunnicut?"

Cassin shook his head. He'd assured his friends when he joined the partnership that, despite being an earl, he knew few men among society's elite. They'd brought him into the business anyway, the poor sods.

Their loose collaboration amounted to Stoker's ownership of a fast ship and his proficiency as captain, Joseph's brains and business acumen, and Cassin's legitimacy as an earl. Albeit an impoverished one. Who hadn't passed time in London in years. But they had been friends since university, and their newly minted partnership, not even a year old, was built on loyalty and shared history.

Their most bankable asset was a shared commodity they'd won in a card game and split three ways. Joseph had played the winning hand, Stoker had loaned him the money, and Cassin had relentlessly pursued the loser, a small-time smuggler and sometime pirate known for shirking his debts. Cassin had hounded him until he'd provided the actual printed deed to the spoils—a small island in the Caribbean Sea, off the coast of Barbadoes.

As partnerships went, Cassin brought the least to the table. But Stoker and Joseph Chance were lowborn scrappers who had risen up in the world, and they were unduly impressed with the title of earl. Stoker and Chance saw Cassin's title as an open door to richer, more influential clients and investors.

Cassin was doubtful, to say the least, but he would be forever grateful they'd cut him in. Especially now, considering the potential of the island they had won on a lucky turn of cards. Especially if he could bag this investor.

"But why the emphasis on foreign work?" Joseph continued, studying the advertisement again. "Says it in four or five different ways."

"Perhaps he's grown weary of the opportunities in England." Cassin pulled out a chair. "Perhaps he himself is of foreign birth. Perhaps, like us, he knows that the future of successful commerce is beyond this island."

"Strong words from someone whose own future in this partnership is limited to the first windfall," said Stoker.

"A windfall I've yet to see." Cassin sighed. He leaned back in his chair and stared down at the advertisement. "I've no doubt that the two of you will eventually become richer than your wildest dreams, but I don't have the leisure of sailing 'round the world indefinitely, waiting for this fortune to come to pass. I've responsibilities, as you well know." He looked back and forth between his friends. "My time is already running out."

Joseph looked up. "But could it be possible? That the money would be this simple to get?" He read from the advertisement: "'A modest fortune,' it says. How much could he mean?"

Stoker sat up again. "Not enough to print this advertisement properly. With a press. On good paper." He ran a finger along the script. "Advertisement's been hand-lettered on parchment."

"So it is," sighed Cassin. He took up the sheet. "So what?"

"Did anyone see you pull it down?" asked Joseph.

Cassin shrugged, rolling up the advert. "It's mine now—the advertisement and the money it will bring."

"It's *ours*, you mean," said Stoker. "The money would be *ours*."

Cassin smiled. "So you are interested?"

"I'm the captain of the bloody ship," Stoker said. "You deal with the investments."

He looked back and forth between his partners. "What's the risk in trying?"

Joseph scratched his head. "Revealing our plans for the island to a competitor. Being made fools if the advert turns out to be a trick or a fabrication, as Stoker said."

"So nothing, effectively," said Cassin. "Low risk—very low."

Stoker laughed. "Aren't you an eager lad?"

"Eager does not begin to describe what I am." Cassin sighed. "I've been away from home for too many months, with too little to show for the time away. People rely on me."

"And now you would add Mr. W. J. Hunnicut to that list?" asked Stoker. "Investors expect returns on their money, don't they?"

"Yes, and the profits from the island are incalculable," said Cassin. "Joseph has done the projections. All we lack is a financier." He tucked the advertisement in his coat. "And now, it would appear we have one. If we're lucky. If we can sell him on the idea."

"He's right," said Joseph. "If it's authentic, an offer like this is exactly what we've been looking for."

"Tell me this," said Stoker. "What is a 'gentleman sailor'?"

"I am," said Cassin immediately. "I am a gentleman sailor. I'm a bloody earl, and I've been sailing with you lot since…what was it? June?"

"Well, I'm no gentleman," said Stoker.

"Nor I," said Joseph.

"Very well," said Cassin, "you are 'Entrepreneurs with International Interests.' You are 'Professional Travelers.' I don't care how you refer to yourselves, nor do I care if W. J. Hunnicut thinks you are gentlemen or sailors or the bloody Spanish Armada. I only care that he gives us the money so we may mine the island before the market floods, and we're too late."

"Why not?" asked Joseph, leaning back, lacing his fingers behind his head. "I can hardly see the harm in writing to the bloke to introduce the idea."

Cassin shook his head. "No. No letter. There's no time to exchange correspondence with an old man in godforsaken Surrey. And Stoker is correct: It's reckless to put pen to paper and describe the potential of the island, only to post it to a stranger." He kicked Stoker's leg and gestured for him to sit up.

Leaning in, Cassin spoke low. "We'll travel in person to Pixham, wherever the devil it is, and see for ourselves. Meet the bloke. Look him in the bloody eye. If W. J. Hunnicut is an honest man with legitimate resources, we'll know it."

"And if not?" asked Stoker.

"If not," said Cassin, "then you may buy me out of the partnership, and I'll return to Yorkshire. With nothing."

CHAPTER TWO

Fifteen days after Lady Willow dispatched Mr. Fisk to London with the advertisement, a lone man arrived on horseback to Leland Park.

"That's odd," Willow said, pausing near the window to her workshop. She wrenched open the pane, watching the rider gallop the long, tree-lined drive that stretched from the lane to the manor house.

Willow had spent the morning in the workshop, directing Mr. Simms as he recovered a library chair with bright puce velvet she had ordered from Portugal. Tessa had come for luncheon and never left. Her friend reclined on the chaise longue that would be next to receive the new fabric. It was a pleasant afternoon, unseasonably warm for October, and Tessa had propped open the door to allow for a breeze. The stone outbuilding had been a falconry before Willow had requisitioned it as her workshop, and warm days still evoked the smell of feathers. A fat mama cat stretched half in, half out of the open door while her kittens bounded to and fro.

"What's odd?" asked Tessa. She dangled a piece of velvet over the alert gaze of a kitten.

"A man on horseback," said Willow. "Approaching the house."

"Calling on your mother at the stables, no doubt."

Willow shook her head. "He is not here about horses, I believe. I've never seen him before. And my mother takes appointments in the mornings, when horses are more spirited and there is less chance of rain."

"Oh, has she bought another stallion? If so, my brothers will call immediately."

"I cannot say," Willow mumbled, looking closer. Now the rider slowed to a canter in the circle drive and stared up at the house. She knew enough about horses to see that his mount was strong and solid, a stallion. The animal spun and side-stepped as the man reined it in with skill.

Not a horse person, she thought idly, watching him. Her eyes narrowed. Of course there was no evidence of this; every manner of equine enthusiast called upon the Leland Park stables weekly, sometimes every day, and the disparity in appearance from buyer to breeder was great. And yet...

Willow looked again. Two grooms dashed to take his horse as he dismounted, and there was Mr. Fisk, rising up from the flower beds to shade his eyes from the sun. Willow squinted too, trying to discern the man's age, the quality of his coat and hat, to see his face.

Surely not, she thought. *Surely, surely* not.

"But is it Mr. Cahill?" asked Tessa, speaking of an elderly neighbor.

"No. Not Cahill," said Willow. Their neighbor was tall but as thin as a leather strap. This man was substantial. Broad shouldered and thick chested. He dropped from his horse with a thud and stood solidly, scanning the Leland Park grounds.

"Then who?" said Tessa. "Willow, you should see your face."

Willow shook her head. "Will you help me pick the sawdust from my hair?" She yanked at her muslin apron, pulling it off, and worked the scarf from her head.

"It couldn't be your brother," said Tessa. "You've said he would not return to England until summer."

"No," she said. "Not Phillip."

Tessa joined her at the window, and they stared as the man clipped up the front steps. Mr. Fisk abandoned the flower bed to greet him.

Thank God for Mr. Fisk, Willow thought. Her late father's valet had the uncanny ability to be everywhere and nowhere, depending on what any situation required. His usefulness was surpassed only by his loyalty.

Tessa cocked her head. "Oh," she said, studying the guest. After a beat, she repeated, "*Oh.*"

So Willow had not imagined it. There was some remarkable sort of…differentness about the guest. Tessa was acutely attuned to remarkable men.

Willow, on the other hand, had trained herself to take little notice of men in general and remarkable men in particular. But she could easily spot the odd or the unlikely, and there was something distinctively out of the ordinary about the rider who now stood on her front steps.

While the man spoke to Mr. Fisk, the massive oak front door swung wide, revealing Abbott, the butler. Willow moaned. Where Mr. Fisk could smooth over any situation and buy time, Mr. Abbott disrupted and dismissed.

Mr. Fisk ignored the butler and carried on, gesturing and nodding and ultimately stepping around Abbott and beckoning the man to follow him inside the house.

Willow's heart jumped again. Now the door shut in the butler's face, and he stood abandoned on the stoop. He pivoted and glared in the direction of Willow's workshop. With a grim expression, the butler began the long, determined glide to her.

Willow jerked away from the window, taking Tessa with her. "Tessa," she whispered, "that man has come about the advertisement." She looked at her friend. "It could be nothing less."

"The advertisement?" whispered Tessa.

"The dowries. The *Gentleman Sailors*."

They hadn't discussed the advertisement in ten days at least. Letters had come by post, just as Willow had promised, but the majority of the applicants were unsuitable. If they did not invite caveats or stipulations, they proposed unsuitable ventures, everything from impractical to improbable to illegal. Illiteracy was rife and illegibility the rule. Willow had elected not to mention these to her friends. Where was the value in discussing the *wrong* applicants until the correct applicants came along?

And now this.

"But have you arranged an interview already?" asked Tessa.

Willow shook her head. "There have been no suitable applicants to speak of. If this man has come about the advertisement, he is here…unprovoked." Willow stared at the open workshop door. The butler would reach them any moment.

"But I don't understand," said Tessa. "I thought…"

Just then, Abbott stepped into the open door, blocking the sunlight and scattering kittens.

"Begging your pardon, my lady," intoned the butler, glancing with distaste around the workshop, "a gentleman from London has called."

"A gentleman?" repeated Willow.

The butler grunted. "Regretfully, I did not ascertain the man's name, but Mr. Fisk may know it." Abbott cleared his throat. "I did learn that he requests an appointment with an individual he refers to as 'W. J. Hunnicut'…"

Here he paused and stared pointedly. Willow blinked, one innocuously gentle bat of her lashes. Shock and wild fear exploded in her chest.

She continued to say nothing, and the butler was forced to go on. "Of his own accord, Mr. Fisk informed us both that 'W. J. Hunnicut' was in the falconry at present." Abbott sneered at the confines of the workshop. "And then he suggested that the man wait in the blue room while 'W. J. Hunnicut' was summoned. I take it to mean that the illustrious 'W. J.' is you?" He added, "My lady."

Willow smiled briskly. "Thank you, Abbott. You'll forgive my oversight. As you may or may not know, W. J. Hunnicut is, in fact, a form of *my* name, Willow Joy Hunnicut. Mr. Fisk is correct."

To this, Abbott had no response. It was now his turn to wait.

"Might I ask," Willow went on, casually folding her scarf, "after the location of my mother?"

"Lady Lytton is on her afternoon ride, I believe."

"Of course." Willow's mother and her grooms exercised chosen horses every afternoon. On a fine day, they had been known to ride the North Downs all the way to Dorking and back.

Willow checked the window. Three hours until the sun set, at least. By some miracle, time was on her side. Not a lot of time. Not enough to conduct any real business. But certainly it was enough time to ascertain whether or not this uninvited man was remotely suitable.

It would have to be enough.

She looked back to Abbott. "If Mr. Fisk has not already done so, please install the gentleman in my father's library. I will attend them shortly."

"I beg your pardon?" Abbott said carefully.

Willow turned her back to him to close the window. "The library, if you please, Mr. Abbott." Her voice was firmer now. She glanced back and Abbott stared. His very posture projected, *I will not.*

"You may send Perry to attend to us," Willow added, grasping at straws. Her lady's maid rarely lent propriety to any given situation, but she would be another female in the room, and Willow was desperate. She added, "Mr. Fisk will linger as well." In her head, she thought, *But you will not.*

Abbott did not voice his objection so much as allow his silence to speak.

Willow did the same, dismissing him by ignoring him. When he was gone, she drew her first breath in what felt like five minutes. She glanced at her friend.

"*What* are you doing?" Tessa whispered. Her voice was somewhere between fear and awe.

I've no idea, Willow thought, but she said, "I'm getting married, and moving to London, and making all of my dreams come true. Just as I've said."

Something, Cassin thought, *is not quite right.*

He turned a slow circle in the center of a parlor that was so blue, it appeared to be submerged underwater. Blue walls, blue furnishings, blue rugs. Every known shade. He'd been held in the underwater room for more than a half an hour. His coat and gloves and hat had not been taken. Tea had not been offered. Unless he was mistaken, he'd been shown inside by a *gardener.*

Up and down the main corridor, doors opened and closed, but no one looked in. A scrum of four or five small dogs, little more than scuttling puffs of fur, roamed in and out en masse, alternately sniffing at his boots or barking.

I should have brought my sword, he thought, leaning against the indigo wall. Another dog admitted himself into the room and tapped over to him on sharp, tiny claws. Man and dog studied one another.

"By definition," Cassin recited to the dog, "golden opportunities feel rare and different." The dog barked once.

His own Barbadoes venture was nothing if not rare and different. He could allow for some strangeness in order to be granted the same.

"And the villagers didn't blanch when I asked for W. J. Hunnicut," Cassin continued to the dog. "Perfectly happy to give directions. No one batted an eye."

This wasn't entirely true. The villagers in nearby Pixham had known the surname Hunnicut, but they seemed oddly clueless about the illustrious "W. J." It had been the first of a growing list of inconsistencies. But the house to which he'd been directed was grand and the grounds expansive. Inside, the art on the walls was valuable, the furnishings fine. The gardener had shown appropriate deference when Cassin presented his card and introduced himself as earl. All of it amounted to precisely what the advertisement had claimed: Here lived an investor with so much money he was looking for new and diverse ways to spend it. If Cassin's reception had been odd, he had turned up unannounced. With no letter of introduction. He'd caught the old man off guard.

Then again, I am a bloody earl, Cassin thought. And an earl called with no forewarning.

"Begging your pardon, my lord," said a cheerful voice from the doorway. Cassin turned.

It was the gardener, extending his hand to the corridor. "Sorry to keep you waiting, my lord. Right this way, if you please. And allow me to take your coat and hat."

Cassin hesitated two beats, exchanged glances with the dog, and followed the man out of the room.

CHAPTER THREE

The surprise arrival of the unidentified man allowed Willow precious little time to prepare. What would she say? In what tone? Would she sit behind the desk while he sat across, like an applicant? Should they both sit in front of the desk? Should she take down notes? These were left unconsidered as she sprinted from her workshop to the kitchen door. She bolted up the servants' stairs and around the corner into the library, scrambling behind the desk and running her fingers through her loose hair. She was still winded when she heard Mr. Fisk's voice in the corridor.

There was a mumbled thank-you, scuffling, a small trio of barks, and then, time stopped.

The next moments played out in Willow's mind with a strange mix of sharp clarity and prolonged slowness, almost as if the earth had stopped spinning, and for a time, life unfolded with a glacial, almost backward, progress. Only her heartbeat raced.

The man was tall—taller than Mr. Fisk, taller even than Willow's brother, Phillip, a rarity indeed. His hair was light brown, streaked with blond by the sun. He wasn't smiling, but his mouth was broad. His nose was substantial—a man's nose, not terrible. Not terrible at all.

She blinked, struggling to keep her face neutral. How silly it had been to worry about where everyone would sit. The struggle now was simply not to stare.

His expression was calm, cautious but not self-conscious. He scanned the library, taking in the floor-to-ceiling book-shelves, the windows that overlooked the garden, the giant book of animal husbandry opened on a stand. His profile was strong, with a hard jaw, eyelashes thick enough to be seen from across the room, hair that just touched his cravat. His coat was a fine, claret-colored wool that stretched over broad shoulders. On his lapel, he wore a small ivory ribboned pin, arranged like the whorl of flower petals. Willow stared at it, her designer's eye captivated by any flourish that introduced dimension or personality.

When finally he looked to the desk and then to her, he froze. Willow felt her breath catch. His eyes were a strange pale green, the color of worn copper, weathered with age. Tingles prickled down the back of her neck.

Far too late, Willow remembered her own appearance. She wore a simple blue day dress, one of many she favored on days spent in her workshop. Her hands were bare. She'd managed to smooth back her thick, unruly mass of auburn hair, but without the scarf, it hung unbound down her back. She looked to Mr. Fisk, hoping for some signal. Too wild? Inappropriate? Ridiculous? The seasoned servant stared benignly down the corridor.

Willow looked back to the man. It occurred to her suddenly, uselessly, that he looked almost exactly like every daydream she had never allowed herself to spin, the hero of fairy tales that happened to other girls. To girls who would grow up and marry and have children and become the loving matriarch of large families of their own. Girls who were not her. The pinpricks on her neck dulled and began to slide, one by one, into a burning pile in the pit of her stomach.

Willow pulled her gaze away. Blank parchment was stacked on the edge of the desk, and she slid a piece before her and took up the pen.

"Good afternoon," she managed. A rhetorical greeting. Perhaps he would not answer. She was not prepared to hear the sound of his voice.

Mr. Fisk stepped forward then, whistling to shoo her mother's dogs into the corridor. "May I present Lady Wilhelmina Hunnicut," he said.

Willow looked at the servant, looked at his extended arm, looked at his tweed gardening jacket. Of course they had not rehearsed this moment; they had not even discussed the possibility of a moment remotely resembling this.

Willow bit her lip and struggled to compose the next reasonable thing to say. He had not replied to her *good afternoon*. He had done little more than stare.

She was just about to say "How do you do?" when Perry, her lady's maid, bolted into the room. Four dogs returned in a wave at her feet.

"Begging your pardon, my lady," the maid said. Perry had nervous habit of tugging at her cap, her apron, and the frazzled curls at the base of her neck. "Mr. Abbott said I was wanted in the library." She waved her hands in front of her face as if the room was filled with smoke. "I was just in the middle of washing your stockings, and I said—"

"*Thank you,* Perry," said Willow. "You may take a seat near the door, behind Mr. Fisk."

Perry made a surprised little gasp. Rarely, if ever, was Perry invited to take a seat.

The maid bobbed a curtsy. "Yes, my lady. Begging your pardon, my lady. I never reckoned that you would *truly* wish me to—"

"*Silently,*" cut in Willow, "you may take a seat."

"But should I—?"

"*The chair,* Perry," Willow said.

Perry took stock of the gentleman, blinking at him as if looking into the face of the sun. Willow cleared her throat, and the maid drew an audible breath, bunched her apron in a fist, and dropped into the appointed chair. A dog hopped into her lap.

Willow returned her attention to the man. "I beg your pardon, Mr...." Of course she had no notion of his name.

Mr. Fisk stepped forward again. "Forgive me, my lady. May I introduce his lordship, the Earl of Cassin."

"Thank you, Mr. Fisk," Willow said, looking back to the man.

An earl? Willow felt her heart stop. *I've elicited an earl?*

"How do you do," she managed, "Lord Cassin."

He did not reply.

Cassin...Cassin... Her mind spun but she could not place the title. All this situation needed was some acquaintance of her late father's or, God forbid, a relative. The plan hinged on

Willow's marrying a man no one knew, a man who, for her mother's sake, would feign affection for her long enough for them to become man and wife.

"Won't you sit down?" she heard herself ask.

"Forgive me," said the earl, "but there must be some mistake. I was hoping to be received by a *Mr. W. J. Hunnicut…?*"

"*I* am W. J. Hunnicut." It felt suddenly appropriate to stand, and she shoved to her feet. "Lady Willow Joy Hunnicut."

"You?"

"Indeed. Me. The very one."

"I beg your pardon," the earl said carefully, "but I've called in search of W. J. Hunnicut, *the investor.*" He spoke slowly, succinctly, as if he wanted to say enough correct things to cause the joke to end. He produced a folded parchment from his jacket pocket. "This advertisement was posted in his name in London. Redmond Street."

She watched him unfold it, knowing, of course, what it was. She held her breath as if it revealed a drawing of her face.

"Quite so," she said. "That is my advertisement. I am W. J. Hunnicut, as I've said, and I have £60,000 to invest with a man of international commerce or travel. My partners and I had hoped for a letter of introduction—"

"You have…*partners?*" the earl said hopefully.

"I should be happy to explain my offer in full, if you would be so kind as to take a seat and—"

"Who?" he interrupted. "*Who* are your partners?"

She felt a flash of irritation. "I prefer not to discuss the specifics of the partnership until I learn a bit more about who *you* may be, sir. And about the venture for which you seek financing." *Was it too much to request that he sit?*

The earl looked from her to the advertisement and then back to her again. "May I assume that all of these partners are...female?" He had an expression of dying hope, as if helplessly watching a capsizing boat slowly roll and sink.

Willow nodded. Words came more quickly now. "Yes, my lord, we are all young women, in fact. Three in total. Together, we offer one investment of £60,000 and two of £30,000."

This declaration was met with silence. The earl blinked at her. "You are...unmarried, Miss Hunnicut?"

"Yes."

"And your father is..."

Now Perry let out an airy, high-pitched sigh from the rear of the room. Perry mourned indefinitely for everyone who ever died, whether she knew the person or not.

Willow spoke over her. "Deceased."

"What of a brother?" asked the earl. "An uncle? Some man must oversee your living and approve of investments of tens of thousands of pounds to...to..."—he looked again at the advertisement in his hand—"gentleman sailors."

It was an accusation, but his voice was more defeated than hard. He was confused, likely not a familiar state. Willow was on uncertain footing herself. It had never been her intention to dole out the terms of their arrangement in vague, one-word answers.

She cleared her throat. "If the arrangement sounds unorthodox, it is. However, you might have lessened your surprise by following the directive on the advertisement. Apply by letter first?" She gestured to the parchment in his hand. "It was never my intention to waste anyone's time."

"A little late for that."

"But it would not have been, if you would have written from the start. The advertisement is very clear."

"The advertisement is as vague as Parliament's Speech from the Throne." He tossed it on the desk. "And now I see why."

"No, you do not see," she said. "But this is by design. It was my intention to evaluate the potential of any candidate before he traveled to Surrey. Much can be discerned from a simple letter or two. You needed only to explain yourself, and I could have done the same, assuming our interests remotely aligned."

"Forgive me if I cannot rely on the *discernment* of a young woman I've never met, when thousands of pounds and an ocean are at stake." The earl's voice rose. "And here's a thought—neither should you. Facts. Figures. *Who* and *why*. These are the bare minimum required to engage in serious business with serious men embarking on a serious endeavor. I've called in person because I haven't the time to trade correspondence back and forth like a girl in school."

"Indeed," said Willow. "Very well. If facts and figures are what you want, I have them and am happy to discuss them. I should be happy to reveal everything when you are equally forthcoming. My God, can I not impose on you to sit?" She was breathing hard, feeling the exertion of a defensive position. She had expected some shock and perhaps confusion to her offer, but she had not expected to have to defend it, point by point. Not to a carefully selected applicant who had been screened by letter first. Irritation crackled. *He* was being considered here, not she.

"I cannot imagine what you have to say," he said, refusing to sit.

"You've made this very clear, and look where it has gotten us."

The maid hissed again, and Willow snapped, "Perry, please." To the earl, she said, "Fine. I will sit. You may stand if you prefer it, and I shall strain my neck looking up at you."

Primly, she lowered herself into the chair. "I speak only for myself; please be aware. However, the scenario I describe may be repeated twice over by my partners if, individually, we deem any other applicant to be…er, appropriate."

The earl said nothing, although he did, at long last, drop into the leather wingback behind him.

"Before my father, Earl Lytton, died, he settled on me a dowry of £60,000." She paused. It was an extraordinary sum. She would not have embarked upon the scheme with anything less. Her parents may not have been particularly affectionate or even present in her childhood, but they had not been miserly.

She continued, "I am prepared to award that sum in its entirety to a man who will use the money for an international venture, just as the advertisement said, and leave England to do it."

"Just to be clear," said the earl, "do you mean the money is your dowry? Because I cannot see how dowry money is yours to invest."

Willow hesitated. Her entire future hinged on his reaction to her answer. "I cannot reveal any more about how the money will be…mine to invest," she said, "until I learn more about you, my lord. And your venture."

"Well, then we are at an impasse because my venture is…rare and untried, and my partners and I are protective of it. In my view, the burden of answering any questions is on the unmarried girl who claims to have £60,000 at her disposal."

Willow looked down at her hands. She breathed in and out. If she revealed nothing more, he would leave and take his very slim potential with him. If she said more, her reputation was at risk. Her reputation already was acutely at risk. Even if she made it to London, she could not be hired, not by respectable clients, unless her reputation was untarnished. This was her reason for endeavoring to marry in the first place. A married woman could do as she pleased.

Before she could respond, he said, "What, specifically, do you wish to know, Miss Hunnicut?"

She looked up. He had not said *no*. A tendril of hope began to climb up the trellis of her heart.

Of course there were dozens of things she wished to know.

Who are you?

From where have you come?

Are you a criminal?

Are you a madman?

Are you a liar or a cheat or a degenerate?

How will you spend my £60,000?

Who else have you approached about this rare and untried venture?

And why, in God's name, would a man claiming to be earl require £60,000 from me?

She opened her mouth to ask any of these, but she heard herself say, "Are you married, my lord?"

The earl narrowed his pale green eyes. "No. What does that have to do with anything?"

"Just one of many bits of information I should like to know." She released a breath. If he'd said yes, then no other question mattered. She pretended to make a notation on the parchment. "You and are I both unmarried, so there you have it."

Perry made a strange sound, and Willow again spoke over her. "Carrying on…my next question repeats my original concern. *What* do you intend to do with the money?"

Cassin stared at W. J. Hunnicut, who was not, as it happened, a man. Or an investor. Or a sane person, obviously.

Staring at her was not a hardship. In fact, the sight of her was so appealing, he found himself reaching deep for discipline, feeling around for self-control he hadn't summoned in years. He couldn't say what exactly her game might be, but the rare coalescence of cleverness and beauty and determination distracted him. By all accounts, he should have already made his excuses and gone, and yet here he sat. Too intrigued to leave.

"I'll tell you again," he said carefully. "Our venture is proprietary. The market is fiercely competitive. Exclusivity is a chief advantage. We don't dole out business secrets to just anyone."

"If you consider my offer to be a viable one, I would not be 'just anyone.'"

Your offer isn't viable, he thought, but something about the slight note of desperation in her tone kept his mouth shut. Instead, he said, "We've only just met. I haven't the slightest idea who you are."

"Lady Willow Hunnicut," she said, "daughter to Earl Lytton."

"Lady *Willow?*"

"Yes, Willow. Like the tree. It's short for Wilhelmina."

"This tells me exactly nothing, I'm afraid," he said, but he thought, *It suits her.* She was tall and solid but also graceful, like a willow. And there was something wholly natural and fresh about her. It was a useless thing to notice, of course. He'd dragged Stoker and Joseph all this way for nothing.

"If you cannot describe the venture," Lady Willow said, undeterred, "can you name the market? In general, perhaps?"

Cassin narrowed his eyes. Then again, he was already here. And he did not relish the task of returning to his partners with bad news. If nothing else, her persistence was a lesson to him. She refused to give up.

"Mining," he finally said. "And farming."

She glanced up from her notes.

He explained, "We will mine a resource that is used in farming."

She nodded slowly and scribbled. He could not look away from the open interest in her face. She scratched notes as if he described the route to a buried treasure.

"And in what country is this meant to happen?" she asked.

"The mining or the farming?"

"*Both.*"

"The mining is in the Caribbean Sea. The farming is in England." Cassin sighed. What he would have given to be taken so seriously by a *legitimate* investor.

She looked up and smiled. Cassin's heart beat double for two heavy thuds.

"The Caribbean and England…" she repeated. "Fascinating. Was that so difficult to reveal?"

No, he thought, *it was far too easy, which is what worries me.* He said, "It was not difficult as much as reckless. And please be aware I will not say another word until I learn more about you and your alleged £60,000."

After a pause and a glance at her manservant, she said, "Very well. I shall say it. But please be aware that what I'm about to tell you may have an inconsequential effect on your life but could very well ruin mine. Please understand. My evasiveness has been only to protect myself. If the arrangement does not interest you, then I ask you, as a gentleman, to disregard it. Consider it irrelevant and leave here, speaking of it to no one."

Well, that was not what I expected, Cassin thought. Did she want something smuggled out of England? Had someone put her up to importing contraband?

He shifted in his seat. "And I caution *you* not to reveal an illegal proposition. I regard myself as an entrepreneur and a taker of great risk, but I am an honest man. My partners and I have a great deal at stake. We will not circumvent the law."

Across the room, her maid moaned.

"*Perry,*" Lady Willow snapped, "tea, if you please."

"But my la—"

"*Now,* Perry."

The maid scrambled from her seat, scattering dogs.

To Cassin, she said, "You mistake me, my lord. What I propose is perfectly legal."

"Very well then; say it."

Lady Willow nodded. "I've said the £60,000 is my dowry." She paused and cleared her throat. "And under the terms of the proposed arrangement," she continued, "that sum would be transferred to the suitable man in the same way that any dowry is transferred. In exchange for marriage." She looked down at her notes. "To me."

Silence fell on the room like a net. Even the dogs ceased their panting. He wasn't certain, but he believed this young woman had just *proposed marriage* to him. She let out a quavering breath. Cassin felt very much like drawing his own quavering breath. He glanced at the silent servant standing sentry beside the door. The man made no reaction. Cassin cocked his head, running the words over in his mind.

"Forgive me," he said slowly, "but do I understand that your entire scheme is meant to engineer your own wedding? You endeavor to *buy* a husband?" His mind reeled. Cassin was in possession of three sisters and countless female cousins; he had been a resident of the earth alongside other females for thirty-six years. He had never heard of such a thing.

Lady Willow nodded and pushed out of her chair. "I am not interested in engineering a wedding or even a marriage. But I do wish to engineer a mutually beneficial union."

"And what does *that* mean?" Now he was up. He ran his hand through his hair.

"It means I am desperate to leave Surrey, the reason for which I will freely reveal to…the suitable man."

"More secrets."

She went on, saying, "Unmarried young women from respectable families dare not build a life alone outside of their childhood homes or families. But a married woman? A married woman may come and go as she pleases."

"Go *where?* Surely you do not mean to travel the world with the man you *buy* with your dowry?"

"Certainly not," she said. "I have an aunt in London who has offered me a lovely home and fulfilling employment—an apprenticeship, the culmination of years of passion and study. It is the occupation of my wildest dreams. And it's no secret. I'll tell you; I would design the interiors of the finest new homes in London. In Belgravia. Do you know it?"

"*No,*" he said. "Let us put aside for a moment the notion that you wish to be *employed*—an ambition I have never before known by any woman of quality—and return to the reason why you must *buy a husband* if your own aunt can sponsor you in London?"

Willow shook her head. "My mother does not get on with this particular member of the family. She has forbidden it."

"And yet she would allow you to marry a stranger?"

"Oh, she will not realize that yo—"

Now she stopped and flushed deep red. Cassin felt his own skin grow hot, and he turned away.

"That is," she corrected, "my mother would not realize that the man who takes my dowry would be a stranger. In her eyes, I shall marry for…traditional reasons. She is not acutely attuned to my, er, relationships. If I suggest to her that I have fallen in with an ear—that is, with an appropriate gentleman, she will not question how well acquainted we are. She will assume a natural affinity if I present it as such."

It is a betrothal plot, he thought. *Plain and simple.* The money was her dowry, and someone would have to marry her to get it. How had he not seen this coming?

"Just to be clear," she went on, "the marriage would not be traditional. When I am married, I will make my own way. And the man who has married me may, likewise, go his own way. All the way around the world. Or wherever…wherever he wishes. Simply…not near me."

Well, he could not have seen *that*. Cassin said, "Do I understand correctly that your plan precludes the traditional shared home of a husband and wife?"

She looked at her hands. "The marriage is to be a business arrangement. The man I marry will take my dowry and be gone. I will take his name and live the life of which I've always dreamed."

"Alone?"

She nodded, although it was a slow, reluctant nod. "I should like to have my friends with me—that is, my partners. My aunt and her husband will be part of my life, of course. I will have clients and collaborate with craftsmen and artists. Beyond these…well, I have always been alone in a manner. I am quite comfortable without the convention of…pairing up."

He blinked at her, struggling to comprehend.

"It's very simple, really," Willow said, taking her seat behind the desk. "I shall marry legally in the eyes of God and man. I shall move to London. Once there, I should have no use for a husband, not when I am gainfully employed and living with my aunt. This allows the man I married to be free—to sail the world, pursuing his own work, living his own life. On the rare occasion that he is in England, perhaps we might…take tea." She paused, nervously biting her lip. "But the arrangement was never meant to be traditional or…constant.

"And so now you know," she finished. "I'm certain you will not keep me in suspense as to what you will do with the offer. Do you have interest in marrying me for £60,000 and a life of freedom? Or not?"

CHAPTER FOUR

Needless to say, the very last thing Cassin expected to encounter in Surrey was a proposal of marriage. *No,* he thought, *that is inaccurate.* The very last thing he expected was a young woman posing as an investor *and* a proposal of marriage.

He smiled, a touchy, cautious smile, the smile he gave to high-strung horses he did not trust.

Her question hung in the air between them.

Do you have interest in marrying me for £60,000 and a life of freedom? Or not?

No, he thought, he had no interest in marrying for any amount of money.

And no, he would also not reveal the details of his venture. And yet...

His brain suddenly refused to form the word. He opened his mouth and then closed it. He tried and failed to conjure a convincingly lordly scowl. He thought of all the things he wanted in the world, essential things, urgent things, things that would sustain not just him but his family and tenants.

Instead of those considerable things, he suddenly wanted something else. Something frivolous and useless and just for him. He wanted her to continue talking. He wanted to hear more of her rationalizing and debating. He wanted to remain seated five feet away from her. He wanted—

"Tea, my lady!" Lady Willow's chattering maid's voice rang from the corridor.

"But where shall I put it?" sang the maid, backing into the room with a tea trolley. She did not wait for an answer but maneuvered the overburdened trolley into the impossibly tight space between the desk and Cassin's boots. Dogs filed in around her.

"By the window will do, Perry," said Lady Willow.

"Very good, my lady," she said enthusiastically, reversing direction with undo force and winding the tea trolley through the small room.

"Will you take tea, Lord Cassin?" Lady Willow asked.

"Ahhh," Cassin said, eyeing the cart. He thought of his partners, cooling their heels at the coaching inn in the village, waiting eagerly to hear the potential of the advertisement's "modest fortune."

He thought of Stoker's brig, bobbing idle on the Thames, generating no money while in port.

He thought of his mother and brother and sisters and their blind faith that he would provide for them. All the while, this trip to Surrey had been a complete waste.

"Yes, thank you," he said.

The maid gasped. "Shall I pour, my lady?"

"That won't be necessary, Perry."

"But I—"

"You may return to your duties, Perry."

The girl tried again but fell silent at her mistress's quelling look. After a deep curtsy to Cassin, she trudged from the room.

Lady Willow smiled gently to the manservant at the door. "Can I trouble you to check on the progress of my mother, Mr. Fisk?"

"Very good, my lady," he said.

And just like that, they were alone. Cassin watched the door close.

"Your mother?" he asked.

Willow shrugged. "She is riding. How do you take your tea?"

"Cream," he said. He was surprised by how cavalier she was about her mother. His own mother presided over his sisters' daily lives with a loving but watchful eye. Never would they regard her with a shrug.

"I must apologize for my maid," Lady Willow said, smiling over the trolley, deftly preparing his tea. *Her face opens up when she smiles*, he thought.

She positioned a delicate cup on a saucer. Her movements were swift and efficient but not careless. Cup and saucer made only the slightest *clink*. She stooped for a spoon. Her hair fell across her face, and she shook it away. Cassin had the unhelpful thought that he had never seen anyone like her, not ever.

In five minutes, I will go, he thought.

"Perry is far cleverer than she seems," she went on, bringing him the steaming cup.

He rose to accept it but studied her at close range instead. He could see her eyelashes, auburn like her hair but shades darker. He saw a faint smattering of freckles at the top of each cheek. He saw—

"My lord?" She nodded to the cup.

He mumbled an apology. Their hands brushed beneath the saucer, and Cassin went very, very still.

"I was not prepared for you to call in person, as I've said," she continued, "and Perry was the only chaperone I could muster on short notice."

He choked on the first sip. "I am surprised that a woman who seeks to arrange her own marriage is burdened with chaperones."

Only five minutes more, he repeated in his brain.

"Propriety is the very thing that prevents me from moving to London of my own accord," she said. "I've no choice but to adhere to it. My plan may be…unconventional in general terms, but I see no reason why, bit by bit, the preliminaries should not follow proper custom."

"Yes, if it were *proper custom* for a woman to dangle money as bait and then buy a husband."

"'Dangle money'? 'Bait'? You sensationalize. The offer is outrageous enough without exaggerating."

"At least we agree on the outrage." He watched her make her own cup and decide between the desk or the empty chair beside him. He held his breath.

"I have seen the face of outrage before, Lord Cassin, and you do not have it."

And now he wondered what she saw in his face. Weariness? Worry? The yoke of responsibility? Fascination?

Desire?

The thick, hot pull of it had been flickering at the periphery of his consciousness, but now that she was close, longing surged. His ears had latched on to the low, husky rasp of her voice. He could just detect the faint, cinnamon scent.

"If you have other reasons," she was saying, "valid reasons, for resisting my offer, I should like to know them. To improve my proposition for the next gentleman who may apply."

His cup hit the saucer with a rattle. *The next gentleman?*

Sentient thought and articulation returned to him in a rush. "I resist because the advertisement is a lie. Your insistence on learning the details of my venture is intrusive. And you are..." He trailed off, searching for a word that would not betray him.

"I am *unexpected?*" she offered innocently, sipping her tea.

"I was going to say *threatening*."

"I threaten you?"

"*I* am not threatened," he lied. "I'm afraid of tipping the scales of your obvious madness into hysteria. There lies the threat." And now he *was* sensationalizing. She hadn't shown the slightest proclivity toward hysteria. But he could hardly say what he truly felt, which was distraction and curiosity and shock.

And mind-blanking attraction, he thought suddenly, honestly.

"I appear mad to you, my lord?"

"I'm not finished," he said. "Your promise of money is unsubstantiated. What if some poor sod does the unthinkable and marries you, only to discover there is no money? No money at all?"

"It takes no effort to prove the validity of a dowry," she said.

This was true, of course. She was the most charming when she raised some truth. No matter what point he made, she always countered with something just as valid. He'd never met another female so willing to challenge him.

"But perhaps you simply feel that you cannot abide me," Lady Willow said. "Not even long enough to quickly marry." She set her empty cup on the desk before them.

"*No*," Cassin said, "I do not know you."

This was true, although he found it surprisingly difficult to say. He knew her hair was the color of an ash leaf in November. He knew her skin was as smooth and pale as cream. He knew her voice was husky, that it washed over him like hot water on a cold night. He knew her arguments, no matter how unacceptable, had made his pulse pound and his brain misfire.

Cassin enjoyed the distraction of a pretty girl as much as the next man, but he also toiled daily beneath the yoke of obligation, an effort that left him too mired down to notice autumn hair or cream skin or a dusky voice.

But he had noticed today. Inconveniently. Uselessly.

He noticed her like he would notice a beautiful sunset when what he really needed was ten more minutes of daylight.

He glanced at her. She appeared to be winding up to explain how it would not matter that they were not acquainted. He found himself suddenly, urgently, wanting to hear it. But there was a soft knock at the door.

"Begging your pardon, my lady," said her manservant.

Lady Willow rose. "What's happened?"

"The countess. She's returned, I'm afraid. Tom can just see them cresting the hill behind the paddock."

"The hill already?" Lady Willow spun to the window.

"Might I suggest that you and his lordship conclude your interview in the garden?" he said. "I can have his lordship's horse and coat brought 'round."

"The garden. Yes, thank you, Mr. Fisk. Excellent idea, as always." She scanned the room. "Will you tell Abbott to clear the tea? Wait—no, he will make more of the request than necessary. Send Perry, if you please. It is not her job, but she will do it for me. Thank you."

When she looked to Cassin, her face was young and flushed and determined. "I'm afraid I must ask you to join me outside the house. My mother is...complicated."

"She knows nothing, does she?" Cassin asked. "You've done this entirely on your own."

Lady Willow nodded. "Yes." She leaned toward the desk and swept up the parchment, pen, and ink pot. "She knows nothing. This way, if you please, my lord."

She filed into the corridor.

Just five minutes more, Cassin thought as he followed her out the door.

CHAPTER FIVE

The risk of discovery by Lady Lytton was a welcome new source of panic, but Willow was too preoccupied to really care about her mother. Against all odds, the Earl of Cassin held great potential. His reserve. His caution. His willingness to flee the house. Very great potential, indeed.

And flee they did, down the corridor, through the ballroom, and out onto the terrace that led to the garden. They did not run, precisely, but they were hardly strolling.

The new location meant there would be less time for everything, of course; no more beating around the bush. He would have to declare himself, yea or nay. But perhaps this, too, was preferred. In Willow's view, she'd already said enough. All the while, he'd said—well, what had he said? He'd done little more than challenge her.

But he did not go, she thought.

Even now, he did not go.

She cast a glance over her shoulder. He took one long step to her two, but he was not far behind.

"This way, if you please," she said lightly, descending the great stone steps that led to the garden. She would lead him down the gravel path, beyond the fountain, and skirt the labyrinth. There, obscured by a thick yew hedge, was a stone bench and bowling green. It was secluded but not intimate, the perfect spot to conclude the interview.

"The grounds of your home are beautiful," the earl said. His voice was not winded. He did not sound the slightest bit appalled.

Please, please keep Mother away, she prayed. She said, "The garden is Mr. Fisk's handiwork. My mother will struggle to replace him when we relocate to London, I'm afraid."

"You will move to London with a gardener?"

"Mr. Fisk is not a gardener," she said. "He is my personal servant, a steward, if you will. Previously, he served as my late father's valet. When my father passed on, the terms of his will provided a salary and pension for Mr. Fisk under my employ. In many ways, Mr. Fisk has been looking after me since I was a girl. My father and I were not close, but he showed his regard for us both when he arranged for Mr. Fisk's future with me."

Finally, she reached the corner of the concealing hedge. She cast a searching look in the direction of the stables and saw no movement, thank God. Her mother would be cooling down the animals for another half hour. She motioned to the earl and slipped around the wall of green.

This is reasonable, she told herself, looking around the secluded bench and stately oak tree. She dropped onto the bench. With hands that shook, she arranged the ink pot and pen and straightened the parchment.

"Now," she began, looking up.

The earl stared down at her. "You are so convinced that you will go to London?"

"Oh, quite convinced," she lied. "But I'm afraid we've no longer the luxury of discussing how I'll get there, or why, or with whose permission." She took a deep breath. "I've said enough—surely we can agree on that—while you have committed to virtually nothing. In the interest of time, may I implore you to, er, contribute?"

"*Contribute?*"

She narrowed her eyes. "If nothing else, I should like to learn the nature of your venture. Only then will we know if our ambitions align."

The earl walked a slow circle around the bench, staring up at the dappled golden light filtering through the canopy of the oak. He ran a hand through his hair.

Willow gritted her teeth and calculated the number of minutes at their disposal. She brushed the feathered end of her pen against her chin. She waited. Finally, she said, "But perhaps you have no venture to speak of? Is that it? Or your business is illegal?" She turned to face him. "Please tell me the venture is not supported by the slave trade? But perhaps this is why you dodge the question. If this is the case, then you have been correct to conceal it. I'm afraid we have nothing more to discuss."

"On the contrary," he said levelly. "We have been very careful to pursue only opportunities that are not supported by slave labor."

She gave a satisfied nod. "On this, we are in agreement."

"It did not occur to me that you would consider this."

"It was our first concern, actually. But if you cannot find words to articulate the industry into which I will contribute

£60,000, then lack of consideration may be better applied to you than me. I urge you to *try*."

"A final question for you…"

"No. Absolutely no more questions."

"Mining and farming," he said, dropping onto the bench. "There, I've said it. In general, simple terms."

"Less general than that, if you please. Do you not know? Am I meant to *guess*?"

Years later, Cassin would look back on this moment and marvel that his life had descended from earldom and castle to *here*. In a garden, hiding from someone's *mother*, being forced by a young woman to justify the great potential and bright future of…

"*Guano*," he said.

Silence.

A loon sang in the distance. A breeze fluttered the leaves of the tree. Lady Willow stared, unblinking.

Cassin indulged the vain, fleeting hope that one word would do it, that she would drop this nonsense of a dowry and proposal and…and force him to go.

After a long moment, she said, "I beg your pardon?"

Cassin cleared his throat. "Guano." And then, because, *why bloody not*, he asked her, "Do you know it?"

She shook her head.

"Guano is a…natural resource," he said. "Found on tropical islands."

She bent immediately over her paper and began to scribble. "Go on," she said.

Cassin stared at the top of her head, her small shoulders, her delicate hands. "The guano, as I've—"

"Forgive me, my lord, but would you be so kind as to *spell* this word?" She looked at him, her pen lifted eagerly from the page, her blue-green eyes both interested and, if he was not mistaken, a little bit excited. He felt his heartbeat kick up.

"G-u-a-n-o," he said, watching her write. Her auburn hair fell around her shoulders, and one particularly perfect spiral spilled deep orange on the page. She whisked it away.

"A Spanish word, is it?" She looked up.

"I don't know," he said slowly.

"*Possibly Spanish*," she said aloud as she made another notation. "We shall look it up. Go on."

Cassin opened his mouth to tell her, *We will not look it up*, but instead he said, "The guano is mined, in a manner. After we have it in barrels, it can be imported to farm-rich countries and sold. As fertilizer."

"Fertilizer?" she repeated, looking up again.

"It's mixed with a farmer's soil to introduce vital nutrients. It transforms the very nature of the earth for the better. When it's tilled in before a planting, vegetation will thrive, despite the quality of the soil or how frequently it has been farmed."

Lady Willow looked into the distance, speculating. "But this is the effect of *any* fertilizer, as any girl raised in the country knows. I also know the most common source of fertilizer. Are you suggesting that this…"

"Guano," he provided.

"Yes, thank you, this guano is something far and away different from what English farmers find in plentiful supply on the ground of any livestock pen? But you mentioned mining. Perhaps this *guano* is a mineral?"

"Guano is a naturally occurring…compound," Cassin said, marveling at her persistence. "It builds up over time on small islands and hardens in the tropical sun. After that, it can be mined by hand, using something like a pickax."

Lady Willow considered this. She scribbled more notes. Cassin held his breath as he watched her. She wrote faster and with more determination than ever he'd seen a woman write. His sisters devoted a full day to a leisurely one-page letter to their cousin.

"It's bird excrement," he heard himself say. He eyed her, waiting for the incredulity, the giggling, the blushes.

"It's what?" she called. Her pen hovered just above the parchment; then she skipped down a space and wrote on.

"Bird excrement," he repeated. "Also bat. And occasionally…seal. But excrement—all of it, the lot. It petrifies to rock hardness in the sun and becomes flaky. The hardened heaps of it form mounds. In many cases, these are as tall as a bluff or hill and can be scaled by men, like the face of a cliff. It's mined by chipping away at the great bloody pile of it, and then it's funneled into barrels. After that, it's moved to the buyer's market by sea. In our case, in the hold of my partner's brig."

Cassin rolled from the bench, crossing his arms over his chest. "Guano," he repeated. "Bird excrement. Imported and sold to the farmers of England. *This* is my venture—well, *our* venture."

"And you need my dowry to…*purchase* the excrement?"

"That's the beauty of it." He began to pace. "My partners and I have come into ownership of an island in the Caribbean Sea that's heaped with it. We don't have to buy it; we *own* it. We need an investor to finance the mining, the shipping, and then the selling of it in England."

Now she looked up. "Come into ownership? Did you purchase this island?"

"No. The island was…transferred to us. Some time ago. Land and natural resources, all ours." He paused and glanced at her. "We won it in a game of cards. The island is twenty miles off the coast of Barbadoes."

The questions came quickly after that, far more thoughtful and serious than any questions from the other investors Cassin had approached.

"How will you procure laborers to do the actual mining?" she asked. "What of the native inhabitants of the island? When do you hope to begin and end the work? Do you anticipate a great many risks? To whom would you sell the…guano? What are the costs involved in mining? And what of your plans for the island after the guano has been depleted?"

Cassin rattled off answers, oddly gratified that someone, finally, cared to ask. She hung on his every word. He watched her nod, and chew on her lip, and scribble notes. He could have watched her for hours, he thought, but with every new answer, he was certain she would tell him to go.

"I shall ask Mr. Fisk what he knows of this *guano*," she said thoughtfully. "His experience as a gardener will be a useful resource."

And now the servants will have a say, thought Cassin.

"This," said Willow, dabbing her pen into the ink, "has been so informative. And was it so terrible? Revealing it?" She stood and gestured to the garden. "I cannot say that this is how I planned to consider applicants or ventures, but the afternoon has not been complete folly."

Folly is precisely what the afternoon has been, he thought, standing beside her. *Indulgent, distracted, mad folly.* Underlying it all was his persistent, thudding reaction to her.

"However," she went on, "I think we've said enough for one day. When my mother returns to the manor house, I cannot guarantee our...privacy. In the meantime, allow me to dispense with formalities. I am highly interested in sponsoring your venture."

He stared down, marveling at her boldness. Even as he evaded her. Even after he explained about the bird shite. Even as...

The relative quiet of the bench was broken by a chorus of barking, and Lady Willow moaned. The thud of running feet followed, along with panting and someone hissing *"Shh!"* There was a squeal and then—

"My lady!" Her maid flung herself around the hedge with dogs spilling at her feet.

"She's come, she's come, she's come, she's come!" The maid jabbed her index finger back and forth in the direction of the house. "Mr. Fisk will bring the earl's horse. He's said, *meet him by the pond.*" The maid wadded her apron in her hands.

"Thank you," said Lady Willow tightly, wading through dogs. To Cassin, she said, "I feared this might happen. This way, if you will, my lord. How lucky for you; now you shall see the pond." She took his hand.

"Lady Willow," he said, staring down at their joined hands.

"The pond is just ahead."

"*Lady Willow,*" he repeated and stopped walking. She endeavored to trudge forward, but he pulled her back. She stopped herself just short of colliding with his chest and turned her face up. Her eyes were large and earnest and the most captivating shade of blue-green. Her pink mouth was parted with exertion. The breeze whipped her hair across her face. A scramble of thoughts raced through his head.

I'm sorry our goals do not align.

Take care posting solicitations for strange men.

How old are you?

Why are you not married already?

Instead, he said, "Your ingenuity and determination do you credit, but please…understand. I am not prepared to marry for the money."

She blinked again and bit her lip, drawing his attention to her mouth. "Why not?"

He let out a noise of frustration. "Do you know, I have three sisters and a mother, and they come part and parcel with a crowd of female friends and relations—literally dozens of women of every age—and I have never met one of them as bold or demanding as you."

"I am not bold and demanding, sir. I am desperate. Why? Why won't you marry for money?"

"Oh." He blew out a breath. "I don't know. There is the small consideration of my pride. And the fact that we have only just met. Also, my very few years as earl have been riddled with what some might term 'misguided leadership,' and I am loath to add 'married a stranger from a dockside advertisement' to the list. Believe me, my lady, the answer to your question is long and complicated and unnecessary."

She scoffed, "More evasiveness."

"But I owe you nothing."

"Why, then, are you still here?"

He opened his mouth to answer but closed it. He tried again. "I cannot think of any man in my acquaintance who would agree to your offer."

Her eyes grew larger. "You're speaking of your partners."

"No. I speak of any gentleman."

"I have two friends," she said, forging on, "and our plan has always been to relocate to London together. If your partners are unmarried, my friends may extend the same arrangement to them…assuming the gentlemen are similar—that is, if the gentlemen are correct."

"No gentleman is correct for this scheme. The *scheme* is not correct."

"*Ask* them," she insisted, and he laughed again. So persistent, so…beautiful and persistent.

"I will prepare my mother for 'callers,'" she assured him. "If you call again, you may expect no hiding or dashing about. Come tomorrow, if it suits you."

"More boldness."

The jingle of tack and a whinny rose behind them. His horse. Her Mr. Fisk. His five minutes were up.

"There are worse things than bold and demanding." She took a step back.

"On this, we are agreed." Cassin sighed. He thought of his castle and family and tenants, of the rapidly approaching winter.

She took another step back. Mr. Fisk could be heard talking softly to the horse. Cassin thanked the man and mounted.

The horse danced and spun. Cassin whipped around, staring at her. Her auburn hair lifted on the breeze. She shaded her eyes with her hand.

"Until tomorrow, perhaps," she said.

Cassin could not find words to say good-bye, so he nodded, promising nothing, denying nothing. Then he kicked in his heels and was gone.

CHAPTER SIX

"He won't be back," Willow told her maid, Perry, the next morning. "Not this morning. Not ever, in fact." In the wake of the earl's departure, reason and reality poured in and Willow's optimism had dissolved.

She paced a straight line from her bed to the dressing table and back again. Perry sat in the window seat, sewing a button on Willow's lavender day dress.

"Gone forever," Willow repeated, pausing to look out the window over Perry's head. "And I cannot believe I didn't see it. But I do see you, Perry, and I see that delicate purple dress. Absolutely not. I cannot work in the purple dress."

Perry shook her head and continued to sew.

"It's pointless to make a fuss when no one will come," Willow went on. "I want practical, not fragile, when I work."

"Practical?" Perry sighed, biting off the thread with her teeth. "Pretty is what matters today."

"Today is no different from yesterday." Willow said, cringing at the memory of the plain blue day dress in which she'd received the Earl of Cassin. "And even if he did come—which he will not——my appearance is of little consequence. An arrangement between us could never work. Yesterday I was...I was carried away. I did not think. How can I marry an *earl*?" This had been the first devastating question to come to her. She took a seat at her dressing table and began to work a brush through the wild curls of her hair, more chaotic than usual after a sleepless night.

"'Course you can, my lady," said Perry, standing up and giving the dress a shake. "You're the daughter of an earl yourself, aren't you? So clever and pretty. I think you are very well matched to his lordship."

"It makes no difference if we are matched, Perry. We are not a pair of candlesticks. But don't you see? An earl will require an heir. All men want an heir, but a nobleman absolutely must have one. It was ridiculous of me to carry on as I did yesterday, considering my unsuitability in this regard. If he returns—which, I feel certain, he will not—he will be sure to leave again as soon as I tell him. Of this I am certain." She held the brush still, watching herself say the words in the mirror.

"I say he *will* come." Perry brought the dress to Willow and began maneuvering it over her head.

"Yes, but you also believe it will snow on Christmas. And be sunny and warm on Easter." Willow's words were muffled through the fabric. Her head emerged. "And it never happens, does it?"

For once, Perry was quiet, preoccupied with the fifty tiny lavender buttons running the length of Willow's spine. Or perhaps Willow had convinced her. Now she needed only to convince herself.

He will not want me, Willow repeated in her head.

She'd said it a hundred times in the night, and she would say it a hundred more. The Earl of Cassin had seemed too perfect because he *was* too perfect. Even if a nobleman could overcome the outrageous arrangement of the marriage—a very substantial *if*—he would never get around the fact that she could not give him an heir.

It was cruelly ironic that she had devised a plan to produce an unaccountable non-husband husband—someone desperate enough to overlook her barrenness—yet the first viable applicant had literally been *born* unable to accept. Even for a marriage of convenience. Even for £60,000.

To Willow's great frustration, unexpected tears began to close her throat, and she squeezed her eyes shut. Really, what had she expected, given the limitations of her body?

"Oh, don't cry, my lady!" trilled Perry. She crouched at Willow's feet and, grabbing hold of the lavender hem, vigorously fanned Willow's skirts in and out, like a sail in the wind. Willow yelped and grabbed the bedpost.

She reminded herself that *this* was why she had avoided men her entire life—this useless, tearful spiral of self-pity. She never moped or felt sorry for herself when she was occupied and diligent. Rarely, if ever, did she think about men and how much happier she always was for the distance.

Until now.

Until the *one man*, literally among hundreds of men she'd ignored and by whom she was likewise ignored, turned up and reminded her why she never bothered. Until now, when suddenly she wanted to bother very much.

A knock at her bedroom door yanked her attention from the bedpost,

"Do you mind, darling?" said her mother's voice from the corridor. The door swung wide to admit her mother, Lady Lytton. "You won't believe what's happened."

"My lady," said Willow, taking two steps toward her. The countess rarely, if ever, came to Willow's bedroom.

"Abbott sent a maid to fetch you," said the countess, "but I sent her away and came myself. It's not every day a gentleman calls on my daughter." She waved a calling card in her right hand.

"I...I beg your pardon?" Willow's voice belonged to someone else.

"'Brent Caulder, the Earl of Cassin,'" her mother read. "Honestly, I wouldn't have believed it if I hadn't seen it with my own eyes. I thought he'd come about the roan mare, but he made himself very clear. He is here for *you*, darling. Your father told you that eventually the gentlemen would come. Oh, and you've worn the purple. So pretty. I'll tell him you'll be right down."

Willow stared at her mother. Vaguely, she was aware that Perry had begun to bounce up and down behind her.

Her mother frowned. "Whatever is the matter with your maid?"

Willow reached behind her and grabbed Perry's wrist.

"Cassin...Cassin..." mused Lady Lytton, looking at the card again. "I have not heard of this family, but I shall look them up. When he spoke, his accent suggested somewhere north. Yorkshire, perhaps? However did you meet an earl from Yorkshire?"

"Ah..." began Willow. A benefit of repelling most every man she met was never having to embellish them. "He is an acquaintance of Tessa St. Croix," she lied.

"Ah, yes, of course," said Lady Lytton. "Their business dealings acquaints the family with a great many gentleman."

Willow needed to hear her say it again. "Lord Cassin is here? Now?"

Lady Lytton laughed again. "But you are overcome with nerves, aren't you? How charming. Of course he will find you lovely; do not fret. And remember…" She lowered her voice to a whisper. "No one can prove what the doctors say about your—about you. It's better left unmentioned, to be sure. Such an awkward, indelicate topic. Mark my words."

Willow made no answer, and her mother turned away. "I was meant to watch the grooms run a new stallion this morning," her mother said. "I have him on loan from Enderby, but I shall put it off."

"W-why?" asked Willow. If the earl really had come, the last thing the situation needed was her mother's presence.

"Do not fret. I shan't hover. But I can hardly leave the two of you alone in the house, now can I? I shall read the papers over breakfast while you receive him in the drawing room. How is that? And Wilhelmina?" prompted Lady Lytton. "Pray do not stare at the man like a fish on a plate. If only you could see your expression. You look terrified. Honestly, I would not expect this from the girl who has begged for months to relocate alone to London. How correct I have been to forbid it, if this is how you react to one young man. His mount is lovely, by the way—a Lipizzan stallion."

"I am not terrified," Willow said, the only thing she could safely assert, despite its being not entirely true.

CHAPTER SEVEN

Cassin had come to Leland Park to tell her, *no, thank you*. In person. Face-to-face.

He came to assure her, also in person, that her advertisement would not be discussed with another living soul. It was the gentlemanly thing to do.

If there was time, he would caution her against future trolling for husbands with misleading advertisements on the docks in London.

After this, he would bid her farewell. Forever. He would not linger in Surrey. They would share no further interaction. And above all, he would not marry her, not even for £60,000.

That was why he'd come.

He repeated this reasoning to himself over and over again while he waited again in the blue drawing room. The dogs had returned, crowding in the doorway to consider him. When Willow's mother strode into the room for an introduction, they'd swept in at her feet. Now the countess had gone and the dogs with her—all except for one, a petite butterscotch-colored puff with a fox's face. She sat before him and stared up as if waiting for the truth.

"What?" Cassin asked the dog. "Shall I tell you that I came because Joseph and Stoker have descended into madness? An affliction hidden from me all these years?"

Instead of laughing at Cassin's description of W. J. Hunnicut and her outrageous offer, his partners had been intrigued. Aggressively intrigued. Startlingly intrigued.

What of the girl's friends? they wished to know.

How old? How much did their dowries offer?

Why were they in such a blind rush to leave Surrey?

Cassin had been dumbfounded by their interest and invoked every logical argument to dissuade it, all to no avail. It was *their* fault he'd returned—their fault and the fault of his own sense of honor. He would decline her offer in person, and he would go.

"Careful," said a female voice from the doorway. "That dog is a known mind reader."

Slowly, Cassin looked up. Of all the promises he had made to himself about the call, the most urgent had been not to stare, not to engage her, not to slide into the same unhinged, boggled-mind reaction he'd had the day before.

Today, he knew what to expect.

She was a woman—a *pretty* woman, yes, but she need not be a woman who caused his heart to pound or his mouth to dry. Not today.

She had not moved from the doorway, and he remembered to stand. She took two tentative steps inside. She wore purple, two shades of it, both bright and unexpected. Not the purple of an iris or hydrangea but the tropical, acrid purple of an orchid. It suited her, he thought. The tart color cast her in a bright, hot glow.

But now she was blushing, the result of his mute stare, and the thud in his throat took up where it had left off the day before.

She'd piled her hair on top of her head in a riot of auburn curls that exposed her neck. She wore small, round pearls on her earlobes. There were freckles on her collarbone.

This is why you came, he thought, his mind otherwise blank. How stupid it had been to make up any other excuse.

"My mother is a lover of animals," she told him, "especially dogs and horses. I have grown accustomed to the great many dogs, but I've never understood about the horses."

He nodded. That voice. Low and husky. She'd talked for nearly an hour yesterday, said outrageous things, impossible things, and he'd hung on every word.

"I've not given much thought to dogs or horses," he said.

He looked at the neat purple trim on the collar of her dress. He looked at her delicate, ungloved hands. He scanned the silk of her skirts to the floor and back up. She blushed again, and he felt a proprietary surge of gratification.

"I did not expect that you would be back," she said.

"No? Why not?" Perhaps *she* knew why he'd come.

"I…I cannot say." She made her way to him. He held his breath, anticipating the cinnamon scent from the day before.

"Will you sit?" she said.

No, he thought, but he held out a hand, inviting her to precede him. He watched her smooth her skirts and settle onto the end of a sofa. He wanted to sit beside her—immediately beside her, thigh-to-skirts beside her—but he took an adjacent chair. The dog jumped into his lap.

She waited.

Tell her good-bye, he thought, staring at the dog.

"Why will you not acquire a husband the traditional way?" he said. "Go to London for a season? Dance, flirt, enter into courtships until you find the right fellow. Or you could marry a well-heeled neighbor or cousin, for that matter. Why...*this*?"

To her credit, she did not fidget or flinch. There were no I-beg-your-pardons or I-dare-not-says. She nodded to herself.

"Yes, of course." A nervous laugh. "How right of you to ask." She paused, composing herself. "I cannot—or will not—acquire a husband the traditional way because..." Another pause. "I have a medical condition that precludes a traditional marriage."

He stopped breathing. "You are...ill?

She shook her head. "No, it's nothing like that. I *was* ill, as a girl, almost eighteen years ago. An infection. I almost died at the time, but now I am quite well. Except for..." Yet another pause. "The infection left me barren."

"Barren?" Cassin blinked. It was rude of him to repeat her, but he'd been unprepared for such a bald truth. He said, "But surely some man would be willing to—"

"Don't," she said softly. "Please do not offer the solution of 'some man.' I reconciled myself to my limitation years ago. It is a private matter, obviously, and I only speak of it with you because we are discussing this...arrangement. Honesty is imperative."

We are not discussing this arrangement, Cassin thought.

"I made up my mind as a girl that I should find some other way to lead a fulfilling life, beyond motherhood and marriage. Luckily, I possessed a…a desire to create—or to be creative, I should say. I…I suppose I might as well explain this now."

She smiled at him hopefully and stood up, opening and closing her fists at her sides. He rose with her, but she waved him back to his chair. "I love to create, as I've said. And I love beautiful objects, beautiful spaces, paintings, textiles, sculpture."

She traced a slender finger up and over the contoured sofa. He followed the swoop of her hand with his eyes.

She said, "I spent hours of my girlhood sketching or curating miniatures, little…oh, I suppose one might call them small windows to little scenes. They were like…tiny displays of fabric and tassels, bits of nature—a leaf or feather or pebble. I would arrange them in the box by color or texture or shape. My aunt Mary—the one I hope to join in London— encouraged me. She saw some talent in my little creations— God knows how—and she believed my interests needed only to be cultivated and expanded to ultimately be very satisfying. Before she married her husband and was, essentially, exiled from the family"—Willow made a bitter expression—"she sent books to me about design. We pored over them on her frequent visits, studying the sketches of castles and great estates from around the world."

Lady Willow prowled the room, speaking with her hands. Each new statement had a gesture—two fingers rubbed together to show texture, or palms open wide beside her face to show delight. She looked to the side when she was thoughtful. She fiddled with leaves of a potted fern when she revealed some fear or hope. Every minute or so, she shot him a careful glance.

Tell her, he thought. But he dare not interrupt.

"After reading and writing and sums," she went on, "these windowed boxes and my own sketching took up nearly all of my time. On a particularly long visit, Aunt Mary conspired with me to repaint my bedroom and select fabric for new linens. After that, I was off. I remade the bedroom of my governess, the nursery, my brother's rooms—on and on it went until I had I made changes to every room in the house."

Cassin glanced around him at the blue walls and back to her.

"I've redesigned the interior of every room in Leland Park many times over. This drawing room, for instance, I've only just finished." She held out her arms and pivoted, indicating the long, blue room.

Cassin thought of the cold stone walls of Caldera, his castle in Yorkshire. Ancient tapestries had hung on the same walls for what must have been hundreds of years, and portraits of identically posed relatives lined the corridors. A belching fire dusted everything with a whirl of black soot. It had never occurred to him that the rooms should look any other way. His mother and sisters had never shown the slightest interest in bringing in so much as a new footstool. The sturdy antique furniture was as natural to the castle as the towering trees in the garden.

She was at the mantel now, adjusting the angle of a vase and lacquered box. "I hope this explains, at least in part, my great desire to relocate to this new neighborhood in London. When I am reunited with my aunt and uncle and am in their employ, I can devote every day to the designs of one beautiful new home after another. All the best craftsmen and merchants are at their disposal." She turned to beam at him. "Leland Park can only be made over so many times," she said. "A few select Pixham neighbors have taken my advice on a room or two in their homes, but to design every room in every house in an entire London district? It is the opportunity of a lifetime."

She looked at him, waiting for some response. The repeat chorus of *Tell her* scraped at the back of his head, but he could barely hear it.

She returned to the sofa, and the dog jumped beside her. "It's why I conceived of the advertisement. I have to get to London, and my mother cannot be persuaded."

"Why is your mother so opposed?" *The last question*, he thought.

"My mother doesn't care that I will never have a family or that I should like to fill my life with something I value instead. She will not listen; she never has. And she detests my aunt's choices for her life. Considering this, I was forced to find a way around her."

"So many secrets," he said.

"Yes, well, you should try to lead a fulfilling life with lively interests and engaging relationships but absolutely no rights, and you'd see how many secrets you are compelled to keep. Better still, try living at the mercy of others who enjoy unlimited rights. What then? Self-preservation quite literally forced my hand. It sounds drastic, but I grow older with every year. Life is passing me by." Her voice broke, and she struggled to gain composure.

"It does not distress you to join an aunt whom your parents have disowned?"

"Well, *I* have not disowned her. Aunt Mary was dear to me as a child. She alone saw that I would not have motherhood to occupy me, and she set me on the path to find satisfaction in another way. I owe her so much. We correspond weekly. When she wrote to say she could make a place for me in their new commissions in Belgravia, I could not help but conceive of some method or means to get myself there."

"Why was this aunt disowned?" he asked.

"Reasons entirely unfounded." She waved her hand, sweeping away the insignificance. "She married a penniless man of no distinction. He is lovely, of course, and completely devoted to her. She viewed him as an artist—he designs furniture, you see—but the family saw him only as a yeoman laborer, toiling away with his hands. Now the two of them create furniture and design the interior of homes. They are quite renowned in London, really. Certainly he is penniless no more. They've made a name for themselves and are sought after by the finest families." She shrugged. "But none of this matters, does it, when she was the daughter of a rich baron, and he was the son of nobody-knows-who." She smiled at him.

"So you would live in the care of this disgraced London aunt. But where? In their…flat?"

She laughed. "Oh no! They live in one of the first townhomes built in Belgravia. Aunt Mary has promised me ground-floor apartments—large enough for me and my man, Mr. Fisk, and my maid, Perry. And if my friends are able to find arrangements for their dowries, they may come too. The accommodations could not be more perfect, really."

She beamed as she said it, looking off as if to imagine the perfection of this collective life with her two bosom friends and a fallen aunt and her carpenter husband.

"Your own apartments," Cassin repeated. "And your hus—" He swallowed what he almost said, what he had come here specifically *not* to say, and corrected himself. "The man you marry is meant to pay no mind to an arrangement that your mother will not allow?"

Her smile fell just a little. Her eyes darted left. "The man I marry will receive a large sum of money to pay me no mind whatsoever. Won't he?" She looked back.

"That would depend on what you would be doing and where you would be going, in and out of your private entrance."

And there it was, the question he'd wanted to know most of all. His primary question. He raised an eyebrow.

She laughed again, although it was an uneasy, cautious laugh. "I will be making my dreams come true. Designing the interiors of these beautiful homes."

He considered this. An answer that was really no answer at all. He wanted to ask again, to press her and make her define the life she intended to lead as a married woman with an absent husband, but…but…

But he was not to be that absent husband, so what could it matter?

She returned to the sofa and leaned to him, as if intimating a secret. "Look, Cassin, I know the scheme is outrageous and unorthodox. And if it was only me and my dream, I probably would have already given up on the idea. It is exactly the life I have always wanted, an alternative to the family I cannot have. Is it worth deceiving my mother and marrying a stranger under false pretenses? Probably not. But it's not only me and my dream, is it? When the lives of my friends became complicated in such a way that they, too, could benefit from a fresh start in London, I thought, *I can do something about this for all of us.*"

She sat up and waited. She added, "I could but act."

Cassin could think of no answer to this, only more questions, and he'd already appeared too interested and too conspiratorial. It was almost as if his time to tell her had come and gone. He sighed and ran a finger through his hair.

He was just about to ask her about the urgency of her friends' flight from Surrey when they were interrupted by a fresh wave of barking.

She laughed. "My mother's dogs again. She allows them free rein of the house, I'm afraid. I'm sorry for the barking yesterday—and today. They are impossible to contain."

"Your mother..." he said, seizing on a topic that neither committed him nor encouraged her.

"Oh yes, I understand that you have met. Thank you for not...er, thank you for playing along."

But perhaps her mother was not a safe topic. Before he could stop himself, Cassin asked, "She will consent to your marriage to a perfect stranger?"

"My mother is only marginally interested in my carryings on, as I've said." She smiled a sad smile. "Her great love is horses, followed by these dogs, followed by my late father. If I tell her I've grown fond of an ea—that is, if I tell her I've grown fond of a remotely suitable man, she will agree to the marriage without much further thought. After that, her obligation to me will be complete. She is acutely adherent to propriety, and she holds me accountable in the same way, but she will be perfectly happy to have me taken off her hands. If I go to my aunt as a married woman, well—she did her best, didn't she?"

"How can you be so sure?" Cassin's sisters endured unrelenting interest from their mother.

"Beg your pardon, my lord? Wilhelmina?" sang a voice from the doorway.

Cassin and Lady Willow spun to see Lady Lytton. She had secured a scarf tightly around her head, and a servant hovered behind her with an open coat. Cassin shoved himself to his feet.

"I cannot be kept from the morning exercises any longer, I'm afraid," the countess said. "May I trust that your visit will draw to its natural conclusion very soon? I shan't wait, but Abbott can show the earl out when you've said your good-byes. It was a pleasure to meet you, my lord. If you are available, I host a dinner every Thursday—the local racing community mostly, but I should be delighted to have you as my guest—"

"I am unsure of the length of my stay in Surrey, my lady," he said. "If...er, business keeps me in the country, I should be delighted to attend." He cleared his throat.

"Lovely," said the countess. "It's all settled, then." And then she was gone, trailed by a line of dogs.

When the front door could be heard opening and shutting, Lady Willow rose. "My mother will believe what she wishes to believe," she said.

He looked down at her. She stood so close their arms brushed. He saw the blues and greens of her eyes. He counted three freckles beside her mouth. Her coiffure had begun to drop curls onto her shoulders. She rubbed her open palm on her skirt, smiling a brilliant smile.

"Dinner on Thursday is not a requirement," she said. "Truly, fewer betrothals could be less of a bother than the one I offer. You may ask her for my hand, the lawyers will draw up the settlement contract, the ceremony will be small and brief. And it will be done."

It was those words that did it.

Willow Hunnicut was pretty and clever and...something more—something he could not quite put his finger on—but this hardly meant he should *marry* her. He did not want a wife. Moreover, he did not want a wife he hardly knew and would never know, apparently. He had misled her and indulged himself long enough.

"I cannot," he blurted.

"Cannot do...which?" She reversed one small step.

"I cannot—will not marry you," he said. "As I said yesterday. Not for any amount of money. It is out of the question."

She took another step back. Then another. "But..."

"It's why I came."

"*It's why you came?*" she repeated. "But...but was it... Have I..."

"It's nothing that you've said or done," he said. Irritation punctuated his words. He was angry with himself for saying too little too late. She took another step back.

"The arrangement you offer is not viable," he said.

"But if you knew this, why did you..." Her voice had gone high and airy. "I've gone on and on. You allowed me to—"

"It was a mistake not to reveal my intentions when I arrived. I apologize."

Another step back, another. She collided with the sofa and tipped backward until she sat. "A mistake? *A mistake?*"

She popped up on a quick intake of breath. The lone, remaining dog jumped and barked at her feet. "You sat quietly and listened to me prattle on and on about my talents and ambitions and my...*health*—even while you knew all along. I told you—" She spoke in profile. "I told you things that I never reveal to anyone."

He held out his hands as if to explain, but he couldn't think of a useful thing to say.

"Good-bye," she said, and she moved to the farthest end of the sofa. "My mother was correct about Abbott. He will show you to the door."

"No, you—"

"Please *go.*"

CHAPTER EIGHT

"I beg your pardon?" said Lord Cassin.

"I would ask you"—she paused, determined that her voice would not break—"to leave, my lord. We have no more business."

You knew better, she told herself. *You knew all along.*

"But I…" he began. "It was never my intention to—"

"Excuses are unnecessary."

His expression had taken on a stricken sort of shock; he actually looked a little afraid of her. It was appropriate. She was a little afraid of herself, teetering on the terrible edge where anger and embarrassment collide.

He had deliberately misled her; he'd sat idly by as she revealed things known to only a handful of people in the world. He'd provoked her with questions, and she'd allowed him to do so, going on and on about her future and her past, the whys and wherefores of it all.

Meanwhile, he'd known all along.

I will not marry you for any amount of money.

He'd known, and she'd known. He was an earl, and she was barren and, well, men simply did not regard her in the wifely way. Even men who would marry her and not know her as a wife at all.

But now she'd revealed the history of her health and every dream she'd held dear since girlhood, and he was pretending to feel remorse while she was pretending not to be mortified.

But the pretense ended now. Her vision swam as she strode to the door, and she walked faster. A traitorous tear slid down her cheek, and she looked right as she turned left to hide her hands swiping it away.

Inexplicably, she heard his footsteps behind her. They were determined, hurried on the marble floor. The remaining dog yipped and jumped at his boots. She walked faster.

"*Abbott?*" she called over her shoulder, invoking every known rudeness to actually shout the butler's name.

"Lady Willow, stop," Cassin called. "Please wait. I should like to explain."

And I should like to disappear. She cut left down the side corridor that ran the length of the ballroom.

At the far end of the corridor, her most current project—a small circular vestibule—glowed from the light of its many windows. It was a reading nook, or it would be when she'd finished. He would not follow her there. She was in shock, actually, that he'd followed her out of the blue room. Even her mother's little dog had not kept pace. At any moment, Abbott would intercept the earl and—

"Lady Willow, I beg you," Lord Cassin said behind her. "*Please wait.*"

His footsteps were faster now. He made the corner.

I will not marry you for any amount of money. The words resounded in her head, chasing her, mocking her, and before she knew what she intended, she spun around. "*What?*" she demanded.

He nearly collided with her. "Forgive me, I merely…it's just that I—"

"That you what?"

Mutely, he shook his head. He held out his hands as if to say, *There are no words.*

Yes, she wanted to shout, *you've made me bloody…cry!* And *Yes, there are no words!*

Pride bade her take a deep breath and school her expression into calm indifference. Mildly, she asked, "What more could possibly be said?"

"Well," he began, "I…I wasn't aware that your heart was quite so set on, er, me."

Finally, thank God, anger darted ahead of hurt. She welcomed the hot, pointed spike of it. "Don't flatter yourself, Cassin. My *heart* is set on leaving Surrey and moving to London. You were a means to an end. Someone else will do just as well."

"You're joking. You cannot mean to continue these… solicitations?"

She spun on her heel and resumed her march down the corridor. "I can, and I shall."

"I hope you know that you're bloody lucky that I was the one who got caught up in your little trap." He was following her. "I'm a gentleman, but the same cannot be said of nearly any other man you'd care to meet on the London docks. You invite every manner of pirate and charlatan to your door, or worse. It's a dangerous game you're playing—to offer tens of thousands of pounds to any reprobate who can read a placard in Redmond Street."

She stopped but did not turn. "*No one* was invited to my door. Not even you—particularly you. Applicants were meant to apply by letter. Everyone has followed the directive, except for you."

"Yes, except for me." He stepped in front of her. "And did you send me away? No, you proposed marriage. Can you conceive, Miss W. J. Hunnicut, of the assumptions I could make about your character, based on this circumstance alone?"

"You would malign *my* character when you've just interrogated me about my dreams and plans and the state of my health simply because you wanted to know? Or...or..." She threw up her hands. "God only knows why you did it. Who can guess your motives? I have been open and honest with you from the start, yet you question *my* character?"

His green eyes narrowed. "*You* are a woman who endeavors to construct her own marriage to a perfect stranger. Not to mention conceal the true nature of the union from her own family and then banish her new husband to the far corners of the globe. I hardly think a return visit for a few unanswered questions was too much to ask."

This would have been true, she conceded, if he had not been so unequivocal with his rejection of her. He hadn't come to weigh unanswered questions, oh no.

I will not marry you for any amount of money.

"Are you suggesting that you did not come here with the express purpose of rejecting the arrangement?"

"I…wanted to know more about you," he said, throwing his hands out.

They were both winded by the argument. She heard him suck in a breath and hold it. He glared down at her. She raised one eyebrow. His gaze slid from her eyes to her mouth.

"Know more—*why?*" she demanded. "If there's *no amount of money* that could compel you to marry me?"

"Because," he said, "I find you…you…"

She laughed bitterly. "If you are trying to sugarcoat your distaste for me, you are failing. If you are deliberately—"

"Distaste?" he cut in; now he was laughing. "Distaste is the opposite of my reaction to you, *W. J. Hunnicut*, and you may be certain that I'm not pleased about it."

She opened her mouth to retort, but nothing came out except, "What?" She took one small step back.

He closed up the step. "You are madder than I thought if you believe I find you the least bit distasteful. But the offer was not to admit that you are a beautiful woman, was it?" Another step. "The offer was to bloody *marry you*. In fact, if I understood correctly, any attraction I may feel would be an unwelcome waste of time, as your future groom is expected to leave the country. I may be desperate for money, but I'm not *that* desperate."

Willow glared at him. "Desperate, are you? Forgive my skepticism, considering you are an *earl*."

He did not answer, no great shock, and Willow shook her head and stepped around him, resuming her march toward the vestibule at the end of the corridor.

He swore and said, "Where are you *going?*"

"To work," she shot back. She strode into the vestibule, winding her way around strewn paintbrushes and draped furniture. *Go away, go away, go away,* she thought, even while she listened for his footsteps.

Distaste is the opposite of my reaction to you.

She heard him stop in the doorway behind her. After a beat, he said, *"Oh."*

For some reason entirely unknown, her stomach reacted with a traitorous little flip. He sounded as if he'd come upon an unexpected surprise. She stole a glance over her shoulder. He was looking around the octagonal little room with wide, curious eyes.

"What is it?" He made a circular twirl of one finger at the room.

"This is where I entertain my pirates and charlatans."

"Clever." He took one step inside. "A solarium?"

She shook her head. "There are a great many windows but not that many." She pointed to another doorway. "It's a retiring room for ballroom revelers. The ballroom connects through there."

"Your family hosts a great many balls?"

She shook her head. "I cannot remember the last time that Leland Park was host to a ball. Not since my father died, certainly. But this is why I'm doing the room over. It's such a unique, bright space; why should we not set it up for reading or taking tea?"

She couldn't recall anyone ever asking about her motivation for redesigning a room before, not even Sabine or Tessa.

He looked around the circle of windows, examining the half-completed room. The paint on the walls had dried to a sweet, warm blush color, almost indiscernible from white. She'd left the black-and-white floor tiles untouched, and the contrast was eye-blinkingly cheerful. Footmen had delivered the two pieces of furniture that Mr. Simms recovered in the Portuguese velvet. They were draped in sheets, and she yanked them off.

"Your mother gives you leave to...change everything 'round as you see fit?"

"My mother does not care what I do, as long as I do not trouble her. We've been all over this; in fact, we've been over everything. I don't understand why you continue asking. But perhaps I am to blame. I answer without thinking."

She lodged her shoulder against the chaise longue and began to scoot it across the floor. He came beside her to help, and together they slid the heavy piece toward the center of the room.

"My earldom is in Yorkshire," he said suddenly.

She stopped pushing and looked at him.

He stared down at the chaise. "My father has been dead for five years, and I am responsible for a mother and three sisters, a brother and his wife, and more than fifty tenant families. There is also a castle, Caldera. Sixteenth century."

"Oh," she said.

He shrugged. "You asked how I came to be so desperate." He nodded to the chaise, and she pointed to its designated spot in the center of the room.

When he pushed again, she asked, "If your home is in Yorkshire, then why are you in Surrey? Besides *not* to marry me?"

He chuckled. "To seek my fortune; what else?"

"Because, you...lost it?"

Another chuckle. "Close, unfortunately. My family and the estate are quite out of resources—because of me. And by resources, of course I mean money. I left home to earn it back—and then some, I hope."

"Out of money because you…spent it?"

He shook his head. "No, I closed the coal mines that formerly supported the estate."

"Oh," she said. Why had he told her this? Even worse, what did it matter? She was suddenly overwhelmed with the urge to ask him why.

After a moment, he volunteered, "The Caldera coal mines have served as a steady source of income for the estate and tenants for generations. They also kept my family in the castle, crumbling though it may be. But a series of accidents in recent years caused me to reconsider the value of the mines, compared to the safety of the miners. I found the mines sorely lacking; more tenants were dying every year. And so I ordered them sealed. I could see no other solution."

"I'm…I'm sorry," she said.

"We have all been sorry, but what choice did I have? Ten miners died in the collapse of one mine last year, and twenty-five miners and eight little boys drowned in another, flooded by the tide. The shafts were not stable; the ocean not predictable. I could not, in good conscience, continue to operate an endeavor that left so many families without fathers and sons." He looked up. "If I'm being honest, even without the accidents, I had always been leery of the dark, dangerous business of mining."

"Good for you," Willow said, "if you felt it was as unsafe as all that." She was captivated by the story, in spite of herself. She had fought so very hard to control her own future; she could not imagine managing the future of an estate full of tenants. And he seemed so thoughtful about it, so agonized. She felt a small prick in the area of her heart.

"Yes, well, good for me, bad for Caldera. Without the coal, we find ourselves largely without a reliable way to sustain the estate. The tenants have tried their hands at farming. I have drained the family coffers to help them, but Yorkshire is not like Surrey." He gestured to the verdant green outside the window. "It is cold and rocky and wet. Our sheep have been blighted with a virus that we cannot find our way around. Farming is not impossible, but at the moment it is not enough. I left home ten months ago to seek out my partners, who are old friends from school. I knew their shipping venture in London was earning some measure of success. They've asked me for years to join their partnership. I thought if we could work together, we might advance their moderate earnings into a legitimate windfall and that I might make enough money to sustain Caldera until we got the farming sorted out."

He glanced at her and shrugged. "And then we won the island and learned the potential of the bat sh—of the guano. I wrote to my family and implored them not to lose heart, that I'd discovered some means to sustain us. It would only take another year or two—"

"And they opposed you," guessed Willow.

He laughed. "You're of a negative point of view."

She shrugged. "My family has not, as a rule, been a great source of encouragement for my professional fulfillment."

More laughter. "For better or worse, my mother and sisters, my brother—they all consider me to be learned and wise and many other things that I am not. They expect me to know what is best. In reality"—he blew out a frustrated puff of air—"I am riddled with uncertainty. Their faith in me is unwavering." Another breath. "And misplaced."

Willow wanted to reassure him; the words were on the tip of her tongue, but she reminded herself that his feelings were not her responsibility. She cleared her throat and went to the newly covered chair and began to bump it across the tiles. "I cannot relate, I'm afraid. My family relies on me for nothing. But my friends? Now, they are a different story."

"My family believes in me," he said. "But our tenants are frustrated and impatient and critical. Mining is all they have ever known. They are dubious of farming. I understand, really I do, but I cannot make them see that mining, although profitable, is simply not safe. Meanwhile, I've a successful uncle—my father's brother—who sweeps in on occasion to suggest to the tenants that I am not of sound mind, that no sane landlord would seal perfectly productive mines. He would steal Caldera out from under me, given half the chance; reopen all the mines; take up as earl. If I cannot ease the general feeling of desperation soon, he may convince them, and I'll have mutiny on my hands."

"But you are earl," she insisted.

"Yes, but I am not a tyrant. What if they charge the castle with pitchforks and torches? What then? It was never my goal to bend them to my will."

Willow chuckled and shook her head.

"Perhaps it won't be as bad as all that," he said, "but can you see my dilemma? I may be forced to choose between what I feel is best and what the tenant families truly want. If I cannot peacefully enforce the mine closures, I may well lose Caldera to my uncle. He would like nothing more. I'm convinced the mines are not safe, but I am the only one, I'm afraid."

I believe the mines are unsafe. The thought emerged fully formed in Willow's brain, but she said nothing. They were veering dangerously close to having a real conversation. He had revealed his own struggles, just as she had. Most impossibly of all, *he was still here.*

She had abandoned the chair to listen, but now she resumed pushing. One of the legs caught on an uneven tile, and she put her shoulder to it and shoved. He came beside her and lifted it.

"Where?" he asked.

She pointed adjacent to the chaise. It was a heavy chair, with fat mahogany legs and a sculptural frame. He set it down as if it weighed nothing. She adjusted the angle.

"Why put the chairs in the center of the room?" he asked.

"It matters less where the seating is placed and more how it is situated. Chairs should face each other to cultivate conversation. But, since you asked, the reason I've put them here is…"

She took a step back and pointed upward, directly above their heads. Cassin followed her gaze, leaning back to look at the ceiling.

And there it was, the centerpiece of the room. A domed ceiling, painted with an ornate mural in pinks, purples, and greens. Vines and tendrils of lush vegetation encroached on a sky of cerulean blue. Sumptuous blooms made up the lively border.

The earl blinked, took two steps back, and looked at it from a different spot. "It's beautiful," he said, straining his neck. "But how did it—"

"I commissioned it," Willow said proudly. "It was stained oak before, which was fine enough, I suppose, but unremarkable. I am of the belief that every room, no matter how small, should have one sort of dazzling element. I'd seen a domed mural ceiling in a design quarterly years ago, and I've always longed to recreate it. The sketch in the quarterly was of the night sky, but I intend this room for daytime use, so I conceived of the garden theme. After plastering over the old wood, I hired an artist to bring the mural to life."

She watched his face as he studied it. "Here," she said, patting the back of the chaise, "sit here and lean your head back. From this position, you can really appreciate it."

He did not hesitate, and her heart seized at his enthusiasm.

"I've never seen anything quite like it," he said.

He reclined on the chaise, lying down completely, and she cast a furtive glance at his broad chest and long legs, now sprawled conveniently for her to see. She had the unhelpful thought that he was not quite like anything she'd ever seen.

"Is that an…insect?" he asked.

She sat down on the edge of the chaise to gaze up. "Oh, but can you see it? The moth? I asked the artist to include several. They are not easy to spot."

"Where are the others?"

She leaned back and pointed. "There. Do you see the hydrangea? Look left from there."

And just like that, she reclined on the chaise beside him. They lay side by side, staring up at the ceiling. She could feel the warmth of his body from her temple to her ankle. If she scooted over, even just a little, she would bump up against him. Her skirts had fallen across his boot. The puffed sleeve of her dress brushed the shoulder of his coat.

By some miracle, she managed to point out features of the mural in a calm, even tone. Her hand did not tremble. Her brain formed cohesive statements about flowers and foliage and light. All the while, her heart pounded in her ears, and her stomach thrummed with an unspecified energy.

She paused for a beat, trying to remember what she'd just said, and she heard him suck in a breath to speak. Her heart stopped.

"Lady Willow," he began, "can I convince you to pull your advertisements from London?"

Can he what? She went very still.

"Seek out some other means of leaving Surrey and joining your aunt. Please. It is not my business, I know, but I cannot, in good conscience, *not* suggest it. Your endeavor is foolhardy at best and unsafe at worst."

There was no demand in his tone, no judgment. It was an entreaty.

Willow spoke to the mural above them. "If I did it only for myself," she said, "then perhaps. But my friends are my priority now. I cannot discuss their situations, as I've said, but they cannot go without me because our home will be with my aunt. I must find them husbands. I must find husbands for us all. So, the answer is no." She dropped her head to the side and looked at him. "I cannot stop searching for

some man." *Although God save me from another man like you.*
"Somewhere there is a candidate willing to trade his name for
my dowry."

She blinked at the closeness of his ear and cheek. She saw
the small lines at the corner of his eye, the thickness of his
lashes.

She wondered how old he might be. Older than she, but
not too very old. Five and thirty, perhaps? Like everything
else about him, his age seemed exactly perfectly right. Not
old enough to be infirm, but not so young that he was rash
or reckless.

After a moment's consideration, she said, "I understand
that you are a titled nobleman. People rely on you. My hope
is to find a suitable man who is not quite so esteemed, someone with fewer responsibilities. Of course you must reject any
arrangement that does not result in an appropriate countess.
Someone who can settle herself in your Yorkshire castle and
bear a passel of children—a male heir, first and foremost, if
possible. You are not a good candidate for my arrangement,
but someone with no castle or title will be."

There, she thought, *I've exonerated him. It was short-sighted
and selfish of me to hold his denial so close to heart.*

Lord Cassin made a huffing noise. "Actually, the burden is
not on me to provide an heir, not really. I've long thought my
brother and his wife shall do nicely at that."

Willow's heart stopped for half a beat. "You...you don't
care about getting an heir?"

He shrugged.

Just to be sure, she repeated, "Your *brother* will do nicely
at th—" Her throat grew so tight, so quickly, she felt like a

marionette whose puppeteer had pulled a string. She laid a hand over her mouth.

So the limits of her body made no difference at all.

He was at peace with not becoming a father, and yet...

He did not want her still.

CHAPTER NINE

It occurred to Cassin that he'd offended her again, and he struggled to make his brain focus on how or why or what.

His brain, such that it was, refused to cooperate. He'd ceased cerebral function in the same moment she had kicked her long legs, so beguilingly hidden in her lightening-purple skirts, onto the chaise and scooted her perfect bottom into the crook of the seat. All function save one had ground to a halt in that moment, while she had casually pointed out the features of the dome mural. Meanwhile, he was rapidly, willingly, losing his mind.

And now he was meant to discern offense? He already worked so bloody hard to keep his hands, his legs, his bloody shoulder, which bumped hers if he rolled *just so*, to himself.

He swallowed hard and tried to determine where he'd gone wrong. It was something about the statement with his brother. Had he been wrong to suggest that Felix and his new wife would, mostly likely, bear the heir apparent who would inherit Caldera? It was a true statement, if nothing else, which was consistent with all the other highly personal biographical information he'd felt compelled, for some reason, to tell her this day.

But truth was not always sensitive or kind, and now she was silent and detached. She'd placed her hand across her mouth—he had become acutely attuned to the location of her hands and her mouth—but what did it mean? Disbelief? Regret? But Felix and his new wife were not *her* relations. He had refused her offer of marriage, so it had nothing to do with her.

And yet…

And yet, he'd remained in her home, telling her the story of his life. Long, pitiful stories about dead miners while he lay beside her on a soft, wide piece of furniture that could have been designed for no other purpose than to ravish beautiful women.

He felt her shift beside him, and the urge to grasp her wrist and hold her in place was almost unbearable. Instead, he tried vainly to further explain. "As for a countess," he explained, "I've long said I might never marry, to be honest."

Silence. She shifted again. Cassin gritted his teeth, waiting a beat. The toe of his right boot fell to the side and nestled in the hem of her skirts.

After a moment, he said, "The thought of adding even one more person to provide for, even if she is my wife, is enough to turn me off marriage for the foreseeable future. If ever."

"And this is the reason you rejected my arrangement?" she asked softly.

"Well," he said, "it is one of several reasons."

"Of course the marriage I proposed," she said, "provided *for you*, not the other way around." Her voice was a little thick.

My God, was she *crying*?

He looked over. She stared at the mural on the ceiling. Her eyes were dry. Her profile was unmoving. This was a valid point. He wondered why her endless valid points continued to surprise him. She'd proven nothing if not cleverness, yet somehow he was never prepared.

He thought a moment and said, "So I'm meant to suffer the indignity of poverty *and*, if I marry you, have all my troubles magically solved because of a wedding?"

"Countless men," she said, "change their fortunes by taking rich brides."

"I did not leave Yorkshire to *marry* my way out of mean times. I intend to earn the money."

"And yet you deny your first viable investment." She sat up.

"Collecting your dowry is *not* an investment." He followed her up.

"It is £60,000 and complete freedom." She swung her legs to the floor.

"It is £60,000 and *a wife*," he said, "who, apparently, I would never see."

"You've just said that you don't want a wife."

"Yes, and you wish to become one tomorrow."

"No, I wish to *marry* tomorrow. Not be a wife."

He made a sound of frustration. "How, exactly, does that *happen*? That arrangement?"

She opened her mouth to say something but hesitated. "I…beg your pardon?" she asked.

"I'm curious," he said, rolling to his feet, "how a married woman goes about her life as if she is 'not a wife.'"

"I'll…I'll do as I please," she told him defensively. "I'll answer to no one. I'll be a bother and a burden to no one."

"Right, right, such isolation. That's not what I mean, and I think you know it."

Answer, he thought suddenly. *Explain it; explain yourself.* It was, perhaps, the morning's first moment of true clarity. To hell with his pride about the source of the money; to hell with his duties as earl. What he really wanted to know was *this*.

"You believe I know *what?*" she asked. "I don't understand."

He studied her face, full of pride and challenge, eyes flashing, auburn curls trembling as she shook her head in frustrated little shakes.

"You're an heiress, yes?" he asked slowly. "With a substantial dowry and an inheritance to boot?"

"Yes?"

"And if you were to marry *an earl*, for example"—he raised his brow—"you would be a countess."

"My mother is a countess, and I'm hardly impressed. I am not a title hunter, if that's what you mean."

"No, it's not. I *mean* that your place in society would then provide you with countless opportunities to socialize. In London. You would be invited to parties and dinners. Balls and theatre. The opera."

"Actually, I haven't—"

He spoke over her. "I've three sisters who talk of little else than London's social whirl. Believe me, you will. You're a beautiful woman, young and rich. There will be no end to the invitations. So, what then? Do you intend to arrive to these events entirely alone? The husband that you've banished to the far ends of the earth will not be there, obviously."

He watched her consider this.

"Allow me to answer for you. You very well may take up with a consort, of course. A companion. A…'special friend.'" He watched her as he added, "A lover."

Her hand flew to her throat. "I most certainly will not."

"Can you say what you will do? Honestly?"

"I believe I can," she said.

"And perhaps you can, but I can also say this. If you wish to know the real reason why I cannot marry you, it's because I'm not sure my pride could tolerate being made a cuckold. Take offense where you will, but it all comes down to this. I'm not sure I could bear having my wife dally around London while I am *paid* to stay anywhere else in the world and turn a blind eye."

Now her cheeks were red hot. "*What?*"

"I know very few men who could bear it, actually."

"But you have no intention of marrying me, so how—"

"You seem determined that someone will marry you. Don't tell me you have not thought of it."

"Well, I have not." She made an exasperated gesture. "Of course I would not entertain men. I shall be too busy in my aunt's studio and looking after my friends to bother with…*lovers.*"

He sighed wearily. "Lovers require very little bother, I'm afraid. It is one of the many convenient ways they differ from husbands."

"If you believe I wish to move to London to carry on with…with 'special friends,' then you do not know me at all."

"This is true, Willow," he said softly. "I don't know you. We've only just met, haven't we?"

"Yes, we've only just met, and yet somehow you've managed to extract highly personal details about my life and my health—but to what end, if your appraisal of me is *adulteress?*"

"I'm merely suggesting that the existence you envision as wife-who-is-no-wife is neither practical nor realistic."

"How lucky for you that we have no future together!" She marched around the chaise to meet him where he stood. "Even so, I feel compelled to make myself very clear. The reality of my...of my barrenness has always precluded me from the social company of men. It has shaped my vision of the future—*also* without any man. In fact, I have long said I would never marry, and it was only my frustration with leaving Surrey and the dire straits of my friends that prompted me to construct a union that would win me a few basic rights.

"That said," she went on, " I am a perfectly happy and fulfilled woman, even while I am unattached and unescorted. And certainly without"—she rolled her eyes—"lovers. And besides, if it was my goal to take up with a, er, 'special friend' when I leave Surrey—which it is not—what man would that be, hmmm?" She laughed a bitter little trill. "Men do not view me in this way."

Cassin drew breath to retort but stopped.

Men do not what?

He scowled. "Men do not view you in *what* way?"

"Surely you do not require me to explain all the ways that men do not view me. I am not the seductress you make me out to be; let us leave it at that. I've proven my point, I think. It is ungentlemanly to compel to me say more."

"Ungentlemanly?" His brain snagged on this word and seized it. "I'll show you ungentlemanly," he said as he reached for her.

She made the slightest little gasping sound before he descended on her mouth and kissed her.

CHAPTER TEN

Willow had never before been kissed. She had also never been alone in an empty room with a man or shared a reclining piece of furniture with anyone. Despite all this, *she'd known*. The moment before he'd kissed her, she had known he would do it.

How? Instinct? Suppressed yearning? She had seen the wild, unfocused look in his eyes, and his gaze darted repeatedly to her mouth.

And then she was hauled up against him, and he paused a fraction of a second, their breath mingling, eyes locking, and he brushed his mouth across her lips once, twice, and then he'd sealed them together.

As realizations went, knowing he would kiss her was not actionable as much as it was a great saver of time. It cut out debilitating shock and useless disbelief. The kiss was real. His arm was locked around her, he put a rough hand on her cheek. She watched his face until it was too close to see, and her hands went to his chest, receiving him, feeling the warm solidness beneath the wool of his coat. She heard herself make the smallest noise of anticipation, and he moaned.

The only real surprise had been how much she had wanted it. Well, she wanted—if not precisely *it* then something that eventually led to it. And after it began, "it" was definitely what she wanted.

When his mouth closed over hers, and she shut her eyes, the swirl of sensations affirmed everything she had suspected for two days. Yes, his body was muscled and rock hard; yes, he smelled masculine and woodsy and like *him*; and yes, she felt the kiss everywhere—her lips, the tips of her fingers, her knees.

And finally—yes, it felt like nothing she'd ever experienced. Kissing was soft and hard at the same time, wet but not too wet, a maelstrom of sensation but also a little like floating in the pond on a calm day.

"My God, Willow, forgive me," he said, breathing hard against her skin. "There is no excuse for it. I never behave like this, honestly."

He had rather pounced, she thought. But she'd been ready, so ready. Too ready? She couldn't say. Later, she would recreate every breathtaking moment in her mind and make some ruling, perhaps, about right or wrong. Then again, maybe she would not. Maybe she would simply enjoy the memory.

"Pull the advertisements from London," he breathed, pressing kisses along her jaw, her cheek, her eye.

"What?" she gasped, reaching for the return of his lips.

"The advertisement. Your appeal to strange men. The promise of money. You *must* stop." He seized her mouth.

This again? She kissed him back, trying to savor and think at the same time.

"It's foolhardy and reckless, and you put yourself in danger," he said on a breath between kisses.

He sounded so…agonized, she idly thought. *Was he—? Did he—?*

The flicker of an idea illuminated the haze in her brain, and she broke away from the kiss.

"Marry me," she said.

He was breathing hard. He stared down at her. "*Oh God.*"

"You repeatedly implore me to pull the advertisement. You've said you are desperate for the money."

"*I've said* I'm not that desperate."

"Aren't you?" She was breathing hard.

"*No,*" he said, but the conviction sounded forced. His hands loosened on her body.

She would not beg him; she wouldn't even ask him again, but she could not resist adding, "It's only pride that prevents you."

"Yes," he said, and his face took on a pained expression, "and thank God I have a scrap of it left." His arms slid away, and he took a step back. "In case you weren't aware, everything just became ten times more complicated." He touched a finger to his lips and turned away.

"It was always complicated."

He exhaled sharply and grabbed the back of his head with both hands. "What have I done?" he asked. He turned back to her and said. "I came here to tell you good-bye."

"Which you've done, several times."

"Yes, but I've not actually gone, have I?" He looked around, as if searching for something. "No, I have not. I've done the opposite—worse than the opposite." He glanced at her and began to pace. "Laugh if you will, but my actions, as inexcusable as they have been, are but a fraction of what most strange men will do if you carry on in this manner. You're...you're utterly unsupervised here." He walked to the first window and followed the curved line of paned glass, like a fish circling a bowl.

She turned to watch him. "That may well be, but I *want* no supervision." He opened his mouth to retort, but she cut him off. "And not for the freedom to cavort around London with lovers. Freedom to *work*. I don't require supervision. I'm not a child."

"Of this, I am well aware." He shot her a heated look, his gaze roaming from her body. Her belly flipped, and she felt an unaccustomed stab of desire. Willow blinked and raised her chin.

"I'm leaving," he announced, resuming his prowl, "and I won't be back. I believe we've said all available words on the matter." When he came to the glass-paned terrace door, he stopped and tested the knob. The door yawned open to the cool morning. He remained where he stood and slammed it shut.

She watched his struggle. He'd said no in so many different ways she'd lost count.

He went on, "Marrying a stranger for dowry money is utterly out of the question." He embarked on another lap of the room. He was a tiger in a cage.

Willow said, "Perhaps you should reconvene with your partners to gauge their current feeling on the matter."

"You've selective hearing," he said. "Or perhaps you think I'm coming 'round."

"What I think," she said, gathering her nerve, "is that you do not *not* like me."

He stopped walking. He was behind her now.

"Is that what you think?" he whispered.

She turned to watch him close the distance, two long strides. Willow did not fall back. Moth wings rioted in her belly.

"Yes," she whispered, looking up at him, "it is."

She saw conflict in his eyes, a struggle, and then he swept her to him again. "*That* is an understatement," he said and dropped his head.

Cassin could not keep his hands off this woman, and it made no bloody sense. He had never lacked self-control, not ever; it was one of his most steadfast qualities, along with making prudent choices and distrusting people he'd only known for one bloody day.

She was archly beautiful, of course; that was indisputable— and not beautiful in a way that suggested, "Oh, look, a pretty girl." She was beautiful in the way that stopped him dead and caused his eyes to blur, focus, and blur again, momentarily blotting out all thought. She was markedly, distinctly unlike anything he'd seen before. She was also clever and an irresistible balance of self-assured and uncertain. She thought very little of brokering her own businesslike marriage, but at the same time, she also doubted her own significant appeal to all of mankind.

Very significant. So significant, in fact, that the impulse *must touch* pounded in his head. Prudent choices and self-control suddenly mattered far less when he'd found himself lying supine beside her (yet absolutely *not touching her*, not even a little) on that damned piece of velvet furniture while she described pink petals and brush strokes and soft buds and verdant bloody creeping tendrils. The rasp of her raw, cracking voice dragged over his skin and snagged on parts that had never before been stirred by the sound of a woman's voice. On and on she spoke while he quietly fell apart. The damned mural had been his only salvation, and he stared straight up—stared unblinking until his eyes watered—because it kept him from gazing into the open earnestness of her face.

But now they were up, and he had watched every feature as she'd soberly informed him how displeasing and not tempting she was, how she was routinely viewed as distasteful by men, and he could not, in good conscience, *not* contradict her.

The more she'd proclaimed her lack of desirability, the more he'd found himself consumed with the need to prove her wrong. Her color had risen, her coiffure had drooped to her shoulders, her breath had quickened, and—God help him—everything about her expression and her words had said, *Prove me wrong.*

And so he had. Immediately, stridently, with actions rather than words. It killed two birds with one stone, illustrating his own decidedly male attraction to her in no uncertain terms, and finally, blessedly, sating his need to taste her. Just once. Before he left.

Except it hadn't. He hadn't been sated; instead, he had somehow been stoked, his desire multiplied—nay, it soared. The first kiss demanded the second. Her innocence awakened some previously unknown urge to possess. Their upright embrace felt insufficient, and the chaise behind them beckoned. More, more, *more*—he could barely recall the self-contained man he'd been when he'd arrived in Surrey, occupied with nothing more than making enough money to save his lands and family.

Thank God some ingrained, honor-bound restraint kept him from toppling down and taking her with him. Two passionate embraces would have to do; a final crescendo before he said good-bye, finally and forever.

But he could not seem to say good-bye. He kissed her mouth, he dragged his lips across her cheek and kissed her temple, he breathed the scent of her hair. Now her mouth again, and he dipped his head and kissed the crook of her neck. "You're taking down the advertisements," he growled when he grazed her ear.

Willow stiffened in his arms.

Cassin swore in his head. He had no right, of course, and (of course) she would not listen. She sucked in a breath and pulled back. Her resistance was an icy splash of water, but he was still loath to let her go. Letting go her go felt like giving up the one frivolous thing he'd allowed himself in years of prudence and planning. *Cannot I be permitted this one thing, just for a moment more?*

But then of course he did release her, and he took a painful step back. He forced his brain to churn back to functionality. He swallowed hard and ran a shaky hand through his hair.

She would be angry again, and perhaps that was best, although he could not, in that moment, reason why.

"I will not take down the advertisements," she said. "As I believe you well know. I could not have been more thorough about my reasons why."

Cassin gritted his teeth. This should not matter to him; this *could not* matter.

Why, then, did it seem like all that mattered?

"You will invite other men to come here?" he asked. "You will marry a strange man to get what you want?"

"I will get what I want," she corrected. "I will get my friends what they want. How it happens interests me less than that it actually occurs."

Cassin nodded grimly and looked around. One part of his brain, the rational and responsible part, bade him to bolt for the door, to simply flee. Run away like a coward. A responsible, self-preserving coward.

Another part, a part he rarely invoked and barely recognized, asked him, *What's the worst that could happen?*

And then, *If I refuse, what is the worst that could happen to her?*

He squinted out the windows into the hazy garden, wet and autumnal, resplendent in every dripping shade of orange, gold, and purple. Had he actually kissed her twice in a room that allowed unobstructed views from every direction, inside and out? He harrumphed. Was it any surprise he now considered the unthinkable?

He glanced at her. She'd crossed her hands over her chest. Her breathing came fast and labored. Her lips were swollen and red.

I did that, he thought, illogically, possessively. *Me.*

When he looked into her blue-green eyes, she raised an eyebrow. *Now*, he thought, *she will slap me*. God knew he deserved it. He held his breath. She sucked in a breath and…giggled.

He glared. "*Don't.*" He pointed to her, daring her to laugh again.

Another giggle. Something in Cassin's chest floated—the breath in his lungs? His heart?

He would've laughed, too, if he hadn't felt so much like howling. He'd come to Surrey for the financing to save his family, and instead, he had...he was...

Instead, his priorities were in such a bloody shambles he could barely recognize himself.

"We've crushed your pin," she said softly, gesturing to the cockade on his lapel.

He glared at the whorl of ribbon pinned to his jacket. "Yes," he said.

"I noticed it yesterday. It's striking, lovely, really. Is it significant?"

He pulled the crushed cockade from the wool of his jacket with stiff, jerky movements. "It is a cockade. Most noblemen from the north of England wear some version on their lapels or hats. It represents the white rose of Yorkshire. It is not beyond repair. My sisters will see to it if I send it home. I have others." He shoved the whorl of white ribbon into his pocket.

"It is important to you," she asked, "your home, your family?"

He took a deep breath. "More than I can say."

"Let me help you save them."

Let me save you from yourself, he thought, and suddenly a question formed in his brain: *What is one more person to save?*

In all honesty? When added to the scores of tenant miners who unwittingly would have buried themselves alive if he had not intervened?

What was one woman, who he also happened to find wildly attractive and who was trying to force £60,000 in his pocket?

In hindsight, the question was short-sighted and flimsy and barely thought through. But it was enough. It gave him an excuse to say yes. For once, he said *yes* to what he really, truly wanted at that one moment in time.

"So this is good-bye?" she asked. She touched a tentative hand to her lips. He nearly choked on a fresh wave of desire.

"I'll do it," he said. The words came out low and fast.

She took a step toward him. "*Stop.*"

"Do not challenge me, Willow," he said. "You have no idea how difficult it is to go against my own better judgment."

Her face lit up with a bright smile. She took another step toward him and then paused, uncertain. She slapped her hands over her face, as if she'd just opened a Christmas surprise. Her excitement was palpable; behind her hands, she made small noises of delight.

He wanted to go to her, wanted it more, perhaps, than he had wanted her all morning, but saying the words out loud froze him in a sort of *what-have-I-done* ramification shock. He needed to think, not launch himself at her. She embodied the opposite of thought. She was impulse.

Go, commanded the self-preserving voice in the back of his head. *You've said it; you've done the precise thing you came here *not* to do; now go. Go before…*

Simply, go.

He felt around behind him and grabbed the knob on the glass door. Not looking away from her, he shoved it open. The first fat, wet raindrops of a storm slapped him in the face, and he ducked his head and hurried down the steps. Stomping through the thick ivy of the garden, he cursed himself, his partners, the bloody island in the Caribbean, and every collapsing coal mine in Yorkshire.

By sheer force of will, he did not look back

CHAPTER ELEVEN

Willow stumbled from the vestibule into the long corridor beside the ballroom to discover Mr. Fisk standing sentry at the far end.

"Mr. Fisk," she said, dazedly stating the obvious.

Mr. Fisk betrayed nothing but the neutral expression of a seasoned servant. "I thought you might wish to know that your mother remains in the stables."

"Does she?" Willow asked. How reckless she had been to forget about her mother. "Oh, well, that is good news. The stables. I am lucky in this. Good sense and caution does not desert you when I...when it deserts me."

He bowed slightly and chuckled. "We'll get there, my lady, you'll see." He touched two fingers to his brow in mock salute and walked away.

We will, indeed, she thought, but Cassin's acceptance was too new to discuss. "Thank you," she called instead, watching him go. His loyalty was a gift she did not deserve, a loyalty he had shown for nearly as long as she could remember.

Alone again, Willow began to drift, walking the beautiful rooms of her home, trying to make sense of the torrent inside her mind. Up the stairs, down the corridors, through the common rooms and servants' passages, in and out of the kitchen. She'd designed these spaces, meticulously selecting every color, the angle of each chair, the texture of the fabrics. Today, she saw none of it. Today, the journey of her life took precedence over the backdrop.

And what an unexpected journey—Yorkshire, London, coal mines, Aunt Mary, Barbadoes, *guano* for God's sake…

She tried to make a guess—a wild, reaching guess—at the possibility that the Earl of Cassin actually meant what he'd said. Regardless, her life would never be the same. He had returned. He had listened. He had shared his story. And he had kissed her. Twice.

It was fruitless to deny or dither or deduce some dual meaning. Her experience with men was practically nonexistent, but she had seen the marked, hungry look in his eye. She'd felt the urgent sweep of his arm when he'd pulled her to him. Nothing about it had been sweet or suave or playful or any of the things that books or, God love her, Tessa led her to believe about kissing men. It had been urgent and fleeting, with an intensity reserved for precious things that had been long lost; for things that had been newly, impossibly found.

And in every way, Willow had concurred. *Yes*, she'd thought when he'd taken her up. *Yes*, as his hands roamed her body. In an instant, Willow had released her insecurities about motherhood and her body and the forced distance she imposed on men. It suddenly seemed to matter so very little;

it had no obvious relation to this moment at all, and she had simply allowed herself to let go.

But now what? What bearing did one kiss (well, two)— and now the acceptance of her offer, however under duress— have on her larger plan to leave Surrey? They shared a mutual attraction. Should she let it be and allow the impulse to go where it willed? Should she squirrel the memory away in her mind and cherish it forever? He may have said he would marry her, but he'd veritably gritted out the words with a terrible frown and then stormed away. If the proposal came to fruition (a significant *if*), would he kiss her again?

She had no idea. Drifting to the atrium, Willow frowned at the tapping rain on the skylight overhead. The usually bright room was cast in eerie dimness. Lavender clouds sailed overhead. A storm. Lovely. She could hardly report this progress to Tessa or Sabine if it rained all afternoon. The wet would also drive her mother from the stables to pass the day inside. She had no wish to entertain Lady Lytton's questions about Lord Cassin. (Or, to be more accurate, she had no wish to learn that her mother had already forgotten about Lord Cassin altogether.)

As if on cue, the countess's voice could be heard from the doorway, calling for assistance up the stairs in muddy skirts. Servants descended from every direction, and Willow slipped into the adjacent stairwell that led to the cellar. If her mother would go up, she would down.

Willow swiped a candelabra from an alcove, pulled the heavy cellar door, and clipped down, down, down to one of her favorite rooms in Leland Park. The only space untouched by her talents—the crumbling, neglected cellar bathing chamber. It was a red-and-orange tiled room (faded now to brown and mauve) that had not been used for generations. The already low ceiling sagged unevenly and dripped with condensation. Loose tiles were strewn with cobwebs, a byway for mice. There was a pervasive smell of algae and something else, something hollow and bone dry. Family history suggested that the bathing chamber had once been a marvel of luxury and modernization, but now it moldered in neglect. Naturally, the only room forbidden to her talents was the one that most called to her, and Willow made the journey down the small stairwell at least once a month to sketch and fantasize about how beautiful it could be. She also salvaged the floor for spare tile, chipping away foggy squares to polish and use elsewhere in mosaic projects or other handiwork.

The centerpiece of the chamber was a tiled bathing pool, ringed with a thick rim. In the center of the pool was a built-in chair, also tiled. As originally conceived, the bather could recline on the chair while taking the waters. None of it had seen water or bathers for decades, but Willow made a habit of stepping over the rim of the pool and lounging in the chair to think or daydream or, more commonly, avoid her mother. It was the one place she knew she would never be disturbed. Even Perry stayed away on account of the mice.

Willow sighed and settled into the chair now, grateful for the familiar solitude. When she leaned back and closed her eyes, she had the ridiculous thought that the last time she'd been in the cellar, she had never been kissed, and now she had. She frowned. The kisses, however lovely, were insignificant compared to the fact that, in the end, Cassin had said yes. She balanced the strange sensations of hope and throat-closing fear. He'd said yes, but then he'd gone; without another word, he'd gone. And there were so very many words yet to be said. If her mother was to be convinced, a wedding was to be planned. She'd need to pack up all the trappings of her existence in Surrey and prepare to relocate to London. The acceptance was an excellent sign, but it was only the first step.

Willow blinked up at the jumping candlelight on the low ceiling, allowing herself to slowly roll back the memory of the kiss, their discussion, the next kiss, and then the moment he said yes. She wondered what caused him to change his mind. He asked her repeatedly not to appeal to other men, and when she refused—

"Excuse me, my lady? Are you in the cauldron?" Perry's voice called down the stairwell. Perry always referred to the bathing chamber as "the cauldron."

"I am here, Perry. What is it?"

"Miss Tessa and Miss Sabine have both just come. Drove through the rain. Miss Tessa's brother brought them. They would see you, my lady."

Willow sat up. "Tessa and Sabine are here now?"

"Yes, my lady. They are speaking with your mother in the front hall."

Willow scrambled up and squinted at the door at the top of the stairs. "Listen carefully, Perry. I will receive Sabine and Tessa in the cellar…"

"Oh no, my lady, not the cauldr—"

"Perry, please," Willow cut in, "do listen. Send the girls down to me, but first remind Tessa that her brother wished to meet with my mother about the horse."

"Which horse is that, my lady?"

"It doesn't matter *which* horse," Willow said, "Tessa will know what to do. Her brother and the countess can discuss horses for hours. It will keep them occupied so I may speak freely with my friends."

"But all the way into the cauldron?" asked Perry tremulously. "I hope you won't be requiring tea. You know I won't sleep if I have to descend down into the depths of—"

"No, Perry, no tea. But you must tell us when the conversation between Tessa's brother and the countess has ended. In the meantime, send the girls down. And Perry, do hurry, please."

After two minutes of pacing, Willow heard whispers and the swishing of skirts on the stairwell. She stood at the base of the steps, extending the candelabra so they could see.

"Is it a good sign or bad—you hiding in the cellar?" called Tessa.

"You won't believe it, even after I tell you," Willow said. "Careful. Sabine, give Tessa a hand."

CHAPTER TWELVE

Two days later, Cassin scrawled out a note and paid a stable boy to deliver it to Leland Park.

28 October

Dear Lady Willow,

I should like to meet you to discuss our upcoming arrangement. And my two partners would like to become acquainted with your friends. I will call on you this afternoon to learn how best to proceed.

Sincerely,

Brent Caulder, the Earl of Cassin

CHAPTER THIRTEEN

Willow awaited Cassin's arrival in her empty workshop. She organized tools, folded fabric, and washed the well-worn brushes of her paint kit. She worked in quick, jerky motions, a speed and dash borne of anxiousness and nerves. When horses' hooves clattered on the long drive, her hands froze. She drew a deep, shaky breath, hung a mallet on a peg, and walked with forced casualness into the afternoon sun.

His horse was nearly to her when she stepped from the door to signal him. He reined in, a tall, broad-shouldered figure on a high-strung mount. He was at ease on the dancing horse, and she thought she could happily watch him spin and rear forever. But she feigned casualness and returned to her workshop, waiting for him to follow.

"Lady Willow?" he called softly, sticking his head through the open door. He'd removed his hat. His hair was wind-whipped.

She waved him inside, trying not to stare. The room fell in shadows as his height and breadth filled the doorway. The perfectly spacious workshop felt suddenly like a doll's house.

His greatcoat, so long it nearly dragged the floor, billowed around his boots. He bit the finger of his glove and tugged it off. Willow forced herself to look away.

"I thought we would convene in my workshop," she said. "Nothing we say will be overheard or interrupted here."

"You have a workshop." He pivoted in a circle, taking in the small, tidy room. She watched him, her heart pounding for his reaction. It seemed imperative, somehow, that he understand how very much her work meant to her. The workshop was a testament to this—shelves of well-worn design books, a long workbench bearing open boxes of distressed tools, a heap of dismantled furniture beneath the window. It was tangible and functional. Her love of design was not a hobby or fleeting diversion. Beyond her friends, her design work was her life.

He had not balked when she'd shared her dreams these last two days, not once. She'd lain awake, speculating about his seeming openness to her work. He may have opposed other aspects of the marriage arrangement, but he appeared perfectly comfortable with her professional ambitions. It was one of the reasons she wanted him so badly. One of the many reasons. Too many reasons.

She'd been alternately stunned and elated when his letter had arrived. She'd passed the time with the odd balance of dazed anticipation and determined task mastery. There was so much work to be done. If his partners, whoever they were, really did wish to meet Sabine and Tessa, she must prepare her friends for their interviews. If, by some miracle, the interviews went well, she must prepare herself to relocate all three of them to London, pulling her friends from quiet country homes and the only lives they'd ever known. After that, she would stage manage the misrepresentations and downright lies of six people, who would marry each other posthaste, in full view of loving (in the case of Tessa) and controlling (in the case of Sabine) family members.

These were the endeavors that should have stolen her breath, but no. Instead she'd lost stretches of time with reading and rereading Cassin's brief letter. Now she watched him read the spines of her books with quiet interest. He looked tired, she thought. No less beautiful, but drawn, with shoulders tight, a clenched jaw, and smudges beneath his eyes. His stare was flat—his entire manner was flat. Gone was the charged, sort of frustrated longing of their first two encounters. He had been so resistant to her in the vestibule, but it had been a lively resistance, tightly wound and begging to be challenged.

Not today. Today, he simply seemed defeated.

Before she could stop herself, Willow said, "Cassin, do not force yourself into this marriage agreement if you do not want it." Hope fell slowly, like a feather, to the pit of her stomach. It could not *not* be said.

He turned to lean his hip against the workbench and crossed his arms over his chest. "Oh," he began, "sometimes that's exactly what's called for—forcing one's self."

She made a sad little laugh. "Why? To what end?"

He shrugged. "To launch the guano expedition. To save my family and my castle. To be a loyal friend to my partners. And, it should be said, to deliver you into this life you so desperately want."

Another laugh. "But you do not even know me. I am hardly your responsibility."

"Oh, but you will be." He sighed. The grim determination on his tired face made her want to cry. He was resigned. He had resigned himself to her. It was worse than rejecting her.

"Willow," he said, his voice careful, "I must ask you: Have you thought about what will happen in two years, or five years, or twenty years from now…if you wish to marry someone else?" He put his hands on his hips and looked at the floor. "You are so very young."

I wish to be married to you in twenty years, she thought before she could stop. Tears stung the backs of her eyes.

"So very young," he repeated softly. "You've so many men yet to meet. Honorable men who may wish to make a life with you."

And here we go again, she thought. Her throat grew tight, and she balled her hands into fists. Anger twisted with disappointment in her brain. She was suddenly so very glad that she had devoted the last ten years to staying as far away from men as possible.

She thought of Tessa and the man who had deserted her in her condition. Willow could not compare Cassin's behavior to the behavior of *that* man, but she now had some small understanding of what it felt like to be rejected.

"You," she said, "are thinking of your *own* future and the marriage *you* may someday want. Which is well and good, my lord, but do not pin the reason on me."

"No. I am thinking about your notion of 'a wife who is not a wife at all.' Despite what you say about independence, I will be responsible for you."

"The dowry settlement, when you see it, will explain that my needs have been provided for without interfering with your personal expenses."

"Even so, our finances will be intertwined. Your care, your safety—this will all become my concern. This is what happens when people marry, Willow, even if we do live apart."

She crossed her arms over her chest. "It's pointless to discuss the financial aspects of this arrangement until you have read the marriage contract settlement. Is it gauche to come out and tell you that I am a very rich young woman? It seems rude, but I will do it if it helps. If my £60,000 dowry does not speak for itself, you'll soon see that I have income from both my father and my maternal grandmother. This money will provide everything I require, including a doctor if I become ill. And Mr. Fisk looks after my safety; he always has. I won't take anything from your voyage and guano mine; I promise. In fact, I am happy to loan you the money if it comes to that."

He made a strangled sound. "I shall try to manage on the £60,000, thank you very much. But one fact still remains. My larger concern. I've made no secret of it. I may be in dire straits, but I have my pride. I'll not have my non-wife 'wife' carrying on with…sponsors behind my back. Even if I am on the other side of the world."

She started to protest, but he held up a hand. "I am convinced that you believe this is not your path, but God willing, life is long, Willow. Who can say?"

"I can," she said. "I can say."

"What is *more* likely," he said, "is that you might encounter an honorable man—someone with no particular need for children—who wishes to take you as his wife. What if you wish to marry eventually, but you've bound yourself to me?"

"I won't," she said quickly—too quickly. She came off as impulsive, as if she hadn't truly considered his question, which wasn't true. He shook his head.

Willow said, "I have known for years—since I was a girl—that I would never marry. Truly, I had never thought of building any other life than single and unattached. It was only when I needed to get to London—when all three of us needed to go—that I considered marriage. And then, only if it could be constructed as another version of living life alone."

"But you may not always wish to be alone."

"And what about you?" she shot back. "Each of your questions may be asked of you also, my lord."

"My need to provide for my family and my estate is greater than any need to attach myself to a wife."

"Yes, well, I've a greater need, too, and that is to assign some purpose to my existence. Believe me when I say that a move to London, with the purpose of legitimate employment, in an actual studio, designing beautiful new homes will have *no effect* on my unwanted and nonexistent romantic pursuits. Quite the contrary. The only effect it will have is to strengthen the devotion to my craft. It cannot be said enough."

Cassin wondered if there was some acute malfunction with his brain and body. The mutinous attraction he felt each time he was within three feet of this woman could not be medically sound. Or sane. It should not persist and grow, and yet—

He wanted to respond *yes* to nearly everything she said—even if he disagreed with her. It was a new struggle, never before triggered by any female or any speech. But Lady Willow talked more than any woman he'd known, with good sense and vivid language, and that voice. That low, crackly, sex-conjuring voice that reminded him of the sleep-deprived rasp heard in the late hours of the night.

His sisters were chatty and accomplished, although their chatter veered dangerously close to the inane, and their accomplishments were limited mostly to the pianoforte or arranging flowers.

Cassin could not, in fact, remember any woman making quite as much sense as Lady Willow, despite the outrageousness of half of anything she said. She got to the heart of the matter, sharing only what was necessary to convince him or defend herself. She looked him directly in the eye. She did not fidget.

In the end, it mattered less what she said because his brain shut down, his body took over, and he was left to simply, happily, listen. All the while he fought the compulsion to—and this was the most alarming bit—reach out and touch her.

He held her gaze as long as he could, one skeptical eyebrow raised (he might have been losing his mind, but he did have his pride), but then he gave in to the inevitable and slid his gaze to her mouth. She noticed because her breath caught. For half a beat, their eyes locked. His heart was an accelerated thud in his ears and throat. And then, damn her, she swiped her wet pink tongue across her bottom lip.

"I've something I need to know," he heard himself say. His eyes fixed on the lip where her tongue had been. She swiped it again, and he swallowed hard. "As designed, will this 'arrangement' include making love as husband and wife?"

Now her tongue froze, a tiny pink triangle on her bottom lip. It disappeared into her mouth. "I beg your pardon?"

"Yesterday, we shared a kiss—two kisses. And, I should warn you, we're about to share another. Kissing is well and good—for now. But it begs the question, as your husband, will I take you to my bed?"

Cassin had come to Leland with two lists. One list contained the things he needed to know, and another list held the things he wanted to know. Dates for the supposed marriage, the location of her aunt's house in London, the name of her family's lawyer. At the very bottom of the second list, before *Will you bring a vehicle into the marriage?* and *Have you taken the smallpox vaccine?* was *this* question, the sex question, a topic he'd assumed they wouldn't have time to discuss.

Instead, he'd damn near led with it.

She licked her bottom lip again, presumably just for the cruelty of it, and said, "I...well, honestly..." She was suddenly less articulate, and damn if he did not find her discomposure just as alluring.

She went on, "We haven't...that is, I had not fully conceived of this as part of the arrangement. I thought I might gauge how...*necessary* the prospective husband seemed to feel about it after...after we'd become man and wife."

He squinted, trying to comprehend a world where the necessity for sex with her would be anything less than extreme. The struggle must have shown, because she laughed a little—a light, teasing sound—and she touched three fingers to her lips.

"Forgive me," she whispered, "I cannot believe we've circled back to this."

Cassin took a step closer. "Yes. And if you find that even the least bit remarkable, you're more naive than I think. Whether you conceived of it or not, the attraction between us is undeniable, Willow."

"I did not plan one way or the other," she said softly, her eyes growing huge. "How could I? I could not begin to conceive of a man like you."

Cassin's control snapped. He reached out, wrapped both hands around her waist, and pulled her to him.

She let out a little gasp.

"Conceive of it," he rasped. "And let me assure you"—he spoke low in her ear—"I will find it absolutely necessary." He gathered his strength and lifted her off the ground. He kicked the door to the workshop closed with the heel of his boot and strode the three steps to the workshop bench, where he plunked her down.

"Oh," she said, scrambling for a hold on his shoulders. And now they were eye to eye, nose to nose. His lips were inches from hers. Her laughter died, and the only sound was their mingled breathing, fast and shallow.

She surprised him by moving first, reaching beneath his coat, feeling her way around his body. She grabbed hold of his waistcoat, leveraging closer, and he sucked in a breath. His coat felt suddenly heavy and superfluous and bloody *in the way*, and he shrugged it off. He edged closer, nudging her legs right and left until his thighs hit the edge of the workbench ledge. The skirts of her dress were pulled taut across her lap, her knees on either side of his hips. All the while, her eyes never left his; she made breathy, intermittent noises—part shock, part excitement. He growled and came down fast, smothering her mouth with a kiss. She received him, meeting his lips, dropping her head. Her auburn curls brushed the backs of his hands. He scooped up a loose handful, tangling his fingers until he cradled her head in his palm.

She made a small, desperate sound and felt her way from his waist to his chest, sweeping her hands around his neck.

He moaned and kissed her harder, every muscle of his body pulled taut. Conscious thought was pitched into the air like a handful of leaves.

His hands left her hair and roamed her back, swooping low until he scooped her bottom and tucked her closer still. With no encouragement, she looped her feet around his thighs, and the new closeness was heaven.

When he broke the kiss to breathe, he dragged his face against her cheek, marking her with the roughness of his emerging beard and kissing his way down her neck. "Willow," he whispered once, twice.

"Cassin," she answered, kissing the top of his head, his ear. "Cassin, if we do this, how are we to remain detached and separate? Before I met you, a romantic entanglement never crossed my mind."

He captured her mouth again, and she kissed him back. He fought for lucidity and lost, dragging in a breath. He had the idle thought that talking took too much away from kissing. He took her bottom lip in his mouth and sucked. So bloody soft.

"If we...make love," she continued, pausing long enough to answer his next kiss, and his next, "will we not become emotionally involved? Will I not be your real wife?" He attacked her neck, and she dropped her head, moaning slightly. She added, "Your wife in earnest?"

"It needn't be so...so serious," he breathed, sweeping his thumbs up and down her sides, learning the perfect curve where her waist gave way to hip, her ribs gave way to breast.

"What do you mean?" she asked, stretching, raising her arms to give him more access.

Ah, she liked that, did she? He broadened his stance, still trying to get closer, swiping delicious circles from her hip to the ticklish spot beneath her arm.

"Cassin?" she said again, turning her face so her mouth was free.

He moaned, frustrated with the conflicting needs, to kiss her and to answer her at the same time. "We needn't become emotionally involved to be intimately, physically acquainted, Willow," he finally managed, speaking around nips to her ear.

He reached behind his hip for her foot, trying to tuck it more tightly around his thigh, but when he returned to her face, her lips were closed and hard and still. She'd gone still all over, in fact. The foot he'd just tucked closer, dropped from his leg and dangled from the workbench.

The change registered somewhere deep in the hibernating recesses of his brain, but his body did not hear. He buried his face in her neck, breathing her in, and said, "Can you not see how right this feels, sweetheart? We could enjoy the...*rightness*—and then walk away. Just as you conceived it, living our own lives. Our hearts need not engage."

And now she wasn't simply still; she was cold and stiff, rigid in his arms. He started, his brain scrambling to catch up.

He pulled back to look at her. "Are you—"

"Why am I surprised?" she said softly. Her arms fell from his neck. She leaned away, propping herself on her hands. He was given little choice but to step back. He gave his waistcoat a tug. He blinked at her. He stooped to pick up his coat.

He searched his brain for what, exactly, he'd just said to her. He couldn't remember the precise words.

But he could guess.

"Willow, I—" He wiped his mouth. "Your inexperience catches me off guard every time."

"I may be inexperienced, but I know enough about myself to assure you that I will grow attached if I consummate my marriage to a man—that is to say, if I consummate my marriage to you." She caught herself and stopped talking. She placed a hand lightly on her mouth. "This cannot catch you off guard, surely. I cannot agree to a physical relationship without an emotional bond." She glanced at him and then quickly away.

He reached out to hand her down, but she leapt of her own accord and then sidestepped him.

"Believe me," he heard himself say, "it can be done. Many, many people enjoy sexual congress with no...other commitment. Women and men alike. This is what I meant when I said that no wife of mine should carry on with paramours behind my back. It happens every day. Right or wrong."

"Just to be perfectly clear," she said, "you believe that a detached marriage should also amount to detached lovemaking?" She turned away. "We don't know each other at all," she said, a revelation. Her voice was soft. "If you believe this of me, you do not know me."

"I've said this from the beginning."

She did not respond, and he watched her float around the room. Reality and conscience began to weigh on him. This is not what he wanted. He was many selfish things, but he was not a coercer of virgins.

"Look, Willow, I was—"

"I cannot," she said, cutting him off. She shook her head. "I don't claim to know much of the passionate dealings of women and men, but I know myself. And I cannot trade intimacies with you and then walk away, feeling nothing. It's not what I intended for the arrangement; it will disrupt our rapport, and I…I would suffer." She glanced at him. "You may not know me, but I know myself. I am nothing if not self-preserving. To a fault, perhaps. It's why I never intended to marry in the first place. We approach the agreement with no expectation of intimacy, or we don't approach it at all. Strictly business. My dowry for the freedom of being your wife and leaving Surrey with my friends."

"Fine," he said. She was correct, of course. It was a pattern with her.

"It's settled, then," she said.

"Settled," he repeated, rasping the word out. It almost hurt to say it. But only a scoundrel would twist her innocent design in order to sate his own need. And anyway, she did not appear open to further discussion. She dropped the hairpins on the workbench and stared out the window. She would not look at him.

"Fine," he repeated. "I…I apologize for the kiss—er, kisses. I cannot…I cannot say what came over me." This was a lie; he knew exactly what had come over him. Another reason to agree to her terms. He was afraid of what had come over him.

Without warning, she spoke again. "I want to be absolutely sure we intend the same thing." She said the words with measured calm, staring out the workshop window. "Are you saying there is no prospect of a future between us? An authentic future? When you return to England?"

Cassin felt himself begin to sweat. He was not saying that, and he could not say that; likewise, he could not say the opposite. "An 'authentic future' was never discussed as part of the deal," he said.

"Neither was detached sex, but you brought it up, didn't you?" She spun around. "You'll have to forgive me. I am a decisive person; I always have been. And I want to be sure I understand. About what you want."

I want you, he thought, surprising himself. *Beneath me in my bed. Braced before me against the wall. On the floor before the fire.*

If he also meant "opposite me at dinner" or "walking beside me on the grounds of Caldera," he could not allow himself to dwell on these. How could he assume, when there was so much left to do? Barbadoes, guano, her life in Belgravia. It was impossible to say what exactly, precisely, their prospects might be in two years or five years or even next week.

"I am saying that I have no idea," he said. "We don't have an accurate idea of how long it will take to mine the guano. And any calamity may befall us while we do it. I may see and do things that will change me forever, make me unsuitable, or miserable, or…I don't know…one-legged."

She wrinkled her nose, and he said, "It happens."

He went on, "*You* may see and do things. You may despise London and move to France or Italy or the far side of the moon. Or you may adore London so much you never wish to be anywhere else. We cannot say." He paused and she looked down at her hands.

"And," he finished, "at the risk of overburdening you with my family obligations, the threat from my uncle becomes more pressing with each passing day. His letters reach me even here, in Surrey. He challenges my leadership and mocks my authority. My mother writes from Yorkshire that he turns up at Caldera, rallying the tenants to his side."

"I...I'm sorry," she said simply.

"Yes. How sorry we both are, but can you see why I dare not speculate about a future until I sort out my present obstacles? A lunatic uncle and starving tenants?"

She raised her head and nodded. Her eyes were bright.

Softly, he finished, "This is why I meant to dwell only in what we could enjoy right now. It was indulgent of me to consider it, but"—he blew out a puff of air—"you test the limits of my self-control."

She nodded again, more to herself this time, and turned away, gathering up a stack of fabric. Her face was suddenly detached and determined and closed.

"I've asked and you've answered," she said briskly. "I'm grateful for your honesty, truly. If nothing else, it allows us to move on. I've a list of logistical considerations that we must sort out in order to get a quick wedding underway as soon as possible."

She paused and looked at him, and their eyes locked. Could she really cast aside the heart-pounding torrent of the last twenty minutes with so little reaction? One minute she was straddling him on the workbench, and now they would sort out logistics?

He searched her eyes for anger or resentment.

She stared back levelly, her eyes flat. She blinked and smoothed the fabric in her hand. Swollen lips and wild hair were the only indication of their passion.

God, that hair, he thought, wanting urgently to reach out and sink his hands into it.

"How can we best acquaint your partners with my friends?" she asked. "I would be remiss if I did not pursue potential for them as well as for myself."

Cassin swiped a hand across his mouth. "Oh yes. The friends. By chance would these partners be called Miss Tessa St. Croix and Miss Sabine Noble?"

She straightened. "Yes, but how did you—"

"Stoker and Joseph have already sought them out."

"They've what?"

Cassin shrugged. "Not called on them, but they have…looked in on them, shall we say. From afar."

Her eyes went wide, and he looked away. "I apologize for their…er, assertiveness. I was as surprised as you by their speed. Perhaps I underestimated how eager they are to get the guano expedition underway. I…" He started again. "They have compelled me."

He paused now, considering this. *They have compelled me.* It was the newest reason in a long list of reasons he'd said yes to Willow's arrangement. Stoker and Joseph wanted so urgently for the guano plot to succeed. He came to the partnership with so little else, and £60,000 was significant.

"But I'd not even uttered their names," she said.

"It was not difficult to learn of your closest friends when we asked in town. It so happens that the villagers are more familiar with 'Lady Willow' than the never-before-known 'W. J. Hunnicut.' And how happy they've been to tell us about her two friends. My partners were intrigued, to say the least."

"But could they not wait until Sabine and Tessa and I were prepared? It was one thing for me to be caught off guard by your interview, but my friends deserve the advantage of fair warning."

"You have one day, I believe," he said, sliding on his gloves. "Stoker and Joseph would like to meet them right away."

Chapter Fourteen

Willow traveled to her wedding alone in a carriage, except for her maid, Perry, and Mr. Fisk. It felt oddly fitting, considering Willow's family's enduring lack of interest in her, and Perry's obsessive interest in her hair.

And then there was Mr. Fisk. Dear Mr. Fisk, whose relationship to Willow defied any label. And today he had ridden hard from London through rain and fog to reach her in time for the ceremony.

"*Mr. Fisk,*" Willow gushed when he poked his head into the parked carriage. Her tight clutch of nerves fell slack at the sight of him.

"Oh no, you mustn't, Mr. Fisk!" Perry gasped, throwing herself across Willow's perfectly appointed gown. "Just look at him, my lady! Wet and muddy, and he smells like a lathered horse."

Mr. Fisk made a face of mock surprise while cold rainwater dripped from the brim of his hat into a basket of the maid's provisions. Perry squealed and nudged it beneath the carriage seat with her shoe.

"Perry, stop," Willow admonished with a tsk. "It's not a real wedding, and we've waited days for Mr. Fisk's return. Climb in, Mr. Fisk, if you can bear your wet clothes an hour longer."

"'Tis a real wedding!" countered Perry, pressing her back against Willow, as if Mr. Fisk's presence threatened them both.

"I feared I would miss it for certain," said Mr. Fisk, "when the weather would not clear. But I dare not leave London until I'd answered every query on my list."

Mr. Fisk had gone to London to prepare for the move: taking into account what Willow could expect to buy and how she should best pack and provision. He surveyed the living quarters and discussed the household with her aunt. He had his own motives too—Willow was sure of it—and so be it. She had long appreciated his watchfulness and forethought. In the last week alone, he'd taken great pains to verify every claim the earl and his partners made about their ship and island, the mining of guano, and the potential of selling it to English farmers.

"You were too thorough, I'm sure," said Willow. "We do not deserve your diligence. Of course you shall ride with us."

Perry, who remained in a protective dive across Willow's lap, made a strangled noise of frustration.

Willow cringed and reached up to feel the braided affair that had taken on sculptural qualities on her head. "Don't be silly. Perry, you may inflict yourself on my hair with Mr. Fisk inside the carriage, the same as you would do if he was out. And I want him *in*." She gave the maid a gentle shove. "In you come, Mr. Fisk."

Mr. Fisk chuckled and climbed into the carriage. The smell of horse, and rainwater, and cold wind permeated the vehicle, and Perry set about lowering windows.

"Real or not," said Mr. Fisk, "I would not miss my lady's wedding." He winked again and tapped the roof of the carriage, signaling the coachman to drive on.

"Oh, 'tis a real wedding, Mr. Fisk," insisted Perry, turning from the windows and rummaging through her basket. She came up with a loose end of wine-colored ribbon and began to unspool it, length by length. "The church is real, the vicar is real, the vows will be real, and the groom is a handsome earl who is very real, I assure you."

With each new reality, Perry unfurled another length of ribbon into a tangle on the carriage seat.

"Yes, well, the *handsome earl* hasn't been seen for almost as many days as Mr. Fisk has been away, has he?"

Cassin had taken himself off to London not long after their conversation in her workshop. He'd sent a slapdash note—*I've business in London but will return in time for the wedding*—and then had not been heard from again. Since that time, Willow had vacillated between anger at herself for caring that he'd gone and anger at the earl for sprinting off. In the end, her feelings amounted to very little. Cassin had gone. It was but a small taste of the months and months he would be gone across the ocean. As far as she knew, it was a small taste of the rest of her life.

"'Course, I've seen the earl, my lady," said Mr. Fisk, blotting his wet whiskers with a handkerchief. "In London."

Willow's steadily beating heart stopped. "You saw Cassin?" Perry loomed close with the floppy end of a ribbon, and Willow waved her away. "But where? Not in Belgravia."

"Oh, precisely in Belgravia," said Mr. Fisk, looking not the least bit alarmed. It was Mr. Fisk's special talent never to appear alarmed. "Standing, he was, proud as you please, on the doorstep of your aunt and uncle's fine home, two days after I arrived. Your aunt invited him inside. Took tea, they did, and chatted for more than an hour."

"*Tea?*" Willow marveled, wincing as Perry knelt on the seat beside her and began to thread the purple ribbon through her elaborately braided hair. "But why?"

Mr. Fisk shrugged. "The earl seemed to want to make the acquaintance of your aunt and uncle. And have a look at the house. Asked questions about the nature of your work and what, exactly, you would be doing when you join their business."

The nature of my work? Willow thought, shaking her head back and forth in disbelief.

"Hold still, my lady," sang Perry.

"I was glad to hear the answers myself, to be honest," said Mr. Fisk, but Willow barely heard him. Cassin had gone snooping around her aunt's home and livelihood?

Willow had assumed that Cassin had gone to London to collect her dowry. The lawyers had finished haggling, and her mother's solicitor had called to Leland Park. Cassin would be expected to appear in person.

"It's not so improper," ventured Mr. Fisk, "for a husband to make certain his wife will be provided for when he is away."

"But he will not be my husband," said Willow, "not really—not in the way you suppose. And Aunt Mary is family to me, this is true, but she will also be my employer. I've told her by letter than Cassin and I had 'an arrangement' but that he would not be part of our lives. What impression is left when he turns up to pass judgment on her home and occupation? After she's already been so generous, taking me in—and my friends too?" She made the palm-up gesture of *why*. In her peripheral vision, she saw Perry's newly pinned ribbon quiver and toss, cascading from her head like a purple waterfall.

Willow snapped, "Absolutely not, Perry. I resemble a kite."

"But this is the way all the ladies will be wearing their hair in London." Perry rummaged in her basket again and produced a fashion plate.

"I don't care about all the ladies in London. Either cut the ribbons, or take them out." She gathered the loose ends in two hands and began to pull.

"No, you mustn't pull, my lady!" pleaded Perry, rummaging again. "I will cut them to your shoulders, but no shorter."

The carriage hit a rut in the road, and the three of them were jolted with a shout. The tangled end of the uncut ribbon flew from the seat and unraveled into flying burgundy tentacles. Perry dropped the scissors and they stuck, points down, into the floorboard of the carriage. The maid screamed, diving for the scissors, while Mr. Fisk held his hat out the window, shaking off more rainwater.

Willow closed her eyes, trying to imagine the conversation between her aunt and Cassin.

"It is natural to be riddled with a few troublesome nerves on your wedding day, my lady," said Mr. Fisk.

"I'm not nervous," said Willow, not opening her eyes. "I'm…I'm…losing control. He made no mention of a call to Belgravia. He barely told me he would leave Surrey."

But then she did open one eye and looked at Mr. Fisk over Perry's head. For once the maid was wisely silent, carefully trimming the ribbons. "Were you nervous, Mr. Fisk, on your wedding day?" she asked.

Mr. Fisk looked wistful. "Oh, not a bit, my lady. But I have it on good authority that Mrs. Fisk was eaten up with nerves." He winked, and Willow laughed. Mrs. Fisk had been a verbose, jovial woman who hadn't the slightest proclivity for nervousness.

"I am glad that you've made it back in time for the ceremony. Even if it isn't a real wedding."

Mr. Fisk looked at the passing parkland outside the window. "Oh, are we ever truly certain what is real and what is not?" He looked back at Willow. "You haven't forgotten what I said to you the day when you and I became such good friends, have you, my lady?"

Wordlessly, Willow shook her head—no, she hadn't forgotten.

She had been eight years old and finally permitted out of bed after months of battling the illness that nearly killed her. Although the infection had gone, the doctor's visits had not, and she'd just learned from a new doctor about the future limitations of her body.

Willow had passed a week thinking about the new term, *barren*, and what it would mean. She thought about why the doctor had been so very grave when he'd explained it and why her mother had refused to discuss it. On the seventh day out of bed, she had requested that a large, empty trunk be delivered to the nursery, where she studied her lessons and played.

Two footmen promptly complied, and Willow had carefully, tearfully begun to pack up her vast collection of beloved baby dolls and doll dresses, their small cradles and prams. Carefully, stoically, she laid their pliable bodies into the trunk, arranged their copious curls and braids, so similar to her own, and tried not to look at their pert faces and long-lashed, unblinking eyes.

Before she'd finished the task, her father's valet—cold, brittle Mr. Fisk—had strode down the corridor just outside the door. She had been mortified to be discovered by a servant in such a private moment, but when she saw that it was only Mr. Fisk—the most aloof and dismissive of Leland Park's staff—she had assumed he would not notice her and would carry on.

To her great horror, he had not carried on; instead, she'd heard his footsteps stop, pivot, and return to the nursery door. Willow had wiped her eyes and held her breath, praying that he would not address her.

"And what are your plans for this lot, my lady?" he had asked, his voice surprisingly gentle, from the doorway.

Willow had looked up, and he had smiled, perhaps his first ever smile for her. For some reason, Willow had found herself wanting to answer that smile.

"No plans, Mr. Fisk," she had said. "I'm packing them away. Perhaps Abbott can send them to another girl who might enjoy them."

"But *you* enjoy them, don't you, my lady? Why should you send them away?"

Willow had sat back on her heels and considered him. His voice was kinder than she had remembered. And certainly he showed more interest in her than anyone else in the household, her parents included. Finally she had said, "Oh, but perhaps you don't know. I've only just learned. The doctor says that I was so very sick that my body will never be able to make a baby. When I'm older. That part of me is broken. This is what the doctors say."

"Perhaps I did hear something about it," Mr. Fisk had said. He had paused then, and Willow remembered wanting desperately to hear what else he might say on the matter. He lingered a moment more, looking as if he could not decide whether he should come in or go out. Finally, he'd taken a step inside the nursery. "But I don't rightly see how your sickness has anything to do with these dollies," he had said.

"Well, I thought," she had said, "why should I play with dolls if I will not one day grow up to be a mother? Or to have a family of my own?"

"Because it is a jolly fun thing to do, isn't it?" Mr. Fisk had answered. "There is fun in make-believe, Lady Willow."

And Willow had said, "No, Mr. Fisk. There is not. Not to me. Make-believe for something that will not happen is no fun at all. And that is why I shall pack away these dolls and discover something else I might do. Instead of being a mother."

And then—Willow would never forget what came next— Mr. Fisk had not objected again. Instead, he'd said, "Very well, my lady. If that is what you wish. And I shall help you. I will even tell Abbott to send these to another young lady who might enjoy them, just as you have suggested.

"But," he had gone on, "I should like to tell you something in exchange. Will you listen to Mr. Fisk while I tell you this one very important, very grown-up thing?"

Willow had considered this and slowly nodded.

Mr. Fisk said, "Did you know that everyone has a job to do in this life?"

"You mean like you are a valet, and Cook is a cook, and father is a earl?"

"In a way," he had said. "But those are the jobs that I do, and Cook does, and even your father does to survive. I am talking about a grander, more important job. This is the job that you do to make some impression on the world, to make it better in a large or small way. Usually, this job has to do with the way you affect other people. Some people are mothers or fathers, and they make a difference in the lives of their children."

"But not me." Willow had sniffled.

"No, not you—nor me, my lady. I'm no longer a father, am I?" Willow had the vague recollection that Mr. Fisk's own young daughter had died when she was a child.

Slowly, Willow had shaken her head.

For a moment, Mr. Fisk had been quiet, and then he had said, "But what I mean is, some men are very wise teachers, and they make a difference in the lives of their students. And some women have the gift of healing, and they make a difference in the lives of sick people. Do you see?"

Willow had not been sure that she saw, but she had nodded.

"What I'm trying to say is that *some* people's jobs are very clear and very set from the beginning. They always know what they will be. But you? You, my lady, do not yet know, do you?"

"Well, I know I will not be a mother," Willow had said.

"Yes, this we know. But what we do *not* know is what other type of person you will become—or who you will meet or how you may help them or bring them joy, or comfort, or knowledge, or whatever you may do. It's not yet been decided, and that is a very exciting thing. Because instead of having your job already set out for you, *you* may pick."

"I may pick?" Willow had repeated, intrigued by the notion of a choice.

"Well, you may not pick Queen of England," he had said, "but you are a very clever little girl, kind and thoughtful, with a high spirit, and pretty as a sunrise. There are so many possibilities, you simply have to be ready to accept whatever your job may eventually be, and then work very hard to seize it. Can you do that for me, my lady? Can you watch and listen very carefully and accept that job that we do not yet know but that one day will be plainly seen?"

"Yes, Mr. Fisk," Willow had said, her imagination already taking flight. "Yes, I can watch and listen. I will pick my own job. That's exactly what I shall do, I think."

It was a conversation that Willow would never forget, and certainly she remembered it now, in the carriage to her wedding, to which Mr. Fisk, now an old man, had ridden through the rain to reach her in time.

"There are many possibilities," she recited roughly, her throat tight. "I simply have to be ready to accept them."

"Very true," chuckled Mr. Fisk. "And now off you go. We're nearly there. Get married to this earl, and see what might happen. You know I would never have been a party to this if I had not believed in a very great many possibilities."

CHAPTER FIFTEEN

Cassin returned to Surrey from London with a two-part plan: marry Lady Wilhelmina Hunnicut promptly, and keep away from her indefinitely. Or at the very least until they'd pulled the anchor of Stoker's brig and sailed safely away from her.

Cassin's sojourn to London proved nothing if not that the longer he remained in the same country, the more he would be tempted to seek her out—and not just to take her to bed, which he urgently wanted to do. He found himself wanting to learn if his proposition for unattached sex had turned her irrevocably against him. To compare her notion of the future to his and weigh the possibility of some compromise. To discover how willing she might be to eventually leave London for Yorkshire.

It was a conversation he hoped, eventually, to have (her body he also hoped eventually to have), but considering the threat of his uncle and the as-yet-unmined guano, his future was too uncertain to make any promise. There was no tangible future he could conjure for them at this point, and to discuss the unknown seemed disingenuous and unfair.

And so he had stayed away, counting the days until the wedding. When the day finally arrived, he steeled himself to be remote, detached, and businesslike to the bride.

But good Lord, what a bride.

She'd worn a deep-purple gown, almost black, and just a hint of plum. The dark silk was scattered here and there with tiny, wine-colored embellishment. Silk rosebuds? Embroidered berries? He tried and failed not to stare, his eyes drawn again and again to the little details clustered just above the swell of her breasts, at her delicate wrists, along the small, tight seam that circled her body just above her waist.

Her hair had been piled high in a profusion of elaborate braids and trimmed with wine-colored ribbon. The effect accentuated the bright, clear beauty of her face and the elegant curve or her neck. Even the perfection of her small ear, dabbled with freckles, bobbed with a pearl, was enhanced somehow by the drama of her hair. Still, Cassin passed the ceremony glowering at the high sculptural mass of it, making a study of exactly how he might dismantle the braids and ribbons if he were allowed to touch it.

Cassin's vague plan for detachment had been to allow himself to stare at her—for this he could not help—but to avoid engaging in real conversation with her. It was the verbal sparring that pushed him over the edge, after all; the debates and teasing and her dazzling cleverness.

Despite the distance of fifty miles, his time in London had only compounded his preoccupation with her, and he'd lain awake at night, burning to return to her. Now that he was near her, seeing her as his bride, working together to perpetrate this…whatever it was…this mutually beneficial collaboration, his desire raged nearly beyond his control.

In the end, it wasn't the wedding *day* as much as after the wedding, the hours between when he married her and when he could steal himself away again. Brevity, remoteness, and formality had been his very loose plan. And for a time, it worked, as long as they were surrounded by clergymen and Lytton relations and, inexplicably, her mother's show ponies. But eventually, inevitably, bride and groom were forced to face each other with fewer and fewer interruptions. And then were entirely alone.

"And so we've done it," Cassin said lightly after the final guest had gone.

Willow answered with a small smile. "So we have."

It was only one o'clock in the afternoon. Her mother had excused herself to look in on a foaling mare. The relations who planned to remain overnight had retired to their rooms to rest. The servants descended on the strewn dining room like ants, clearing the table settings, flowers, and food with swift efficiency. At Caldera, his family tended to lounge around the drawing room after a party, enjoying the last of the wine and gossiping about the guests, but not at Leland Park. Instead, bride and groom stood in the deserted entryway, watching through the door as the last carriage rolled away.

The impulse to reach for her was so great that Cassin heard himself speak instead. "Lady Wilhelmina—" he began formally, feeling like an idiot. He'd referred to her simply as "Willow" since he'd agreed to marry her.

She laughed at him, a reaction he deserved, and softly shut the door. "You may address me as 'Countess,'" she said.

While he gaped at her, dazzled by her laugh, she turned and began to make her way down the corridor. Her mother's scrum of small dogs scuttled from surrounding rooms to follow at her feet.

For a long moment, he watched her. From the very first, watching her had been one of his favorite occupations. She was always engaged, mindful of even the smallest details of her surroundings; now she picked at the festive garland strung on the banister, touched the base of each ivory bust in a succession of candlelit nooks. A servant with a heaping tray dropped a linen napkin, and she stooped to collect it. His hand itched to reach out for her, to steady her by the waist, to linger there and lean in close enough to smell the warm cinnamon scent of her.

Cassin began to trail behind her, admiring her as she admired the beauty of her home.

Brevity, remoteness, and formality, he reminded himself. It was unfair to encourage an intimacy that he could not reciprocate—possibly for years.

She glanced over her shoulder. "It was nice of Tessa and Joseph to attend the wedding. It shouldn't matter, not really, but I missed my friend Sabine."

"Yes," Cassin agreed, cautiously following. "Besides your servants and your mother, Tessa and Joseph were the only guests with whom I was acquainted."

While he was in London, Cassin's partners, Joseph and Stoker, had both agreed to marry Willow's two friends. The combined income from the girls' three dowries was more than £100,000. This meant the partners had the money they required for the guano expedition and he could now comfortably provide for Caldera through winter.

"It's sweet, really, how well Joseph and Tessa get on," Willow was saying. "But I'm not surprised. She has always been acutely attuned to falling in love. A love match was at the forefront of her mind, even when I was writing the advertisement."

"Well, I was shocked. Joseph enjoys a pretty girl as much as the next man, and there have been many girls in his life, but he's had a very rigid stance on marriage. It was a goal, but a very distant one. Now he claims three weeks was all it took to fall madly in love."

Willow had wandered down the great hall to a sweeping stairwell that rose in a gentle curve to the next floor. Cassin followed five steps behind.

"They were inseparable at the wedding, weren't they?" Willow said. She reached the stairs and began to climb, whispering to the dogs. "Beaming. Mostly at each other."

"Yes, I saw that," he said. He paused at the bottom step and watched her. He called, "Joseph had been the most anxious to reach Barbadoes, and now he'll be the last to leave England."

"The wedding Tessa's parents are planning cannot be rushed. They've invited all of Surrey and half of London."

"Meanwhile, Stoker and your friend Sabine were married alone before a vicar. After just two days."

"Also not a surprise," said Willow. She paused at the top of the stairwell and looked at him. Slowly, warily, against his better judgment, he began to climb. *Brevity, remoteness, and formality.*

"I believe there was some real urgency there," he said, "considering the abuse of the uncle."

"Yes, and thank God," said Willow. "We knew Sir Dryden was hateful, but Sabine had concealed how violent her uncle had become."

"Apparently the man had her locked in a cupboard on the day Stoker called to meet her," said Cassin. "Well, we needn't worry; this will not happen again. Stoker rarely makes a fuss. When he is motivated to assert his displeasure, it is typically not with words. And it is not soon forgotten."

"I know Sabine was grateful, even if she asked to be taken to my aunt in London and left alone. There again, I am not surprised. She has been so cautious and solitary since her father died. Despite Mr. Stoker's assistance, she is distrustful of strangers."

"Hmmm," said Cassin. "Stoker himself is solitary soul. He is naturally suspicious of everyone, especially women. I would have been glad to see him at the wedding, but he detests social gatherings, and he would have been a foreboding presence, alarming old women and frightening children."

Cassin stopped climbing two steps from the top. He looked up to her. "Where are you going?"

She gestured down the corridor. "Perry has fallen behind on packing. I've no choice but to lend a hand. I am anxious to get underway as soon as possible."

Cassin looked down the corridor. He'd already followed her too deep into the house. Now he was upstairs, facing a corridor lined with what could only be family bedrooms.

Packing, he thought. Packing had the ring of monotony and labor. This was…endurable. And he'd learned quickly that any scenario including her maid, Perry, was as devoid of sexual tension as Christmas morning.

Willow and the dogs began down the corridor, and he took a deep breath and followed, passing a series of closed doors. *Brevity, remoteness, and formality*, he chanted again in his head, but the words had lost their meaning. He could think of little more than the nearness of her.

"Willow?" he called suddenly. His voice was too loud. He cleared his throat. "I plan to return to London tonight."

She froze, mid-step. Her shoulders tensed.

"You've said that your move to London was well in hand," he said. "That Mr. Fisk would drive the wagon with your trunks, and you would travel in the carriage your mother has given you. I took you at your word and planned to ride ahead tonight."

She did not respond.

"Will your mother find it odd that I don't stay the night?" he asked the back of her head.

Finally, she turned, searching his face, her wide blue-green eyes looking for something, perhaps, that she hadn't heard him say.

"My mother will be in the stable all night with the mare," she said, and then she turned away. There was a closed door behind her, and she pushed it open. Dogs filed into the room at her feet.

Cassin squinted into the brightness of the room beyond. It was airy and light, pale walls bathed in midday sun. White, so white.

"Congratulations, my lady," sang a cheerful voice from the floor. Perry knelt over a trunk. "*Oh, and your hair…it still looks so beautiful.*"

"Go to the kitchen and have a piece of cake, Perry," Willow said quietly. "The footmen will devour it, and there will be nothing left for you."

The maid's head popped up at this suggestion, and she scrambled to her feet. She bobbed a curtsy to Cassin as she darted out the door. Five dogs followed in her wake.

Cassin stared back at the room. A bedchamber. His wife's bedchamber.

His knees locked.

I should run, he thought.

I should follow the maid and leave for London now, just as I've said. She will be angry and disappointed but not heartbroken.

Instead, he took a step inside. And then another, and another, and another, until he was in the bright, white room, which was dominated by a bright, white bed.

He looked around as if in a daze. Every non-wooden surface was of the purist white or softest ivory. The bed—tall, wide, almost square, he'd never seen a bed like it—was a profusion of gauzy lace, fluttery canopy, and folds and flounces of heavily draped material. Cushions and coverlets abounded, white on ivory on white, velvet on linen on cotton. It was a like a soft platform designed for no other purpose than—

He swallowed hard and looked away. Fluffy white carpets stretched across the floor. Low-slung eruptions of fluff, barely distinguishable as chairs, reclined before the fire.

Taken together, it was an oasis of cool, beckoning, bedlike surfaces. A pasha's tent, bleached to colorless layers of softness. The image of Willow's bright auburn hair flashed in his brain, splayed out against all of that soft whiteness.

He ran a hand through his hair, continuing to walk inside, step after thoughtless step. He was hit by the distinctly cinnamon scent of her. His mouth began to water; he heard his heartbeat drum in his ears.

Willow, meanwhile, ignored him. She paced the floor in an energetic line, biting her fingertips to loosen her gloves. She yanked them off and tossed them on the back of a chair. She strode to a bureau and yanked the doors open wide. The shelves were bare except for a stack of folded yellow fabric, and she snatched it up, crossed to the open trunk, and deposited it carelessly inside. Each movement was quick and jerky. She did not look at him.

"You're cross," he said, but he thought, *Thank God. If she gave me even the slightest invitation…*

She returned to the bureau and yanked open a drawer. It was filled with what appeared to be silk stockings. She scooped up an armful and returned to the trunk.

"*Cross?*" she asked slowly, affecting an expression of exaggerated confusion. She went back to the bureau for another armful of silk. "Would I describe what I'm feeling as *cross*? No, I don't believe I would. What I am feeling is…weary. So incredibly weary." She was back at the bureau, yanking open another drawer.

"Because of the wedding?" he guessed.

"No. Not because of the wedding. I'm *cross* as you put it, because I am *always* the *last to know*," she said loudly, scooping up a limp tangle of something silky and pink and striding to the trunk.

"The last to know?" he repeated.

He was trying to follow the conversation—honestly, he was—but he was transfixed by the strident, energetic, almost incandescent vitality of her. Her cheeks were pink; her bosom rose and fell. Her sculptured coiffure was beginning to erode under the agitated jerking and stooping and flinging. First one auburn tendril, and then another. Burgundy ribbon slipped loose and slid to the floor. A lock of hair fell across her cheek, and she blew it away. Cassin licked his lips.

"Yes, the last to know," she said, gathering up another armful from a drawer. "I am the last to learn of what…what…*thing* will happen to me next. Even now—*especially* now. After I've taken such great pains to make my own way. Meanwhile, you and every other man I know may do as he pleases."

She fished an empty velvet bag from the tangle of silk in the trunk and hauled it to the mirrored vanity. Pulling open the drawer, she began to drop brushes, hairpins, combs, and loose ribbon into the bag.

"If you wish to go to London tonight," she said, "you shall do it. When you wished to go to London after the proposal, you went."

The vanity drawers were full, and she removed every article without discrimination, tossing them all into the bag. When she leaned to dig deeper in the drawer, he was treated to a generous view of her straining neckline.

"I sent you a note," he managed to say.

"Oh yes," she said, "the thoughtful and informative *one-line* note. Thank you so much." She dragged the velvet bag, now full, to the trunk and dropped it in. She marched to a small writing desk near the window and flung open the drawer.

"If you wish to call upon my aunt," she went on, "and interrogate her without my knowledge, *you may*."

"I could not leave the country without knowing you would be settled in suitable accommodation, Willow. Safe and provisioned for with the comforts to which you are accustomed here at Leland Park, and that is no small thing."

She pulled page after page of parchment from the desk drawer, scanned it, and then stacked it into one of two piles. "If you wish to sail Barbadoes and muck around in the bird droppings," she went on, "you may do *that*. My brother has the same freedom. He's gone to India, and we may not see him again for years. Sir Dryden may beat my friend Sabine until her eyes are black if he wishes."

"Careful, Willow, I'll not be put in the same lot as Sir Dryden."

She continued as if she hadn't heard. "Even Mr. Fisk comes and goes as he pleases. My late father, may God rest him, still lends his reputation and name to my mother. She relies on these to conduct the business of the stables, *and he is dead*."

She tossed the last of the parchment into the first stack and looked at him. "Meanwhile, I must ply, and wheedle, and wait and wait and wait, and pay you £60,000, and promise to take no lovers—ah, but wait! God only knows if *you and I* will ever be lovers. It's out of the realm of possibility to apply some supposition to this."

One of the ribbons in her hair flipped across her nose. She made a shrill noise of frustration and took it by the end and yanked. This set off an avalanche within her coiffure, capsizing the highest braids. Long, roped plaits tumbled down her back, molting pins as they fell. She squeezed her eyes and pulled the ribbon again, harder this time, letting out an angered cry.

"Willow, wait," he said, and he crossed to her. "Stop. Allow me."

He was beside her in three strides, gently tugging the ribbon from her frustrated grip, running his fingers along the silk until he'd located the last tenacious pin. Working swiftly, gently, he removed every other offending pin, massaging as he went. Braids were loosened and released. Heavy, creased locks of hair dropped down to her shoulders. Gently, he scratched her scalp.

Willow let out a soft, breathless sigh. Molten desire, which had hovered oppressively just outside Cassin's consciousness, hit him with throat-closing force. He was swimming in the scent of her, the heat of her, the closeness of her lips, just a breath away.

"I'm sorry, Willow," he rasped, his best answer under the circumstances. His brain function was growing dimmer and dimmer. And then, "Turn around."

By some miracle, she complied. He reached for the braids and pins in the back of her head.

"Yes, you are sorry," she said softly. "And I am sorry. And we're all so very sorry. And you are leaving Leland Park tonight—alone."

"I am trying to give you what you want," he said. He could barely hear his voice over the rush of blood in his ears. With hands that shook, he sifted through her hair for more pins. "I am trying to get you to London."

"Yes, I suppose you are, and I should not be selfish. If I wait long enough and accept whatever *last thing* anyone deigns to tell me, then I shall eventually get some part of what I want. Lucky me. I should not be bothered that you get what you want, always, in every instance, on your terms, and in your own time."

He heard himself laugh—a coarse, bitter sound. "Is that what you think?" he growled, leaning down to whisper the words into her ear. "That I have everything that I want?"

She sucked in a breath. The room was bright, and he could see the jumping pulse point in her pale, slender neck. It took every scrap of his weakening self-control not to drop a kiss on the spot, to feel the skin throb beneath his lips.

"If that's what you believe," he went on, his voice a rasp, "then you are not paying attention. Or are more innocent than I thought."

She listed a little, swaying toward him, and let out a little sound of desperation or surrender.

Cassin snapped. In one swift movement, he dropped his hands to her waist and spun her around to face him.

"Because what I want," he said, "what I *really, desperately* want has nothing to do with going to London or Barbadoes or the far side of the moon, and everything to do with picking you up, tossing you on that bed, and making you my wife in earnest."

Chapter Sixteen

Willow rarely, if ever, indulged in temper fits.

Fits of temper solved nothing; they were largely illogical, and honestly, who in her life would indulge her? Her parents didn't care, and Mr. Fisk cared so much that no temper was necessary.

But today? Today, she bumped up against some unforeseen limit and burst through.

Willow was a lifelong planner, a writer of lists, a packer of umbrellas on cloudy days, a tester of three shades of black paint before she committed to the perfect ebony. But how could she plan her life if she was only provided with the most pertinent details in the last moment?

If only Cassin had mentioned that he would not spend *even one night* at Leland Park after the wedding, she could have prepared some excuse for her mother and relatives or planned to leave at the same time.

It wasn't a catastrophic oversight, but it was the straw that broke the camel's back. And the more she raged, the angrier she became.

As a rule, her packing technique was orderly and thoughtful, but now her trunk was in shambles. It would have to be redone. Poor Perry. She'd veritably shouted at the maid to get her out.

And now…this.

"Are you ready to be my wife in every way?" Cassin breathed, looking at her through half-lidded eyes. "Is that why you've led me here?"

"What?" she rasped, breathless. "I've led you nowhere. You *followed* me."

"We were *having* a conversation," he said, "and you continued walking away." His mouth was so close she could feel his breath on her skin. Shivers rolled down her arms. She listed toward him, and he wrapped his large hands around her waist.

"No," she said carefully, fighting for lucidity, "a conversation would be something like, 'Now that we've had the ceremony, how should we manage these next few days?' And I would say, 'I cannot say for sure, Cassin. What do you think?' And you might have said, 'Let us weigh the—'"

He dropped his mouth to hers and kissed her.

Consciousness took flight, spiraling upward, while their bodies snapped together like magnets.

One minute she'd been having two sides of a hypothetical conversation, and the next he was kissing her, and *oh good lord, yes*…

How she had missed the all-consuming feel of his kiss, the strength of his body pressed against her, the steadiness of his large hands gripping her. Without hesitation, she looped her arms around his neck.

"In case you haven't noticed," he panted, "I am incapable of conversing with you, sweetheart, because every sensible, provoking thing you say makes me stupid with lust."

"And all this time, I thought you were just stu—"

He cut her off with a throaty laugh and another kiss. She laughed, too, laughed and kissed him, tangling her fingers into his hair.

"Your bedroom is like a harem enclave," he growled, pulling away to breathe.

"It's merely white…virginal," she countered, seeking his mouth.

He pulled away to laugh. "In no way is it virginal." He widened his stance to grab her by the bottom and rake her against him, descending on her mouth again.

The embrace was almost immediately familiar. The rare and precious contact they'd stolen before informed him of where his hands fit, of how to slide them down the curve of her waist until he reached exactly the right spot, of how to squeeze and grind her against him until she cried out in pleasure. She knew the angle at which to tilt her head, she knew that if she dropped her head back, he would move to her exposed neck, kissing and sucking and scraping her with the roughness of his beard.

Faintly, in the back of her mind, there was so much more to say. She had been earnestly angry about being the last to know. And she would hear more about his visit to Aunt Mary's. But this…*this kiss*…seemed to take urgent precedence over any words that could be effectively spoken, almost as if every non-kissing thing they'd managed that day had been a half effort, playacting, until the urgent business of what they really wanted finally collided them together.

After, she thought idly, holding his head to hers. *After the kiss, we will speak.*

"I've wanted you since the last time," he breathed, sweeping his hands up her body to cradle her face. "I wanted you every moment in your workshop. I thought I would expire from wanting you."

I'm expiring now, she thought, and he scooped her up by the bottom, higher this time, entirely off the ground. He bounced her once to slide his hands from her hips to her thighs, urging her legs around his hips.

She complied without thinking, laughing at how natural it felt, and he carried her, face-to-face, to the bed.

And now he dumped her backward into the fluffy white coverlet. The lace canopy swung into view above her, but only for a moment because he followed her down and fell on top of her.

She laughed again and reached for him, reveling in the hard, solid weight of him. She buried her fingers in his hair and kissed him as if he would sail for Barbadoes in the next five minutes—*which,* she thought idly, *he might do.* She whimpered at the thought and kissed him harder.

"This is madness," he mumbled, grazing his fingers beneath the shoulder of her gown, nudging the fabric down. Lower still, just beneath the top of the bodice, his fingers sliding to the neckline. She arched, willing him to feel lower, deeper. "*Yes,*" she said.

He groaned and followed his fingers with his mouth, kissing first her shoulder and then licking his way down to her breasts. Willow whimpered and raised her knees, wanting urgent closeness. He grabbed her leg through her skirt and hitched it higher on his hip and held it there, aligning their bodies in a way that caused Willow's eyes to fly open. She blinked at the canopy again, seeing nothing, and raised the other knee. Cassin laughed and nudged the neckline of her gown lower, setting her skin aflame with his whisker-bristled chin.

She was just about to wrap her legs around his waist, to hook her feet at the ankles and arch up, when they heard a scream from the doorway, followed by a chorus of barking.

The sound shattered the haze of pleasure and desire, and they froze.

Perry stood in the open doorway with her hands clasped over her eyes. Her mother's five dogs milled at her feet.

Cassin swore, breathing hard, and rested his forehead against her temple. She dropped her legs, and his hands slid away. He rolled off of her and lay beside her, panting at the canopy. Willow bit her lip and tried to steady her breath. Perry pivoted to run, but Willow called out to her. "Perry, wait!"

Cassin swore again, louder this time.

She sat up. "*Perry, wait.*"

The maid reappeared in the open doorway, her hands still clasped over her eyes. "Begging your pardon, my lady," she said.

Willow slid from the bed and smoothed the shoulder and neckline of her gown. "You may open your eyes, Perry. It was unthinkably rude of us to…forget ourselves with the door open. But we are recovered now." Cassin remained splayed across the bed with his arm over his eyes. She kicked his boot.

"But my lady," said Perry, walking into the room with her eyes still covered. "What about the silk negligee? From France? With the silver lace and matching slippers?"

Cassin groaned softly.

"No, no, it's the middle of the day, and the earl was just leaving, actually. You caught us in a good-bye kiss that happened to…tip over. I apologize."

Carefully, Perry dropped her hands from her eyes. "I told you it was a real wedding," she said.

"Never mind that," Willow said in a rush. "I've made a mess of the trunk, I'm afraid. We'll need a second one for these last things from my bedchamber. Will you ask Abbott to send a footman with another? There should be more in the attic."

Perry was staring down into the pile of possessions heaped into the open trunk, shaking her head. "Yes, my lady." She shooed the dogs into the corridor. "Should I close the door, my lady?"

"Yes," Willow said in the same moment that Cassin said, "No."

"Is that what this was?" Cassin asked, sitting up in the bed, dropping his head in his hands. "A good-bye kiss?" His body was so hard he was in physical pain. He gritted his teeth against the impulse to reach for her hand and pull her back to him.

"My attitude toward consummating the marriage has not changed, Cassin," she said. "I cope with things I cannot have by separating myself from them entirely."

"You consider *this*"—he gestured to the bed—"to be separating yourself?"

Willow blushed. "I…I was carried away, but I did not intend to…that is…" She cleared her throat. "Yes, it was a good-bye kiss. Ten minutes ago you were leaving Surrey within the hour. I'm *fond* of you, Cassin. Surely this is obvious to you."

Something in the area of his heart shifted, a barricade held together by responsibility and fear. He knew he should interject, to stop her from saying things that he was not ready to reciprocate, but he could not. His gaze remained locked on her face. He waited like a prisoner awaits news of his parole.

She shrugged. "Every time you kiss me I grow, er, *fonder*. So there you have it. I deny us the consummation not to be tyrannical or prudish but to protect myself. We will have a business relationship until…well, until we do not have one. Whether that is because we have no relationship at all or whether you acknowledge some fondness for me remains to be seen."

"Willow," he said, "I am so blindingly *fond* of you that I nearly took you on your girlhood bed with the bloody door open."

"This is not my girlhood bed."

"The bed is not the point," he ground out. "The point is that I can easily concede *fondness* for you, Willow, it's simply that…"

He ran a hand through his hair and shoved off the bed to pace. He would tell her about his uncle, he thought. It was no explanation, but it was…something.

"I had a visit from my uncle when I was in town." He stopped and stared at her. She stepped away from the trunk into the light of the window, and his body surged again to full possessive attention. He resumed pacing. "It is more important than ever that the guano expedition begin as soon as possible and succeed as spectacularly as possible."

"But what did your uncle want?" she asked.

"I've no wish to trouble you with him, but I cannot leave the country without giving you some awareness. There is a very small chance that he may seek you out, try to make your acquaintance. God knows what he might do."

"But surely he has no notion of me."

Cassin made a scoffing noise. "God forbid. Still, he managed to extract the news that I planned to marry and also that I would depart the country almost immediately afterward. His questions were endless. 'What of this fresh supply of money? How do you plan to provide for Caldera after her dowry runs out?' If he turns up, cut him immediately, Willow. Can you do that?"

She nodded, her turquoise eyes huge, and Cassin's heart clenched in the earnestness of that look. She had been correct, of course. She was always correct. She deserved to know what drove his decisions and how they affected her.

"His threats to Caldera persist," Cassin added. "In fact, they are mounting."

"He would endeavor to take the earldom from you?"

Cassin shrugged. "If he knew a way, I'm sure he would."

"So he wants…" The question trailed off.

"Coal. Always coal. At any cost, even the safety of the men who descend into the earth to pound it out. He seems to have accepted the fact that I will not open the existing mines, but now he hounds me to excavate newer, deeper mines on the land—deep-shaft mines, they are called."

"But Caldera and its mines, new or old, are not his to decide," she said.

"One would assume. But he seems to believe that I can be convinced by a chorus of his like-minded coal hounds in London. He's drawn up a proposal to form a joint-stock company to finance a deep-shaft mine on my land. He's gone so far as to rally six or seven investors and counting. As if his lot of coal-rich bourgeoisie could sway me."

She made a snorting noise, and he looked at her. "What?"

"You do see the irony?"

"That virtually anyone will invest in a death-trap coal mine, but the only person willing to invest in the guano was you?"

"Yes, that," she said softly. She gave a little shrug. He was overwhelmed with the urge to take her up and kiss her again. He forced himself to turn away.

"It's a wretched combination," he said, "of my uncle's boundless ambition and his refusal to take me seriously. I lie awake at night, worrying about his lust for Caldera. It's his boyhood home; he had already begun to salivate over it at the end of my father's life. So avaricious, despite the mines he already owns throughout all of bloody England. His greed burns brightest for Yorkshire. It tortures him that I've closed the mines."

"Can I help you deter him when I am in London? I should like to do more," Willow said.

He laughed again. "You've done so much. Your dowry may very well save the earldom from ruin. Looking back, I cannot believe I resisted you for so long." *I cannot believe I resisted you for even five minutes*, he thought. *I cannot believe I am resisting you now.*

She shrugged and glanced at the open door. "You were being responsible," she said, "when you resisted."

I'm so weary of being responsible, he thought.

Willow added, "That is why we are not consummating the marriage. We are too responsible."

Cassin laughed. "I am not that responsible." He raised an eyebrow.

She blushed more deeply and took a step closer, studying his face. It was a look he knew well, one he dreaded as much as he adored, because it gave him little choice but to stare heatedly back.

Mercy, please, God, he wanted to say. *Aquamarine eyes, auburn lashes, porcelain skin. I see it. I see it all, and what good does it, except to stop my heart?*

If he wanted to kiss her again, she would allow it—of this, he was certain. But where would one kiss lead? He was not in a position to make promises, and she would accept nothing less. And rightly so. Never did he think her unreasonable; simply that she was not what he had planned for this moment in time.

He sighed and turned away, clearing his throat. "I have prepared a dossier for you, Willow, and I have left it in the care of your aunt and uncle in London. Please look it over when you've reached Belgravia. It lists the names of my solicitors and banker, my mother and brother and sisters and their direction at Caldera. They know of you and are curious, naturally. I would not put it beyond my mother to write you and venture some introduction—that is, through the post. You may decide if you care to reply. But be careful; she can be an aggressive correspondent."

He glanced at her. It was a huge confidence, giving her leave to write his mother, but he trusted her to be contained, and respectful, and to restrict language to well within the bounds of their current agreement.

"The papers in London also include the details of where I will be and how to reach me by post in the Caribbean. The Royal Mail delivers twice a week on the island of Barbadoes— although we can expect five weeks from when you post any letter for it to reach us."

He forced himself to stop just shy of asking her to write to him. Her face was unreadable, and he could only imagine that his own expression held something akin to tired misery. He was so very tired, exhausted from mustering inhuman self-control and miserable from wanting her.

He finished, "I've explained these details to your aunt and uncle as well. London is so very different from Surrey, but they will help you make your way. I would not have abandoned you to them if they had not convinced me of this."

She nodded once, raising her eyebrows, another unreadable gesture. It occurred to him that she now suffered through yet another moment of being the last to know.

"This is a lot of information in a short amount of time, I am aware," he said. "I thought a dossier would be the most succinct way, considering my rushed departure. I…I hope you can allow for all of it."

"I don't see how I have a choice," she said.

He sighed. "I see your point about being apprised of things at the last minute, Willow. But honestly, I'm only discovering how to manage our very odd relationship myself. It's not that I—" He paused, searching for the correct word. "It has never been my intent to subjugate you. On top of everything else."

She nodded again. "There is a very great distance between leaving me to my own independence and subjugating me, Cassin. This was the vast territory I wished to explore."

Cassin dropped his head back and stared at the ceiling. She spoke of their potential future. A future for which he could promise exactly nothing.

Willow spoke again. "It is not my nature to leave something undefined; I've said this before. But that is the very essence of our relationship, isn't it? *Undefined.* Not quite business, as I designed it, but also not intimate—not fully. You have shared your reasons for withholding anything more, even if I was forced to wait until we part ways to hear them. They are valid reasons, I grant you. We are at an impasse. I'm not sure what more can be said."

If Cassin was meant to articulate this more-ness, he could not. She was five seconds from showing him the bloody door. He could sense it. He'd be forced from this heavenly room, from her bewitching presence, from the passion that had, just moments ago, blazed. Of course he could not speak. He could barely breathe.

She dropped the gloves into the trunk and walked to the door. "Good-bye, Cassin. And good luck. I will make some excuse to my mother and her guests about why you have gone."

She stepped into the corridor and gestured that he should walk out. Her blue-green eyes were bright with unshed tears, but the set of her jaw left no question.

Cassin swallowed hard, rolled his shoulders, and left the room. "Good-bye, Willow," he said, breathing in the scent of cinnamon.

Chapter Seventeen

25 December 1830
No. 43 Wilton Crescent
Belgrave Square
London, England

Dear Cassin,

I write you on the evening of Christmas, sitting alone in the attic studio of my aunt's home in Wilton Crescent. Just a few lines I hope, after which I'll pen notes to my mother and brother.

Happy Christmas, my lord. Our hasty farewell has weighed heavily on my mind, but it has taken me these many weeks to muster the wherewithal to put pen to paper. What better time than Christmas?

I struggle to imagine Christmas morning on a tropical island, but with any luck you have arrived safely and are settled in. I hope you have managed to take a special meal and have a song or two to celebrate. This letter will not reach you until late January or possibly February, but *please know even now that my thoughts were with you on Christmas, et cetera, et cetera.*

After a day of window-rattling winds and intermittent sun, the night has gone cold and still. I can scarcely make out the trees and pathways of Belgrave Square. My aunt has arranged a workbench for me in their studio, and I drift to the window so frequently they tease me about laziness. They do not know the spectacular view of trees and parkland to which I was accustomed in Leland Park, nor how intrigued I am, even after weeks in London, at the rush of city life on the street below.

How correct you were to warn of the differences between country and city life. London is as different from Surrey as night is from day. But I am quite taken with the pace and crowds of it all, dazzled, you might say. From the crush of street stalls to the museum exhibits and theatres, I devour each new sight and experience.

Tessa and Mr. Chance are married now (more on that in the postscript), and his paddle steamer should be nearly to you. Now that I have both friends with me, exploring the city at my side, I can but marvel that my dream actually came true. Never fear about homesickness, there's none of that here. Well, with the exception of dear Perry. I have suggested that she may eventually view the noise and the commotion as vital and progressive, but I cannot say that she values vitality or progress as I do. She is a country girl at heart. I would not say that I prefer the city to the country, but I do so relish the discovery of a way of life so different from what I have known.

And of course the access to craftsmen and artisans in London is far greater than ever I had dreamed. My aunt has included me in calls to what surely must be every workshop and studio in the city, and I am astounded at the variety and splendor of the fabrics and carpets, the art and stonework. And the international markets! Spilling over with furniture and decorative pieces from around the world. I feel we shall never see it all, and new ships arrive daily with more treasures. I can scarcely sleep at night for the colors and textures spinning in my head. I cannot take down notes or sketch quickly enough to record the onslaught of inspiration. Best of all, the new Belgravia homes in which we might place these treasures are blank canvases just waiting to be adorned.

But I will not bore you with my wide-eyed wonderment. London is all that I dreamed it would be and more, rest assured. I doubt I shall ever find the words to thank you for making it possible for me. (My mother has discovered my intention to live and work with her estranged sister, by the way. Her reaction was one letter, very nasty in tone, declaring that she would not visit. Precisely what I had expected, and so be it.)

But since I am speaking of letters, I should let you know that I have received a missive from your mother and sisters, as you suggested I might. I've taken you at your word that I may respond in kind, and we have begun a lively correspondence. Never fear; I go to great pains to be vague about our relationship and gloss over their requests that I might visit Yorkshire.

Your mother's letters demonstrate her very great affection for you, Cassin. I was careless in this regard, I fear, but my eyes are opened now. Our convenient marriage was a betrayal, in a way, of a hopeful and loving family. Even now, their confusion and disappointment is so clear. It is but another reason you struggled with the decision. For this, I am sorry.

I can also add that, in the days and weeks since our wedding, I have come to regret the awkward and terse manner in which we parted ways. I could say more—my defenses and assumptions, et cetera, et cetera—but the truth is I evicted you from my bedroom… and when your intention had been only to review plans and logistical matters. Of course these were topics to which I had endeavored to restrict us all along. Here, too, I am sorry.

I hope you and Mr. Stoker have found the mining to be speedy and effective (and tolerable). Certainly I would welcome a letter from you, if you have the opportunity to write us. As for this letter, please forgive the length and, if it offends you—the personal tone. I am sentimental, perhaps, on this day. Happy Christmas, Cassin.

  Sincerely,

  Lady Willow Caulder, the Countess of Cassin

PS: By the time you read this, likely you will have learned of the circumstances of my friend Tessa St. Croix—now Tessa Chance. Yes, 'tis true; Tessa is expecting a child. I am not at leave to discuss the father of the baby, but you may be assured that he is no longer a consideration and has not been for many months. We do not expect to hear from him ever again, and good riddance. We will welcome a new baby here sometime in the month of May.

I find myself quite without words to explain or justify Tessa's condition to you, and it is my great hope that you can view both her secret and Mr. Chance's revised future with some measure of compassion.

Although loyalty to Tessa prevented me from discussing her condition with you at the time (Surrey, etc.), please believe me when I tell you that I was unaware that Tessa had not revealed her condition to Mr. Chance. Sabine and I were led to believe that he knew all along. Only after their wedding did Tessa tell us that she told him about the baby for the first time that very night.

The deceit was unforgivable, although it appears that Mr. Chance has, God bless him, managed some manner of forgiveness. At the very least, he did not annul the marriage or flee England in a rage. Nor did he betray her to her family. The wild sort of amorousness of their courtship has now ceased, obviously, and I cannot speak to their plans for future contact. It has been very difficult to coax the details from Tessa all along, but she is heartbroken, that much is clear.

I cannot think of more to say on the matter, except that we all had our own reasons for leaving Surrey, and Tessa's was perhaps the most pressing, followed by Sabine's. My reasons seem insignificant and almost selfish when compared to the dire circumstances of my friends, and yet... And yet I have realized my dream just the same, and oh how I relish it. It was always a reckless and outrageous scheme, Cassin, but please know that I never meant to go so far as to keep secrets from you. I will conclude here by simply saying that we are all so very grateful.

***

Monday, 1 January 1831
Bridgetown, Barbadoes
British West Indies

Dear Willow,

I write to inform you that Stoker and I have arrived safely in Bridgeport, Barbadoes, a fortnight ago.

We set to work almost immediately, taking rooms for ourselves and letting a small warehouse for the provisions we brought from home.

Next, we set about hiring able-bodied men to work as our mining crew.

The work, such that it is, will be hot, grueling, and monotonous. Wretched, in other words. But we intend to pay wages high enough to interest anyone willing to take on the work. Recruiting solid men who will work hard, keep out of fights, and won't steal us blind is worth our time, we believe. Our goal is forty laborers, a cook and medic, and perhaps a few interpreters. (Between Stoker and me, we can manage French and some German. When Joseph arrives, he will add his fluency in Italian and Spanish. However, we'll need a translator for Dutch, the West African dialect of Bajan, Vietnamese, Chinese, and Arabic, just to name a few.)

Because our island can only be reached by a half-day's sail from Barbadoes, any man we hire must also commit to make camp at the mining site for seven days at a stretch. After seven days of work, we will return the men for a two-day furlough while we replenish supplies. The island (which we have dubbed "New Pixham," in honor of its patronesses) could not be more primitive.

But I risk boring you with tedious detail. A shorter version of this explanation is this: The mining has not yet begun, but we are otherwise underway.

Although the work is arduous, and life in the tropics is far removed from cool, predictable England, we remain optimistic about the venture and eager for what progress each new day will bring. We anxiously await the arrival of Joseph, however useless he may be, considering what is surely malaise-inducing lovesickness. He was very caught up, he and Miss St. Croix, when we left, and marrying her could have only accelerated this condition. I regret that I could not attend what was surely the wedding of the century. I am still in disbelief that their pairing became a love match.

It feels imprudent to add the next bit, but I shall do it anyway. How often I think of you, Willow. I hope you are safe in London, that you are happy and well. I hope the city is all you dreamed it would be. I hope that you enjoyed a warm and spirited Christmas with your aunt and friends, and that you were not lonesome for Surrey or…

I hope that you are never lonesome for anything.

And finally, I hope that if (and when) your thoughts turn to me, they are not bitter or regretful. The more I think of the weeks before we set sail, the more I see my own selfishness. For this, I am deeply sorry.

Certainly I would welcome some brief word about how you are getting on…if you have the time.

> *Sincerely,*
> *Brent Caulder, the Earl of Cassin*

***

15 January 1831
No. 43 Wilton Crescent
Belgrave Square
London, England

Dear Cassin,

Pray forgive a second letter so quickly on the heels of the last, but I felt it would be prudent to inform you that your uncle, Mr. Archibald Caulder, has called on me in my aunt's home. Three times, in fact. Do not be alarmed; we have managed him, but the letters I receive from your mother suggest that he is badgering your family in Yorkshire as well. I could but write with this news.

The circumstances of his visit(s) were as follows: I was out of the house on the occasion of his first two calls (thank God), touring new construction with my aunt and uncle. He left his card with staff. His third call, however, caught us unprepared. He discerned from a careless butler that I was at home and demanded to be seen. I saw no way to get around receiving him.

Based on your own descriptions of Mr. Caulder, I believe I can say without offense that he is a wholly unpleasant person. His voice alone unsettled our otherwise quiet household; the length of his stories; the rap of his cane on my aunt's marble floor—jarring, all, and this says nothing of the tediousness of the topics he addressed.

He presented me with a belated wedding gift, which he insisted I unbox while he watched and over which I was clearly expected to gush. (A pair of ceramic ostriches with jewel-encrusted beaks; see sketch below; I could not resist.)

After we praised the ostriches at length, he embarked on a treatise about the great profitability of coal mining. It was a topic so randomly selected (and yet also so pointed directly at you) that I could but nod. Next he described what he had eaten for breakfast and luncheon in detail and then ticked off the names of his sons, their wives, their children, and homes.

Honestly, I could not discern a purpose for his visit other than to make my introduction (the stated reason) and otherwise appraise some potential in me (unstated). Potential in what, I cannot guess. He asked direct questions about my family, my life in London, you, your business in Barbadoes, your mother and brother and sisters, and what I knew of Caldera.

Never fear, I was as discreet as possible, walking the fine line between vagueness and ignorance. He left here with little if no new information other than the personal introduction to me and whatever his shrewd scrutiny of my aunt's drawing room may have provided.

I can only hope I have dealt with him correctly. I have instructed the staff to turn him away, should he ever call again, and Perry has cleverly fashioned the ceramic ostriches into small planters for two indoor ferns that she is cultivating. I am quite fond of them now, actually.

If you have further instructions regarding Mr. Caulder, please advise.

Oh, but Cassin? Please do not worry. Distressing you was not my purpose in writing. I am unharmed and unfazed. The meeting left me little more than annoyed, although I do take offense at his keen interest in your business matters and in Caldera.

In closing, I hope your progress is brisk and your health is well. Time and distance emboldens me, I suppose, and so I shall raise my "suggestion" that you write me to a "request" that you do so. Please send some word, if you have the opportunity. I hope that you are remembering all that you see and hear so that you may, assuming our reunion permits this sort of thing, relay it to me.

As for me, we continue to devour all that London has to offer. My aunt has promised to take us to Vauxhall Gardens before Tessa's confinement. We are counting the days.

>   Warmly,
>   Willow

* * *

Sunday, 30 January 1831
Island of New Pixham
via Bridgetown, Barbadoes
British West Indies

Dear Willow,

I am writing you from the dim interior of my rattling shanty tent on the wind-whipped isle of New Pixham. The persistent island gales, although far less noticeable in the baking heat of the day, make it nearly impossible to sustain candlelight, even with a glass lantern, but I persist.

We have only just returned from our furlough to Bridgetown (a weekly sailing that I have timed to the arrival of the mail packet from Falmouth), and beside me on my trunk is your letter dated Christmas Day.

I am gratified to learn that you are safe and contented. My visit with your aunt and uncle in November assured me that they would welcome you in every way.

Thank you for writing to my mother and sisters. Judging by the sheer number of letters I, myself, receive from Yorkshire, my mother must put pen to paper twice daily. Any correspondence diverted to London is a welcome respite.

As you noted, Christmas has come and gone, but I can relate that Stoker and I celebrated the holiday in high style, taking a full meal in an actual tavern. Quite a switch from our miserly practice of buying produce from market stalls and eating in the warehouse. We were surrounded at the tavern by inebriated sailors (inebriated sailors are our constant companions in the Caribbean). While we ate, the owner's pet iguanas, which are lizards larger and more prodigious than your mother's dogs, prowled the sandy floor at our feet.

Thank you for your willingness to receive letters from me. I shall endeavor to be less prolific than my mother, although no written description, long or short, can do justice to the challenges we face on New Pixham.

The island is small, measuring little more than a mile in every direction, an easy thirty-minute walk from one side to the other. Its topography, assuming it bears any distinctions beyond sandy flatness, is entirely obscured by the great, hardened heap of guano, which rises like a large bluff, two hundred feet into the sky.

In its current state, the bluff is as hard as rock, and the top is too steep to climb. This means it is also impossible to get at it with an ax. So our first orders of business have been to discover (1) how to ascend the bloody thing, (2) how to safely work at the top, and (3) how to remove the guano we chip away without losing half of it to the wind or the sea.

The first week we spent on the island was devoted to studying these problems and then ultimately constructing a network of scaffolding and chutes.

Now we dig terraces up the side of the bluff, working the full detachment of hired men including Joseph, Stoker, and me. The lot of us—forty-five in all—swing the axes from sunrise until sunset. (And yes, I see the irony of sealing mines on my own Yorkshire estate only to become a miner myself halfway across the world, perhaps the first ever nobleman to have done so.)

Certainly I am the only earl to mine bird excrement. Doubtful this is an irony my tenants would enjoy, nor should they, but when I write to Caldera, I have new insights and sympathies that my brother might pass along to them. If nothing else, I hope they can see that I am trying. I did not seal the mines and leave them to struggle without making considerable effort to provide some other, safer way.

And now comes the portion of this letter where I risk both my pride and your impression of me, if ever it was positive. You'll indulge me, I hope, as I've little else to occupy me here but thoughts of you.

You are always on my mind, Willow. Constantly, it seems. The memory of you is with me in the heat of the day, when my arms are so tired I cannot lift the ax again, when my hands bleed through my gloves. And you are with me in the night, when I am alone outside my pathetic tent, staring up at an endless sky, frosted with endless stars.

I entertain myself by guessing what you might be doing in that exact moment. Your impression of London, as described in the Christmas letter, captured the spirit of a great explorer, and I have read it more times than I can count. Looking back, I think how I might have—how I should have—remained in London, even for one day, to accompany you on one turn 'round Mayfair or Hyde Park. The blind rush was my loss, obviously, as you have clearly made your own way (a triumph I never doubted), but I am jealous of your friends. They share with you the pleasure of discovery; they know the delight of turning the corner and seeing some unexpected tableau, distinctly, timelessly London, and yet so new to you. I wonder what you have made of the British Museum. Of Green Park, which is my favorite park, the green openness most like Yorkshire. Have you seen the new London Zoo or London Bridge?

For all my loyalty to Yorkshire, I have always quite enjoyed London. My father made it a priority to convey the family there several times every year. We did not visit enough to justify a residence, but enough that I could confidently orient the city by the time I traveled there as a student in university.

But I digress. I hope your next letter brings further details about your explorations of the city and continued delight.

On the topic of Tessa St. Croix, now Mrs. Tessa Chance, I, too, find myself at a loss for words. Joseph was in a very bad way when he arrived in Barbadoes after the wedding. Angry for the deceit, disheartened, frustrated with his prospects for the future. Worried. I must confess it is an upset (if not an anger) I share; I am loyal too, after all.

Stoker and I are not accustomed to quiet sullenness from Joseph; he has been irrepressibly cheerful, one might say annoyingly cheerful, since our first meeting in university, some fifteen years ago. It is alarming and worrisome to see him so detached and angry and unforthcoming. He refuses to discuss the circumstance of Tessa's condition and will only say he learned of her secret on the night of their wedding. He was taken completely by surprise—we all were.

I appreciate that you addressed the topic in your letter. I believe you when you say that you were never apprised of what Joseph did and did not know. I understand your loyalty and your discretion. It is a very delicate situation indeed. I am responsible for three sisters, and I shudder to think of one of them in Tessa's condition, although I pray God that my sisters would come to me rather than marry a stranger. It does not appear that this was an option for Tessa in her own family, and how lucky she is that the stranger she married was Joseph Chance.

Although Joseph's life has been forever changed, I am, in no way, surprised that he did not abandon her when her secret was revealed. He has not intimated as much to me, but I have every confidence that he will provide for her and the child. He is a gentleman of the highest order.

I conclude by saying that we said all along the scheme was outrageous. And yet you seem to be happy in London, the mining has become a reality, and my estate in Yorkshire survives the winter because of you.

So much good, I have come to think, has happened because of you.

If I sound selfish and unconcerned about my friend or your friend, perhaps I am, in a manner. You have made me that way and for the first time in my life, perhaps. And I don't regret it.

But I may regret speaking so freely here, so I shall close.

> *Warmly,*
> *Your husband, Brent Caulder*

***

1 February 1831
No. 43 Wilton Crescent
Belgrave Square
London, England

Dear Cassin,

Your letter of 1 January arrived yesterday, a day so cold and wet I could scarcely tear myself from the fire. I did not expect a letter—I have not known what to expect from you—but it was a welcome bright spot in a truly abysmal day. How grateful and cheered I am to hear from you.

I read parts of the letter out to the girls. We eagerly await more news and to learn how goes the mining when you are underway. (And we wholeheartedly approve of the name of the island!)

We are all still quite well here in Belgravia, having settled into a daily routine with purpose for us all. After breakfast together with Aunt Mary and Uncle Arthur, Tessa and Sabine discover some diversion in the city—shopping or gardens or tea in a cafe—while I join my aunt and uncle on morning calls to homes under construction or newly completed. The pace of new-home construction in Belgravia is maddening, with entire blocks of lavish residences put up as fast as workers can build them. The master builder even fires his own bricks out of the mud excavated from the very marshland drained to build Belgravia itself. But I digress.

We call upon at least one of these new homes each morning, sometimes several, and Aunt Mary and Uncle

Arthur consult on paneling and plaster for the walls; carved and forged decoration on banisters and balustrades; wood or even marble for the floors; paint; fixtures and fittings for lanterns and chandeliers; and eventually tapestries and rugs. They've not hesitated to make me a part of every meeting, an inclusion for which I am incredibly grateful, and I follow along beside them, taking detailed notes. Frequently they even ask for my opinion. (For better or worse, I am never without one.)

After we have seen the homes under construction, we return to the studio, where I file my notes, and the three of us render sketches and draw up commissions for craftsmen. If there is time at the end of the day, my aunt and I may call upon an artist or auction house to consider furniture or decorative pieces, while my uncle works in his shop to handcraft his own highly sought-after furniture.

The days pass in what feels like five minutes, truly. And then it is suppertime, and we are together again around my aunt's lovely table. Tessa and Sabine bring their stories of the day, and we share ours. The meal rapidly devolves into a jumble of exclamations and questions and laughter. My aunt and uncle bear it so nobly, bless them, and they boast to their friends how young we make them feel. I pray this is true because I adore our new life too much to worry that they regret taking us on.

They send their best regards to you and the other men, by the way—Mr. Fisk too.

And oh—I feel compelled to report that Perry has become more accustomed to London life. I have learned to forestall much of her rambling complaints by allowing her to style my hair to her exacting specifications. If she is exceedingly homesick, I enlist Sabine and Tessa for the same treatment. Whether we are on the forefront of fashion or victims of an indulged country maid, I cannot say.

As this overly long letter finally draws to a close, let me say again how gratified I was to receive your first letter. By no means do I think of you or our last time together with bitterness or regret; please be assured. Quite the contrary. If I'm being honest, I relish every moment we shared together, and I am bolstered by the knowledge that you think of me. When I said I am fond of you, it was true—then and now.

Oh, and please do not hesitate to write me. The post is painfully slow but it seems to be reliable. I continue to exchange weekly letters with your mother and sisters, and they report also to have heard from you. Any word is awaited with impatience and hope by us all.

Your wife,
Willow

***

10 February 1831
Island of New Pixham
via Bridgetown, Barbadoes
British West Indies

Dear Willow,

I have just received your letter dated 15 January regarding the visit of my uncle. Thank you for writing to alert me. It is clear from your description that you handled the situation deftly, despite the unpleasantness, and I am mortified that Archibald has imposed himself. Please accept my most sincere apologies. As you make your new life in London, you've certainly no use for a verbose relation sniffing around with repeated calls and thinly veiled interrogations.

It is my great hope that by the time you receive this, his visit will be all but forgotten and that he has not been heard from again. If for some reason he does return, please reiterate to your aunt's staff that he should be turned away without backward glance. Invoke Mr. Fisk to be ruthless, if you must.

At the risk of boring you with family politics, Archibald appears to be hounding my mother and brother in Yorkshire as well. He and one of his sons have made the journey to Caldera for an extended stay, and they seem disinclined (as of her last writing) to leave. They've installed themselves in the family wing of the castle and make repeated visits to tenants and the sealed mines. My mother is at a loss for how to evict him. My brother is a mild and bookish young man, far more suited to his work as a historian than family protector, and he, too, seems powerless to drive our uncle out.

I would return to England and deal with him in person (and I may do this yet), but we are making such progress. We've tweaked the system of scaffolding and chutes, eliminating nearly all waste. We are sealing thousands of pounds of guano in barrels. We may have double the haul we expected.

Each of us has fallen into informal roles in the operation—Stoker manages anything to do with the ship, Joseph coordinates the logistics for making port in London and distributing the guano to buyers, and I oversee the actual mining, but we all swing a jackhammer, we all shoulder barrels of cargo, we all toil daily, and no man can be spared. With every new threat from home, I curse Archibald's name.

Then again, he did give you cause to write me, and for this I am grateful. If I'm being honest, I live day to day for any word from Belgravia. I welcome any reason you may have to write, even news of Archibald.

Although my work here is for my family and for Caldera, it would be a lie to say that I do not also believe that, somehow, if you will allow it, I work also for you and me. This is either folly or selfishness or both, because we've made no promises—or it should be said that I made no promises—and you are obviously making precisely the life you wanted in London, but still, it could not go unsaid.

And so now I've said it. And now I will cease, except to reiterate how very much I miss you, Willow.

Yours,
Cassin

***

15 February 1831
No. 43 Wilton Crescent
Belgrave Square
London, England

Dear Cassin,

Please overlook another letter so rapidly on the heels of my last and forgive my brevity and haste.

I am trying desperately to seal this and see it carried to the Barbadoes mail packet that leaves the General Post Office in St. Martins Le Grand on the first Wednesday of the month. (Yes, I have committed the schedule to memory.)

But here is my urgent news. I pray God it is inconsequential, but only you may be the judge of that.

Your uncle has returned to Belgrave Square, several times in fact, although I have refused to receive him. I keep out of sight when he calls, but the staff summons me so that I may listen to his exchange with the butler without being seen.

Yesterday he called late in the day, oddly late, a new level of rudeness, and my aunt's butler struggled to remain cordial before I intervened. Archibald was wildly insistent, biting and impatient. He was so set on seeing me that I finally emerged and demanded to know his purpose.

He claimed that he required a signature—your signature—on "important documents" pertaining to Caldera. When I asked how I might provide such a signature, considering you were half a world away, he said that he himself intended to sign on your behalf—"by proxy," he said—and needed only to view some other official paperwork that bore your signature.

Cassin, I believe he meant to forge your name.

When I pressed for more detail, he said that he had just recently returned from Yorkshire, and the situation at Caldera had grown very dire indeed, that the winter had been punishing on the castle and your family. He bemoaned your absence and your (alleged) "indulgent lack of interest" in your responsibilities. That said, he assured me that he had discovered a new and inspired strategy to save us all. (Clearly he includes me in Caldera's dire state, whatever it may be.)

In the beginning, his manner was breezy and light, and he suggested the documents for your signature were inconsequential. But the more I questioned and resisted, the more impatient he became. When I asked that I might read the paperwork for myself, he flashed a thick portfolio of official-looking documents, literally pages and pages of text, and then quickly snapped it shut.

Ultimately, my refusals sent him away. He was angry and sputtering, bemoaning the ride to Yorkshire he would now be forced to make. I can only guess he means to approach your family for these "proxy signatures." This leads me to fear for your mother's wherewithal and stamina against him. At the risk of alarming you, I can recount that he came very close to grabbing me up and shaking me, Cassin, just to make me see. (Never fear; Mr. Fisk hovered just outside of view. I was in no real danger.)

As soon as he'd gone, I dashed off a note to your family and sent it to Yorkshire by private courier. Hopefully this warning will reach them, and they will stand firm against him.

Regardless, I worry for whatever scheme he may have concocted. I worry for paperwork signed "by proxy" that may bind you or Caldera to God knows what. I worry

for your dear mother. I know you are committed to the
island and whatever windfall the mining may bring, but if
you can be spared, even for a week, I believe that nothing
short of your physical presence in England may waylay
your uncle and whatever he has planned.

By the time you read this, it may be too late, but I
could not, in good conscience, not report it to you. I will
await word from your mother and, if necessary, travel to
Yorkshire myself to endeavor to help in any way I can.

I await your direction in the meantime.

And I miss you.

    Yours,

    Willow

Chapter Eighteen

By the third week in April, with no reply from Cassin, Willow made the decision to travel to Yorkshire and look in on Cassin's mother and siblings herself.

It had been nine weeks since she'd mailed her urgent letter to Barbadoes and, in theory, some response could arrive any day. But intermittent letters from Cassin's mother, Louisa, Lady Cassin, painted a miserable picture of Archibald's return visit to Caldera, his departure in a huff, and now a third visit, this time with wagonloads of materials and equipment.

And then last week came the most alarming news of all from Caldera. Cassin's younger brother, Felix, had been injured—how badly, it was difficult to say—by a herd of grazing cattle. Felix's dog had darted ahead on a country walk, startling a bull. The herd was spooked into stampeding, and Felix was badly hurt trying to save the animal.

Now, according to Lady Cassin's latest letter, Felix convalesced in bed, drifting in and out of consciousness, while his wife nursed him, and she and Cassin's sisters managed the uncle on their own.

It was unconscionable that Archibald repeatedly forced himself on Caldera, but now Felix's accident? Willow saw little choice but to go.

"But Willow," said Tessa, watching as Perry tucked Willow's warmest gowns and heaviest boots into a trunk, "word from Cassin may arrive any day. What if he does not wish you to go?"

"Likely, he does *not* wish me to go," said Willow, examining a fur-lined bonnet. "But I cannot ignore the distress I read in his mother's letters."

"A distress you can discern despite never having met this woman?" ventured Tessa, shifting in her chair to be more comfortable. Her petite body was now large and cumbersome with pregnancy.

"I've not met her in person, perhaps," said Willow, "but I have four months of her genuinely lovely letters, not to mention the loyalty borne of marrying her son."

"Oh, but you married her son for convenience, not loyalty," said Tessa.

"Listen to yourself, Tessa. You could be Sabine for all your skepticism."

"Perish the thought. My point is not to dissuade you, Willow; it is to demonstrate that yours was *not* a marriage of convenience after all."

Despite the deterioration of Tessa's own relationship with her husband, Joseph, her passion for matchmaking had not waned.

"My decision to go is unrelated to the nature of the marriage," sighed Willow. She retrieved a stack of glove boxes from a drawer and spilled them onto the bed. "It is the decent thing to do. Cassin's responsibility to his family is chief in his mind and heart; this I know. He is not here, but I am, and I am his wife, convenience or not. As such, I shall go in his stead. Perhaps I will be of little help, but I can lend support, if nothing else. Cassin's mother and sisters know very little of the work he's doing to save the castle. Doubtless, they come across as adrift or unprotected. But *I* shall not come across as adrift or unprotected. And no one may take advantage of me."

"Oh no, they will not," cheered Perry, kneeling before an open trunk.

"Thank you, Perry," said Willow. "I can always count on you, and it gratifies me more than you shall ever know. But let us pack everything we can today. Mr. Fisk wishes to leave tomorrow morning at first light."

"And you're certain you will feel safe, Willow? Traveling alone?" Tessa asked.

Perry interjected, "Oh no, 'tis very dangerous!" in the same moment Willow said, "Yes, of course."

Willow made a face. "We shall keep to well-traveled roads during daylight hours. I cannot tell you the sheer *exhilaration* I feel at being able to simply set out. To embark on a cross-country journey alone, without worrying about a chaperone or the suitability of it, or whether my reputation will be ruined because I'm a female alone on the road. And here we see another benefit of marriage. I relish coming and going as I please."

"You do see the irony," said a voice from the door, and they turned to see Sabine leaning against the jamb, "of riding merrily away because you are married."

Willow smiled, passing a pair of leather gloves to Perry. "What? Because I am married, I am free to go? But also, the *reason* I go is because I am married? Yes, perhaps. But if it is irony, I embrace it. I love the freedom, and I love—"

She stopped herself and made a little cough, turning back to gloves.

"What?" asked Tessa. "What else do you love?"

Willow considered this, surprised at what she'd nearly said. Eventually, she said, "I love being part of a family, even a family I've not formally met. The letters Cassin's mother has written me have moved me to tears. And his sisters send pages of questions about my life in London and the work I'm doing in Belgravia. I am not accustomed to the attention from anyone beyond the two of you. I would be lying if I said I didn't like it."

"You mean you *love it*," corrected Tessa, watching her closely. "You said you love—"

"I love the idea that I might be able to help them," Willow cut in. "How's that?"

"Silly me," sighed Tessa, "I thought you meant to say that you loved your husband."

Willow refused to answer this, but she did roll the notion around in her head. It was useless to deny that she had begun to fall in love with Cassin. It came slowly, letter by letter; memory by memory. It came like the shadow of an approaching man on a sunny day. Step, by step, by step.

"And what do I know of love?" she heard herself ask. "Even if I fancy myself in love with Cassin, I might have misdiagnosed it. Or misconstrued it."

Tessa laughed. "Good lord, Willow, it's not a rash—it's a rush of feeling."

"Yes, and what if I believe it is love, but in reality, it is little more than my first taste of male attention?"

"You know what I believe?" said Sabine, stepping into the room. "I believe you allowed Cassin to be the first because you knew." She raised an eyebrow. "You knew he was correct from the start."

Tessa made a low whistling noise. Willow shook her head. "Love at first sight?" she said. "From you, of all people?"

"Obviously, he suited you," said Sabine with a shrug. "Even I could see this. Do you believe for a second you would have married him if you did not see some potential?"

"Yes, of course I would have," Willow said weakly. "That was the whole of the plan. 'Any groom will do.'"

Sabine crossed her arms over her chest. "Believe that if it pleases you, but I know you, and I know that you would have never gone through with marriage to a man less perfect than Cassin. Less perfect for you, that is."

"Because I loved him?" Willow laughed, pretending the notion was ridiculous.

"Because you *could* love him," her friend said.

"And now…" Tessa added, gesturing to the elaborately staged trunk, "now, you do."

By some miracle, Cassin managed to catch a steamboat bound for England just two days after he received Willow's urgent letter. He had been in Bridgeport for their two-day supply run, and he departed Barbadoes without bothering to return to the island mine.

Neither did he take time to write Willow or his mother to inform them that he was on his way. The steamship would have him to England a week and a half before the mail packet would arrive. And besides, it was to his advantage to take his avaricious uncle by surprise.

Stoker, Joseph, and Cassin had been speculating for weeks about the best time for one of them to return to London. They needed to follow up with the buyers Joseph had managed to procure before he left England. Strictly speaking, account sales fell into Joseph Chance's purview in their partnership, but Joseph had yet to establish more than an uncertain peace with his new wife in Belgravia. He changed his mind daily about the best timing for a return trip. When Willow's letter arrived, Cassin made the decision for them all by boarding the London-bound steamboat and not looking back.

For four weeks, he paced the deck of the steamer as it pushed across the Atlantic, worrying about Caldera and dreaming about Willow.

If his suspicions were correct, his uncle had ignored his denial for more mining on Caldera land and gone ahead with the unsanctioned idea of excavating a new mine. Not alone perhaps, but if he involved numerous investors, a new mine would be more complicated to shut down, not to mention financed by money pooled among many men.

However, multiple investors meant the creation of a joint-stock company, and joint-stock companies, thank God, could be formed by only one means, a bloody act of Parliament.

If this had been Archibald's plan, Cassin's physical presence in London and official calls on members of Parliament should be enough to put an end to it.

After that, the situation would want only an explanation to Caldera tenants. He could only guess the promises his uncle had made them. Cassin could do little more than beg their patience and promise them a better, safer life.

When he wasn't thinking about his physical presence in London and a better life, Cassin thought about his physical presence before his wife.

His wife.

Fantasizing about Willow was hardly a new diversion. Months of back-breaking labor in the mine had provided ample and fertile time to fixate on every conjured detail of his new countess. The irony was not lost. He had not needed her—not really, truly *required* her—until she was inconveniently out of reach. Now the need was single-minded and unceasing, and sometimes it took his breath away. Worry about his uncertain future faded when held up against his desire for her now, every day, forever.

When at last the steamer made landfall in Falmouth, Cassin wasted no time purchasing a fast horse, new clothes, and boots and dashing off a note to his mother.

22 April 1831

Madam,

It is my great pleasure to write you from the shores of England, only a few days' ride from home. I am in Falmouth at the moment, having just made landfall this morning.

I look forward to seeing you and the girls and Felix very soon, but I cannot say exactly when. My priority is to settle this business with Archibald; as such, London must be first call. I will also look in on my wife.

Please write to me at her aunt's home in Belgravia as soon as you are able. I will require the most current and relevant news of Archibald's interference in order to properly shut down whatever he has done.

I look forward to my return to Caldera very soon.

Your son,

Brent

After he posted the letter, Cassin faced two days of hard riding to London, with little sleep in between. The spring sky hung low and dark, dropping intermittent rain, but he raised his collar, leaning in to the first proper chill he'd felt since he'd left England.

Two days later, with only an hour before dusk, he found himself, wet and sweaty but exhilarated, on the doorstep of Willow's aunt's home in Belgrave Square.

"The Earl of Cassin to see Lady Cassin," he told a liveried butler, ignoring his alarmed scrutiny.

Before the man could answer, Willow's small, frizzy-haired maid darted to the door.

"Oh, your lordship!" said the maid, her eyes large. "You've come! Oh, praise be, and just in time. Lady Cassin is set to travel to Yorkshire in the morning!"

"Yorkshire?" Cassin repeated slowly. He scanned the empty parlor behind the butler.

"Oh yes, the very place, if you can believe it," said Perry. "Planning to look in on your mother and sisters and brother. Quite set on it, cannot be swayed. I am to be left behind, of course."

"Look in on my mother?" Cassin felt like an idiot, repeating every statement, but he'd devoted so much imagination to seeing Willow, the possibility of *not* seeing her was difficult to comprehend.

"Yes, my lord," continued Perry, "on account of your terrible uncle. And your brother taking ill. She intends to be of help to the dowager countess, even though they have never, ever met…" Perry's voice trailed off dreamily.

Cassin blinked at her, still trying to catch up. "But at the moment she is in London? She has not yet gone?"

Perry nodded importantly and shouldered around the butler. "Well, she's not here in Wilton Crescent at the moment. She's gone on an errand to one of the new homes. Paint. Three colors, all of them *beige*."

"Gone on an errand at dusk?" Cassin glanced around.

"Oh, dusk is the most important time for paint," lectured Perry. "The tones change when the light fades."

"Please tell me she's taken Mr. Fisk or a footman. Please tell me she does not wander the streets alone at this hour."

"Oh, but 'tis a music room, not the street," said Perry. "But she is alone, I'm afraid. Mr. Fisk is preparing for the journey. She's been most insistent about leaving, but he would not consent until the weather—"

"Where, Perry?" asked Cassin, shoving on his soggy hat and tightening his gloves.

"Yorkshire, my lord," Perry repeated slowly, as if the notion was complicated.

"*Not* the journey; where is my wife now?"

"Oh, *right*. Well, I cannot say precisely, as she does not te—"

"It's number four, my lord," said a voice blocked by the door.

Cassin craned to see. Sabine Stoker stepped into view.

"In Chapel Street," Sabine said. "Not far. Just around the square and to the left."

Cassin nodded to her. "Thank you, ladies," he said, already turning toward the square.

CHAPTER NINETEEN

The knock on the door caused Willow to jump. Her head shot up, and she stared down the corridor at the heavy front door to the Chapel Street house. She squinted. The sun rapidly slid from a soggy grey sky, and the last of the workmen had gone. It was far too late for deliveries or a call from the owners. Willow had assured Mr. Fisk that she would be perfectly safe in the deserted house, which was a short walk from Wilton Crescent. She'd been in and out of the new construction on Chapel Street at least four times today, as she was most days, endeavoring to pin down as many measurements as possible before she departed for Yorkshire. She hadn't even bothered to lock the front door when she'd slipped inside for a final peek at the swatches of paint sampled on the music room wall.

The knock sounded again, and Willow took two steps back.

Silence.

She stopped breathing to listen harder.

Walk away, walk away, walk away, she chanted in her head, speculating wildly about who would pound on the door of an unfinished home at sunset. She was just about to shout, *Is anyone there?* when the knock sounded a third time, louder, so loud that timber rods propped against the wall jumped and rolled to the floor.

"Who's there?" she called out. Fear diluted her voice, and she cleared her throat.

She took two more steps back. Wildly, she scanned the room for a weapon near to hand.

"Willow?" came a muffled voice from the other side of the door.

Willow's heart stopped. In an instant, she forgot about the house and the paint and every other thing she'd ever known. She stared at the closed door.

But that sounded like…

She tried to suck in breath.

But that sounded like *Cassin's* voice.

"Willow, it's Cassin," said the muffled voice again. "Will you—"

And now she launched herself. Her world shrank to the door at the end of the corridor and its heavy brass knob. She grabbed hold with both hands and jerked, throwing it wide.

And there he was.

Her husband leaned against the jamb of the door, his right arm above his head, his forehead on his arm. He'd been looking down, speaking to the keyhole.

She saw the top of his head, dusty-blond hair, sun-bleached to almost white. She saw massive shoulders. Large tanned hands.

He looked up, and her heart burst. Green eyes, tanned face, a surprised smile. It quirked up on one side, a little bit uncertain, a little bit…delighted?

Willow sucked in a shaky breath and tried to speak. She fought her first impulse, her only impulse, which was to throw herself into his arms. He had come home, but she didn't know why. He'd traveled halfway around the world. Someone was dead or in grave danger. Something horrible had happened.

He rose from the door jamb. When he stood at full height, she had to look up to see him.

"I'm here about the advertisement…" he said calmly, his smile hitching up a notch.

Willow laughed. "You were meant to apply by letter, sir." Her voice felt weak and uneven, but she couldn't hear it over the pounding of her heart.

"I was compelled to apply in person," he said. "For efficiency's sake."

She laughed again.

Horses' hooves clomped up the street. A bird called. In the distance, thunder boomed softly.

Cassin cleared his throat and raised an eyebrow.

"Oh, forgive me." She laughed nervously. "Come in. Please."

She stepped back, and he ducked inside. She reached for the door, but he kicked it shut with his boot. He bit off his gloves and looked around.

Willow stared, coming to terms with the living, breathing sight of him just three feet away. She could smell him. Rain, sweat, horse. *Cassin.* He was wet and wrinkled and mud-splattered. His hair was wild. He had not shaved. He shrugged from his greatcoat.

"You've ridden here from Falmouth?" she guessed. "But the weather has been dreadful."

The weather has been dreadful? Willow cringed.

He said, "I did ride. But first I took a steamship." A smile. "In very fine weather. I received your letter. There was no answer but to come."

"Oh yes, the letter." Willow forced herself to think of his family. His brother had been injured, his uncle endeavored castle intrigue. Important matters, all. She planned to leave London out of worry for these people. They should discuss them like measured adults; they were far more important than his closeness or his largeness or his...wet clothing, which he seemed intent on peeling off, layer by layer. He tugged at his soggy cravat and unbuttoned the top button of his waistcoat.

"I did not write to alarm you," she said, "but honestly, I was alarmed myself. Your mother's letters had become so infrequent. And then your uncle behaved so strangely about your signature, only to set out for Yorkshire again."

Cassin grimaced and nodded, running a hand through his wild hair. He dropped his hat, greatcoat, and gloves on a workbench beside the door. Willow stared at his discarded things, piled in a heap. He began a slow prowl of the dim corridor, rubbing his fingers over his jaw.

"How long have you been in London?" she asked.

"I rode to town directly from Falmouth. I've just called to Belgrave Square, my first stop. Perry was very informative."

Willow chuckled serenely—*Oh yes, Perry*—while a mix of nerves and delight fizzed beneath the surface of her skin.

He called to Belgrave Square.

His first stop.

He said, "She told me about your impending journey to Yorkshire. But Sabine told me you could be found here."

Willow nodded—*thank you, Sabine*—glanced around at the empty shell of the house. It was cold and dark and unfinished, an odd place for a reunion. *But oh so private…*

"This house is one of several for which my aunt and uncle will design the interiors," she said, trying to sound calm and informative. "It's difficult to see at this time of day, but the carpentry and appointments are the finest I've seen. Aunt Mary has assigned me the ground-floor music room to outfit entirely on my own. It's a small room, but the wife of the owner is an accomplished musician, and the room is very important in the house."

"I should expect nothing less," he said. "And what a lucky woman she will be." He looked up and down the corridor. "I suppose husbandly worry about your roaming empty houses at dusk has no place. You've come and gone as you pleased for months, haven't you?"

"Indeed," she said. "I have done." She paused, watching him. "I am cautious when on a work site at any hour. I needed to look in on three samples of paint in the fading light. A ten-minute errand before I left for the north tomorrow."

He stopped prowling and turned to her. "Yes. The north."

A pause. Willow held her breath.

"I cannot express how grateful I am for the effort you make. More than grateful, I am humbled," he said. "I am…in your debt."

"Well, I haven't gone yet, have I?" She breathed again. "I hope you aren't displeased with my plan to go. Obviously I had no way to ask you. I put it off until I felt they absolutely required an ally."

He shook his head. "Not displeased. The opposite of displeased. What can you tell me of my brother?" he said. "Your maid mentioned some illness?"

"Not an illness. An accident, I'm afraid." She told him what she knew of Felix's altercation with the stampeding cattle.

"Your mother's letter about the incident rambled aimlessly," she finished. "I could scarcely make sense of it. The tone of the thing was very frantic, and this alarmed me most of all. I could but endeavor to give some aid, even if it was only to make them feel less alone."

"Yes, well, calling on unknown relations in a crisis was hardly part of our arrangement, was it?"

And there it was. "The arrangement." Willow's heart slid from her throat to the pit of her stomach.

Perhaps they would not require the privacy of the empty house. Perhaps it made no difference where they reunited.

An awkward silence settled around them, and she searched for something else they might say. She had no wish to appear meddlesome. Likely, her presence in Yorkshire would no longer be required. She could remain in London. She could see this house to completion. She would be with Tessa when the baby came. For no known reason, tears stung her eyes.

"Can you show me the room you've been charged with designing?" Cassin asked.

Willow blinked at him. "I beg your pardon?"

"The music room, this commission of yours. I should like to see it, if you are willing to show me."

"Of course," she said, her voice strangely faint. She did not move, not for a long moment. She said, "It's the last room at the end of the corridor."

He bowed his head and gestured for her to precede him. Willow felt herself move forward, barely seeing the doorway ahead.

"It would be too dark to see at this hour," she said, "but I had the east wall torn down and rebuilt with towering windows. If the clouds allow for us to see the sunset, you may get some idea."

"Will there be a domed mural?" he asked.

She missed a step. A memory flashed in her mind, Cassin lying with her on the chaise at Leland Park, staring up at her floral mural.

She cleared her throat. "No, no mural. The ceiling is coffered. I met with the owners at length about their expectations. I've had to be mindful of how instrumental sound will resonate in the room."

They reached the music room, and she stepped inside. He came to a stop beside her. "And where is this paint? I would see it before we are alone here in the dark."

The buzzing beneath her skin fizzled back to life. Willow pointed out the wall with three rough squares of paint. "There. They are all lovely in the full light of day, but I need the precise shade that will not appear dingy, or worse, taupe, in the fading light."

"Not dingy or taupe," he repeated slowly. He crossed his arms over his chest. "I shudder to predict your reaction to the walls of Caldera."

"Oh? And what color are they?" she said. *Because I may or may not ever see them.*

"I've no idea."

She laughed. "You don't know?"

"I've never given it a moment's thought, actually. Grey, perhaps? Ivory? Much of the castle is stone, which is definitely a greyish, brownish, blackish color. But there is plaster that is surely…some other shade."

She stared at him, reminding herself that *her* focus was not *everyone's* focus.

"Is it wrong," he speculated, "to admit that each of these samples looks exactly the same to me?" He gave her a boyish look that caused her stomach to flip.

"No, it is not wrong, simply…well, it's not your purview, is it?"

"No. And let us thank God for that. It's fascinating to see the work you're doing." He settled his eyes on her, smiling, and then glanced around the room.

Willow watched him take note of the windows and high beams, the boxed coffers of the ceiling. It felt so validating to share her work with someone besides her aunt and uncle.

"I've scarcely begun," she told him. "I have very high hopes for it, indeed. You can see the exposed timber beams there and there; those will be stained a dark chocolate brown. The smooth plaster in between will be the fawn color. The correct shade is the middle one—there." She pointed. "I quite like it in the dusky light, I must say. The ceiling beams will be stained the same brown, and the coffers, a lighter shade of the fawn. I'm hoping for the rare balance of dramatic but also neutral. The pianoforte and harpsichords are meant to be the showpieces."

"It will be breathtaking, Willow," he said. His voice was so soft that she turned around. He had ceased looking around the room and stared now only at her. It was a half-lidded stare, soft and hot at the same time, like the last embers of a fire.

Willow felt her own eyes grow large. She felt a burst of energy, doubts giving way to nerves and hope.

"This room posed a challenge," she heard herself say. She began to walk the room. "It will be used in the daytime to practice but also in the evenings, when the couple entertain. I've worked with my uncle to design custom-made furniture that will serve as traditional chairs and sofas but also rows of seating, as in a theatre."

"Willow?" Cassin called, his voice still low.

"You'll note the doorway at the far end of the room"— Willow pressed on, rambling now—"that leads from the dining room? 'Tis but a short walk from dinner to chamber concert."

"Willow?"

"Even so," she went on, speaking so very fast, "it was impor-tant to the owners that such spontaneous concerts not appear staged. The wife has significant talent, but she is timid about it, apparently. The husband is an ambassador. There are quite a few ambassadors, actually, taking residence in Belgravia. This wall will be devoted entirely to bookshelves," she said, gesturing behind her. "Apparently their collection of music is extensive."

"Willow?" he said for the third time.

She breezed past, intent on describing how bookshelves would line the passageway from the dining room, but he reached out and grabbed her hand.

Willow froze.

"*Willow*," he said again, so softly she could barely hear him over the thundering of her heart.

"Yes?"

She couldn't look at him. Hadn't he looked enough for them both? Her cheeks burned under the ferocity of his stare. Their combined gazes would ignite the room.

"Willow, forgive me," he rasped, and she had the sudden choking fear that he was about to say good-bye.

He tugged on her hand, pulling her to him, but she resisted. She stared at the floor.

He said, "I want to hear about this room; truly I do. I want to hear about everything you've accomplished and experienced in London. However..."

He paused and tugged at her hand again. This time she allowed it. She fell two steps in his direction.

"However," he repeated, "if I do not kiss you in the next second, I will perish."

Her head shot up, and she searched his face in the dim light.

"I am wet and filthy from the road," he said softly. "I haven't shaved or bathed. I apologize, but in my urgency to see y—"

Willow launched herself at him.

Later, Cassin thought.

Later he would berate himself for kissing her when he should be discussing Caldera, and his uncle, and learning about bloody Felix's bloody cock-up with cattle.

Later.

First, he would commit fully to this kiss, however indulgent. She was in his arms, finally in his arms, and he had wanted her so bloody long. Willow. Against him, kissing him back.

Now he would do it properly, he would bloody devour her, which was the thing he'd wanted to do since she'd swung open the door.

"Willow," he breathed, leaving her mouth to bury his face in her hair. He inhaled her familiar cinnamon scent. "My God, how I have missed you."

"I thought I would die from missing you," she whispered back, kissing his jaw, his ear, his neck. She pawed at his loose, soggy cravat, searching for more bare skin.

He wrapped his arms around her, gathering her up, filling his hands with yards and yards of her dress. When his hands reached the firm curve of her hip, he flattened his palm, feeling the perfect shape of her through the fabric. He sought her mouth again, and she met him halfway, kissing her as he'd taught her to kiss. Time reversed. It felt as if he'd never left. She was just as intoxicating, sweeter now, perhaps, because he wanted her. But it had always been sweet; she had always transported him.

She made a whimpering noise, stepping on his boots to get closer to him, and he put a palm beneath her bottom, collecting her to him. Without warning, she gave a jump, leaping up to straddle him. He caught her beneath the hips with a grunt.

"My God, you are killing me," he said between kisses. She wrapped her arms around his neck as if they weren't close enough. Cassin staggered, weakened by desire, laughing between kisses.

Down, he thought. *Must lie us down.*

He opened one eye and searched the room. Horizontal surface? No, they were in an empty music room. Chair? *No*, the whole bloody house was empty.

He spun, still kissing her, and saw a heap of fabric near the half-tiled hearth.

It will do.

With uneven, meandering steps, he carried her to the mound of cloth, kissing her all the while. Slowly, he lowered them, straining with pickax-hardened muscle, and still he fell the last foot.

"*Oof*," he said, and she laughed, and he turned to sit flat with her astride his lap. He leaned back on the hearth, and she crashed against him with a fresh rain of kisses.

He had known more comfortable positions in his life, but he could not remember when. He could scarcely remember his bloody name. Desire swamped him; his hands could not explore her body fast enough; his mouth could not kiss her deeply enough. She sat on him, sat on the most urgently seeking part of him, and still it was not enough.

When they'd kissed until he could barely breathe, when he was seconds away from rolling her down on the floor and taking her, Cassin leaned his head back on the wall and gasped for breath, closing his eyes. He felt her rise up on her knees to follow his mouth, and he laughed, turning his head.

"Have mercy on me, Willow—please, I beg you." He kissed her forcefully and then dropped his head again. "I am ravenous for you, trust me, but I can only take so much." Another kiss. "You will kill me with pleasure."

"You are pleased?" she asked, falling against his chest, breathing hard.

"I am beyond pleased. What is more than pleased?"

"Your heart is racing."

"So many parts of my body overachieve in this moment, darling, it would be impossible to take store." He bucked up just a little, allowing her to feel his desire. The two of them moaned at the pressure. He felt her go limp against him. He kissed the top of her head.

"But," he said, forcing out the words, "we cannot continue without a discussion first. And a bed. Preferably. Also, a fire. But first, we must talk."

Her head shot up.

"Spare me the reproving looks, Countess; you adore discussions, and I know it. I've never met a woman who loves to discuss more than you do."

"I don't want to talk about the arrangement," she said into his chest.

"Nor I. I would be quite gratified, in fact, never to talk about it again."

She raised her head and studied his face. "What do you mean?"

"I mean that I am an arse, Willow. An arse and blackguard and every overused sentiment you can imagine, and this is why. Something…happened to me when I went away from you. Good lord, I was eons away, it seemed—"

"You contracted malaria," she guessed. She scooted closer to him, setting off a cascade of sensations that blurred his vision.

He cleared his throat. "Possibly. But no, I contracted the life-altering realization that I wanted you."

He paused. Coward that he was, he watched from the corner of his eye. Reactions played across her face. Delight, then thoughtfulness, then narrow-eyed skepticism.

"Believe it or not," she said, "I have not doubted that you *wanted me*."

He cleared his throat. "Indeed. Well said." She was so close, so beautiful. He squeezed his eyes shut, fighting for lucidity. "Perhaps *wanting you* has never been the issue. I am guilty of kissing you, twice, only a day after we first met, aren't I? I have always *desired* you. More, certainly, than ever I've desired any woman."

She raised one beautifully auburn eyebrow, and he could not resist dropping a kiss on her nose. She sat perfectly still. He followed that kiss with a nuzzle, his nose to hers, and a kiss on the lips.

She accepted the kiss but did not kiss him back. She waited.

Cassin rolled his shoulders. "What I'm trying to say is, perhaps it took my going away for me to realize how much I wanted you in every way, every day. Not simply in my bed, but in my life. I want you as my wife, Willow. If…if you will have me."

His racing heart actually stopped when he gritted out the words. He held his breath. He'd made the admission with a playful mix of self-deprecation and smugness, but he was terrified inside. She could refuse him. She had every right to refuse him.

"But nothing about your situation has changed, Cassin," she said. "In fact, the threat from your uncle has grown since you've been away. Your letters claim the mining is going well, but is your future not still uncertain? Forgive me if I am afraid to trust your newfound regard."

Cassin took a deep breath, considering this, considering her honesty and innocence. "I am not surprised, honestly. And that is why..." He ran his hands up her thighs and over the dip of her waist, relishing the feel of the perfect line of her leg and curve of her hip, and then he pulled back one side of his waistcoat to reveal a pocket.

While she watched, he unfastened the pocket and pulled out the tiny velvet pouch that had made soggy journey to London against his heart. "And that is why, I should like to try to bribe you. *Bribe* you to believe me."

His fingers shook as he held up the pouch between them, and he said, "Take it, my lady. It's a gift."

She eyed him and slowly reached out her hand. Without pulling the string, she massaged the velvet to discern what it might contain. The ring would be easy to predict, and when she knew, she went very still. She stared up at him.

"You are correct about my uncle and my future," he said softly. "He is a problem, and I cannot say if the guano will save Caldera. But—and I am ashamed to admit this—it took a journey around the world and months of hard labor in a bloody mine to make me realize that none of that mattered if you are not in my life. God forgive me. It feels selfish of me to insert you into the madness of my current uncertainty, but for once in my life I cannot resist. Being away from you has penetrated my notion of right and wrong."

"Had you thought it was *wrong* to marry me?"

"Never. I have thought it was hasty, and improbable, and dangerous for both of our hearts and our futures, but I never thought it was *wrong*. When I went away, however, I came to realize how exactly, perfectly, essentially *right* it was. And is. How authentic my feelings for you are. How authentic our marriage could be, if you will have me." He rushed to finish. "That is why I have no wish to speak of 'the arrangement' ever again. I sought you out in Belgravia only to find you embarking on a trip to rescue Caldera. This only proves how right I am.

"*You* don't seem to regard our union as simply 'an arrangement,' God love you," he said, "and my only regret—my very great regret—is that it has taken me so long to realize it. But in my defense, I was prepared to admit it after the first week at sea, sailing to the Barbadoes. Inconveniently, you were not available in the middle of the Atlantic."

He'd said enough, he decided, and nodded to the velvet pouch. "A proper wife should have a proper wedding ring. You've gone without every flourish or romantic gesture owed to a properly courted heiress, and I should like to rectify the matter over time. Beginning now. And do not think I've done it with money from your dowry, if you please. Joseph managed to sell our first shipment of guano in advance, before he even departed England. I can afford to spoil you a little now, if you will allow me."

Willow stared at him, her large blue-green eyes filled with a heart-wrenching mix of disbelief and hope. Cassin resisted the urge to throw himself, prostrate, at her feet to beg her to consider him. But he had picked up a thing or two about women over the course of his thirty-six years, and he cocked an eyebrow instead. "Off you go," he said. "Open it."

While he held his breath, Willow tugged the drawstrings and turned the pouch upside down over her palm. The ring fell out, a simple gold band with a colossally large emerald surrounded by diamonds and orange garnets.

She let out a little gasp, staring down at the ring in the fading light.

"I bought it in a shop in Bridgetown, Barbadoes, if you can believe it." His voice was thick and unsteady. He cleared his throat. "The spoils of some pirate's daring high-seas raid, no doubt. I come bearing more romantic drivel, I'm afraid, if you will allow me." He cleared his throat again. When next he spoke, his voice was a whisper. "The emerald reminded me of your eyes, and the orange garnets of your hair. I wanted it for you from the moment I saw it. I bought it months ago, in anticipation of seeing you again."

"It's magical," she whispered reverently, and then she scrambled off him, nearer to the waning sunlight from the windows. Cassin reached after her, loath to let her out of his lap. The linen of her gown slipped through his fingers, and he sighed. He bent a knee and pulled up a leg, watching her study the ring. She slipped it on her finger and held out her hand.

"I am very discerning, Cassin, as you may remember," she said. "Beauty is my vocation, and I cannot tolerate the look of anything expected or boring or garish." She smiled at him, and his heart felt as if it might burst. "And this may well be the most beautiful setting I've ever seen. I adore it. And not simply because it came from you. It's truly remarkable. Well done, Cassin."

She picked her way back to his lap, and he held his arms out to her.

She leaned in to kiss him, and he hesitated, turning his face away. It was almost painful to resist her, and she made an adorable protesting cry.

"What is it?" she demanded.

"I feel compelled to unburden the two of us of one more thing," he said, "er, before we go on."

"Speak for yourself, Cassin. I've no burdens between us."

"Ah, yes. So goes the existence of the pure of heart."

"I've waited an age to be less pure. What is it?"

He laughed. "I simply wanted to say that you were correct to deny me your body until I came to this realization, as tortured a journey as it has been. I know now that I would've come to my senses either way, but you were wise to protect yourself from what must have appeared to be a very fickle, indecisive man."

Willow made a face, and he forged on. "That said, I want to assure you that I'm not saying a lot of pretty words this night so that I can dance merrily into your bed—er, onto this painter's cloth." He grimaced at their nest on the floor. "You have my word that I have no intention of resuming the detachment of our former 'arrangement' tomorrow."

"Hmmm," Willow said, gazing at her ring. "I appreciate the clarity, but I know that you would not betray me." She looked up and tossed her head, shaking errant curls from her shoulders. Her bun had dissolved into a glorious halo of auburn.

Cassin smiled, relief flooding through him, and he took up a handful of the soft curls, squeezing them gently in his fist.

Willow tugged away and flipped the wild, heavy weight of her hair onto the opposite shoulder. "You have declared yourself sufficiently, I would say. And now we shall go to bed."

Cassin's lust surged, and he squeezed his eyes shut and then open. "One more thing…"

"You're joking." She grabbed him by the lapels and brought her mouth to his.

"No," he laughed around kisses. He reached behind her until he caught up her ankles. Pushing up, he raked his fingers along her stockinged legs beneath the hem of her gown.

"You complained before," he said, speaking around another kiss, "about always being the last to know, and I wanted to make sure that"—another kiss—"this late declaration of mine did not leave you to feel—"

"If you do not cease talking," she said, "and take me to bed, I shall be the last virginal wife in the history of time. I will be forced to ravish you myself, in the same way I was forced to propose to you."

He laughed. "You mean, in your father's library, accompanied by Perry and Mr. Fisk and your mother's hounds?"

"No." She laughed, kissing him again. "Without the slightest idea of what I'm doing. Although less paperwork."

And now he growled and swept her up, vaulting to his feet with her in his arms.

"Agreed. But not here. I'm sorry. You made your own proposal, endured a forgettable wedding, and received a ring five months late. I will make love to you properly if it's the last thing I do. In a bed. With a warm fire. Behind a locked door. Please tell me you have your own room in Belgrave Square."

"Yes," she said, kissing him. "Yes, yes, *yes*."

CHAPTER TWENTY

Cassin strode down the corridor with Willow in his arms until they collided with the front door. He released her, sliding her between the door and his body, pressing her into the smooth wood without breaking the kiss.

"My coat and hat," he mumbled between kisses and tried twice to lean sideways to collect them. Willow swayed both times, woozy from the kiss, and he laughed and lunged back to kiss her again. The third time, she pushed him away, desperate for progress, and he scooped them up and crowded behind her as she made her way out the door. Looking right and left, she locked the empty house and stole one more kiss. He growled and then took up her hand and led her down the steps.

"I came by Wilton Crescent," he told her. "Is that the quickest way to return to your aunt's house?"

"Yes, the quickest," she said, and he squeezed her hand and tugged her along.

"Wait," she laughed, "I cannot walk so fast. I take two steps to your one."

"*Try,*" he breathed, his voice pained and comically impatient, and he pulled her along. A lone carriage rumbled past them on Upper Belgrave Street, and he hustled her into the shadow of a high stoop and kissed her until the carriage rolled away. They were across the street after that, around the square and to her aunt's home in less than ten minutes.

"Willow, I'm warning you," Cassin said, his voice low. "I haven't the endurance for pleasantries with friends and relations. I avoid rudeness when I can, honestly I do, but tonight is not one of those avoidable occasions. I want you; I want a bed; I want a *locked door*. And nothing else. Can we possibly gain these things without running the gauntlet of well-wishers and explanations?"

Willow laughed and pointed to a walkway that led through a garden around the side of the house.

"We have our own entrance—there, behind the roses. Tessa and I rarely use it, but Sabine slips in and out every day. With any luck, it will be unlocked."

Their luck held, and the unlocked door swung open to an empty corridor. All along the wall, fresh candles burned and the jumble of umbrellas and shawls beside the door had been straightened. Willow heard a door shut briskly when they spilled inside; after that, racing footsteps on the stairs. Willow smiled and took Cassin by the hand, leading him to her bedroom. He trailed behind, walking at a civil pace only long enough to breach the door and shut it behind them. When they were alone, he yanked her to him to resume their kiss.

"Where are we?" he asked, gasping for a breath.

She laughed. "Not the parlor."

Between kisses, he said, "Your room, then?" He looked around.

Willow blinked over his shoulder, squinting into the room. A fresh fire had been laid and was jumping in the hearth. The curtains were drawn and the coverlet was pulled back on her bed. A candle glowed on a trolley of bread and cheese, setting crystal goblets of wine to twinkle. The silvery French negligee, never worn, had been draped over the arm of a chair.

Oh, Perry, she thought, her heart expanding at her thoughtfulness. She squeezed her eyes shut.

"Oh, lovely," Cassin said, "a bed."

She laughed. He stooped to kiss the smile from her mouth and lifted her in the same deft movement. He carried her to the bed, breaking the kiss long enough to deposit her in the center.

"Boots," he told her, stepping back. "I need five seconds to pull my boots."

"Oh, they are lovely boots." she said.

"Lovely, perhaps. Hurt like the very devil. But thank you. I bought them in Falmouth to impress you."

She thought of this; she thought of all of his clothes, damp and caked with mud but clearly new. She'd not considered his attire before, not really, and she thought of him making landfall in Falmouth and then dashing about, outfitting himself with her in mind.

She looked down at her own ivory day dress. She was too old, not to mention too married, to wear white, but the fabric was a rich oat-ivory, pretty for spring but thick and expensive enough to not appear flimsy or juvenile. It wasn't practical on rainy, muddy days or days when she maneuvered through the construction of an unfinished house, but she'd worn it today anyway, on a whim. It was unique and made her feel pretty; it set off her auburn hair. She was glad she'd worn it. And now she was glad she would wear it no more.

She asked, "Are we to…remove all of our clothes?"

He was balancing on one foot, and he tipped. "Yes, Willow, all."

She considered this, slipping off her own shoes. She wondered if she should undress now, or if he would do it.

"Don't worry," he said, reading her thoughts, "removing our clothes is something we will venture together. But I'll save you the bother of my boots. Too much mud and the new leather has no give."

He grimaced, pulling, and Willow watched in rapt fascination at the entirely male ritual. His hands were so large, his muscled leg so long. After his boots, he stripped off his waistcoat and tossed it on the chair. The thin white fabric of his shirt was billowy and loose. He reached for his shoulders to pull it off.

"No, let me," she heard herself say, coming up on her knees.

He eyed her, a flash of conspiratorial green that flooded her with pleasure. He let the shirt to fall back over his chest. "Let's take off your dress," he said. "Let me see what irresistibility awaits me underneath."

She looked down at the dress and wondered if she should have made time to change into the silvery negligee. "You've missed my wedding-night frock from France, I'm afraid." She pointed to the chair. "One detriment to waiting five months to determine whether you like me or not."

He growled and came to her, leaning a knee on the mattress and sweeping her to him. "I always liked you, Willow. I liked you too bloody much."

She fell against him, burying her face in his neck. *He always made me feel beautiful,* she thought, *despite anything else he may have done.*

It was true, he'd wanted her from the start; he seemed unable to resist her. It was a fervor she struggled to accept after all the years of feeling so very...neutral in the eyes of any man.

She lifted her head, allowing the heavy weight of her hair to fall down her back. He sighed as if she'd touched him and skimmed his hands down her shoulders. When he found her hands, they locked their fingers, squeezing, only for him to disentangle them and cup her face. He kissed her, the first deep, real kiss since he'd declared himself by the fire. Willow's mind went hazy, doubts and questions floating away, and she succumbed to his command of her body. He caught her up and lay her back.

"You've not delivered on the promise to relieve me of my shirt, madam," he said, his voice low in her ear.

She reached up, only to discover that her arms were like straw. She fumbled at his shoulders, taking up loose, ineffective handfuls of fabric. He laughed and sat up, pulling the shirt over his head and tossing it to a chair.

At the sight of his bare chest, Willow gasped. She propped up on her elbows. "*Cassin,*" she began, and then she trailed off, stunned speechless.

"Yes?" A small, prideful laugh.

"You're so...*strong.* And your skin is so tanned."

"Like that, do you?" He laughed again. "Compliments of pickax mining under the blazing Caribbean sun for twelve hours a day."

"But you must never wear a shirt again." She laughed, running her hands along the firm pockets of muscle on his stomach and chest. His skin twitched and jumped beneath her touch and she went back, retracing every contour. His arm bulged with muscle. She wrapped two hands around his bicep, and her fingertips barely touched. He looked like an Italian marble sculpture. "You look like a statue," she said.

"I feel like a statue." He grimaced, unbuttoning the top buttons of his breeches.

"*Oh*," Willow said, wonderment stealing over her. She looked lower. "Oh," she repeated, darting her eyes away.

"Less bold now, I see," he said, laughing. "Never fear, Countess; we'll get to that. But first, off with this dress."

He reached behind her and deftly unbuttoned the dress and then slid it from her shoulders while he kissed her neck. She swam in the sensation, barely aware of her chemise, which slid down next, nor her corset, which was unlaced with five or six urgent tugs. All the while he nuzzled and kissed her neck. She whimpered and listed backward, but he righted her—three times, he nudged her upright—and returned to unbuttoning, unlacing, removing.

When her corset drooped in her lap and her dress and chemise were in a bunch at her waist, he gently laid her back on the bed and gave her three firm kisses on the mouth. She reached for him, trying to keep up, but he slid away, pulling the gown and chemise down her legs, taking her drawers with them.

When he'd finished and she lay naked, except for her stockings, he leaned back on his haunches and stared. The night was cool and the bed was some distance from the fire, but when Cassin explored her body with his eyes, she *burned*. The impulse to cover herself came and left almost in the same instant. Some unknown instinct propelled her to slide her hands through her hair, to preen. She dropped long wild curls on her shoulders and across her breasts. The green of Cassin's eyes went three shades darker.

"You're beautiful, Willow," he whispered. His voice was a reverent rasp. "So beautiful. I cannot believe that you are mine."

"But what will you do with me?" she whispered, instinct driving her again. She reached for him.

"*Everything*," he growled. He pulled away long enough to shuck his breeches and drawers. He kissed her, gathering her close, and sensation exploded in her body. The first skin-on-skin contact. All of her nakedness bussing up against all of him. She sighed, arching into him like a cat, reveling in the feel of his hands sliding possessively down her back and bottom. He answered her sigh with a moan, burying his face in her hair.

"Oh God, Willow," he said against her neck, "I am trying so bloody hard to go slowly. Perhaps if we had one of your lovely chats. Would you like me to tell you what's about to happen?"

"Oh, I know what's about to happen," she assured him, digging her hands into his hair. She would hold his mouth against the skin of her throat forever.

He looked up. "Who told you? Not your mother?"

She shook her head. "Tessa," she said.

"Of course," he said, dropping back to her neck. "At least you're not the last to know."

He kissed her shoulder next, and then her throat, and then lower, to her breast. Willow's sighs turned to moans, and the slow, undulating arch of her body turned to a maddened squirm. She was a strange combination of listless and driven. She wanted to float in his arms, languishing in each touch, but she also felt a thrumming sort of propulsion, a search. Each kiss, each touch, set off a small fire that burned a little brighter with each repeated touch.

"My God, you are responsive," he sighed.

"I want, Cassin," she cried, hearing her lack of articulation but not caring. "I want…" She was at the mercy of her unnamed need.

"Then we are in perfect accord," he growled, kissing his way back to her mouth. He rolled, centering himself on top of her, and the weight of him pushed the air from her lungs.

"Careful," he breathed, rising onto his forearms. "I don't want to crush you."

"No," she gasped, pulling his shoulders down, "I want…I want to feel all of you."

"Lucky," he managed, groaning, and he sunk a knee into the mattress between her legs. "Careful, darling," he whispered into her ear. "Can you raise your leg? Remember, after the wedding, when we fell onto your bed at Leland Pa—"

Her knees came up on either side of his body. He chuckled into her neck, seeking out her hands and entwining their fingers.

"Ready, then?" he whispered into her ear. "Breathe, darling."

And then he moved, and she felt a fullness…and then even more fullness…and then almost too much fullness…

"*Breathe*, Willow," he whispered again.

Willow breathed, and then she gasped, and then she breathed again. By degrees, her body relaxed.

Cassin kissed her, and she had the idle thought, *Oh, there is more kissing,* and she kissed him back.

For a while they kissed, almost until she forgot he was inside of her, and then he made a guttural sound, and she blinked up at him. His face hovered above hers, his eyes closed, his expression anguished. He looked so anguished, in fact, that she almost asked him if he was quite alright. But then he moved, and the agony eased from his face, and she felt a snap of sharp pain.

She sucked in her breath, and he froze. She looked again, opening just one eye. The jokes and the intermittent conversation had tapered off. Everything had tapered off except the incredibly close, incredibly intense feeling of being so intimately joined. And now they felt locked, fused together, his face a mask of discomfort. Willow considered the onslaught of new sensations—the fullness, the pain, and now the ever so small, ever so persistent impulse to move—and decided to hitch her hips up, just once. An experiment.

As she did it, she watched his face. Cassin's eyes were squeezed shut, and he made an indistinguishable sound—pleasure or pain?—and bit his lip.

She thrust again. He opened one eye and stared down at her. She smiled.

"You're alright?" he asked on a breath.

Willow nodded and thrust a third time.

Cassin growled and swept his arms beneath her, pulling him to her, and resumed movement, far more demonstrative and powerful than she had been. But she met him, push for push, and he leaned down and kissed her.

When the explosion happened, Willow pressed her head into the pillow and cried out. No warning could have prepared her for the complete incineration of every nerve, inside and out. No warning could have prepared her for the floating, the tingling as she floated, the slow drift back to earth, the tiny shocks, the blissful feeling of release.

Cassin paused, understanding somehow, that it had happened. But he did not pause for long; in fact, she would have happily indulged in more pausing, more floating, but she understood now; he sought an explosion of his own, and the drive for this goal was nearly unstoppable.

He cried out when it happened, calling her name, and then he collapsed on top of her, and she gathered him up in her arms, however weak, and held him. He buried his face in her hair. Idly, she stroked the bands of muscle that formed his powerful back. He relaxed within seconds, growing heavy, drifting to the same, boneless state in which she now reveled…and she savored it.

I love him, she thought.

And then, *I almost missed it all.*

If we hadn't needed to leave Surrey, and if marrying had not been the only way, I would have missed all of this.

But she hadn't missed it.

He was here, and she was here, and he—

Well, if he had not yet said he loved her, he had said many other things. Things about the authenticity of their marriage and being together every day and for the rest of their lives.

And she had not said these precise words either, not yet, but she would.

Chapter Twenty-One

In the five months since the brides had moved to London, breakfast in Belgrave Square had settled into a lively, communal affair.

Willow would rise early, eager to be ready for whatever her aunt and uncle might require of her.

Naturally diligent and purposeful, Sabine, too, was an early riser, and she would be up, dressed, and ready to explore the next quadrant of the city on her ever-ready list.

Since girlhood, Tessa was the friend most prone to sleep late into the day, but her pregnancy put an end to this practice, and now she would frequently be up before them all, too uncomfortable to sleep.

And so the brides would convene each morning, filling the small, windowed breakfast room with laughter and chatter. A buffet of fried eggs, toast, fresh breads and jams, sausages, and fruit with cream was laid by staff on a sideboard. Uncle Arthur did not take breakfast, but he always presided at the head of the table, drinking coffee and reading the news, while the women spoke around him.

The morning after Cassin arrived should be no different, Willow told herself. Eggs, coffee, chatter. And the unexpected presence of *a man*, fresh from her bed. With him, a thousand unanswered questions.

It only prolonged the awkwardness to be cowardly about it, she thought. Together, the two of them had survived the potentially awkward scene of awakening to the bright light of day with him sprawled, naked, beside her in her bed. The scene had played out so shyly and sweetly, eventually giving way to hilarity. They had laughed until they became too occupied to laugh any more. Now Willow had very high hopes for breakfast. The only way to surpass the strangeness of the situation was to face it.

"Can I trouble the footman to lay a place for the earl?" Willow said brightly from the doorway to the breakfast room.

The tinkle and hum of conversation in the room stopped. Four faces turned to the door, their expressions frozen mid-chew.

Cassin stood behind her, washed and shaved and dressed in dry clothes. Willow had struggled to stop staring at him.

She cleared her throat and took a brave step into the room. "As you may know, Cassin has made a surprise journey home from Barbadoes. He was my guest last…"

Now she lost heart. It had been a glaring breach of manners not to approach her aunt and uncle about Cassin's installment in their home as a guest. She'd simply been so overcome, and he was her husband, after all, and—

"I beg you, forgive the intrusion, Mr. Boyd, Mrs. Boyd," said Cassin, stepping around her. He presented himself to Uncle Arthur with a deferential bow.

The middle-aged man smiled up at him, stirring his coffee. After a long moment, he tapped the spoon and stood, extending his hand. Aunt Mary rose beside him.

"Do not interrupt your breakfast, please," Cassin said, taking Uncle Arthur's hand. "I am so grateful to be your guest. I've returned to England on urgent business at my home in Yorkshire, but my first stop is London. I was also…urgently motivated to call on my wife."

Tessa dropped her knife, and it landed with a clatter on her bread plate. Willow winced but did not look.

"Of course you are always welcome in Wilton Crescent, my lord," said Uncle Arthur. Cassin bowed over Aunt Mary's hand.

"But you must join us for breakfast," said Mary. To Willow, she said, "We've already laid a place for the earl, dear. There, next to you."

Willow released a breath and led Cassin around the table. Slowly, the clink and scrape of silver on china resumed, but the chatter did not. A rare silence descended in the sunny room. Her friends and aunt cast sidelong glances while Willow unsteadily poured two cups of tea.

"Mrs. Chance?" said Cassin suddenly, speaking to Tessa. "I've a letter for you. From Joseph."

Tessa's knife clattered a second time. Cassin reached into the pocket of his waistcoat and produced a letter. Tessa stared at it like a stolen jewel.

"My decision to sail home was hasty and unplanned," Cassin went on. "Joseph had time only for a page or so. This was scrawled, I believe, on an overturned barrel outside the fishmonger's."

Tessa glanced from the extended letter long enough to nod at him. She rose and took the letter, studying the inscription. And then she was gone, dashing from the room as quickly as her swollen condition would allow.

When she was gone, silence reclaimed the room.

"And I've also one for you, Mrs. Stoker," Cassin said.

Sabine's head snapped up. "I beg your pardon?"

Tessa received occasional letters from Joseph—their contents never discussed—but Willow knew of no correspondence between Sabine and Jon Stoker.

"From Stoker," said Cassin, extending a second letter. "Also hastily written, I'm afraid. Even so, I've promised to deliver it."

Sabine paused a moment and then smiled tightly and reached for the letter. She tucked it smoothly in the pocket of her skirts and returned to her blueberries. "Thank you, my lord," she said.

"What? No letter for me?" asked Uncle Arthur, weary, perhaps, of the tenseness around his table. "I dare say, I might cry."

Willow laughed; Aunt Mary, too, and Cassin made for the sideboard with his plate.

Through her chuckles, Aunt Mary asked, "How long will you be in London, my lord? You've come at a beautiful time of year."

"Yes," he mused, "how I enjoyed that beauty as it dripped down my neck, all the way from Falmouth." He shot her a wink, and Willow's heart clenched. "Thanks to my wife," he continued, "I've learned that my uncle endeavors to dig a new mine on my land in Yorkshire—a dangerous undertaking that I do not want, nor have I sanctioned. My purpose in London is to stop his intrusion. I will call on him first, although my suspicion is that he is not in London at all, but in Yorkshire instead. I also have a brother there who has fallen ill. Some accident in a field. For this reason, I cannot tarry long in town. But before I go, I must approach my uncle's mining investors and, depending on his progress to form a joint-stock company, relevant members of Parliament."

"Quite so," said Mary, sounding impressed. "Not quite a holiday, is it?"

"No, I'm afraid not." Cassin returned to the table with a heaping plate. "I've written to my family in Yorkshire and expect a return letter any day. I'll rely on your staff to send for me if some word arrives. I am anxious to hear of the progress of my brother, Felix."

"Oh yes, Willow has told us about your dear brother," said Aunt Mary.

And so the conversation tripped along, leaving Willow calm enough to serve her plate. She was halfway to the sideboard when Cassin said, "I should also like to make time to see Willow's work while I am in town."

Willow turned and blinked at him. "You would?"

"If I won't be an intrusion." He took a bite of crescent bun and made an expression of bliss. "We eat cold fish for breakfast in Barbadoes," he said.

"Cook will be delighted to indulge you," said Aunt Mary. "But my lord, would you have time in your schedule to accompany your young countess to something like a garden party? To the benefit of Willow's work, of course. Well, *our* work."

Willow paused with a piece of toast hovering above her plate.

Aunt Mary shrugged. "It cannot hurt to ask, darling."

"That remains to be seen," said Willow with a nervous laugh. "*What* garden party? When?" She looked back and forth between her aunt and uncle.

"A small gathering tomorrow, I've been told. The Eaton Square townhouse."

"Lord and Lady Landfair's house?" gasped Willow. "But we only finished that house last week."

"Indeed. And the baroness has wasted no time showing it off. We didn't mention the party because you intended to be in Yorkshire. I hesitate to bring it up even now, not knowing when you'll away to Yorkshire…" She trailed off and looked at Cassin.

"I am not certain that I will travel with the earl to Yorkshire," said Willow, taking a step to the table. "Cassin and I have not discussed—"

"I should like very much for you to join me in Yorkshire," he said plainly, "if your schedule permits."

"Of course," Willow said, gratification rising in her chest. "I had always intended to go. But you didn't—that is, we had not…" She looked at him.

Cassin folded his napkin in his lap. "It is my goal to discuss everything we might do, well before we might do it," he said softly, looking only at her. "But I may fall short of that goal for a time. The notion is new." He smiled a boyish smile, and Willow drew her empty plate up to her chest, shielding her heart.

"It had been my hope," he went on, "that you would make the journey to Yorkshire with me. I should like you to meet my family. I should like you with me."

Willow could but nod.

Aunt Mary said, "Lovely. It's all settled then. The party begins at four o'clock."

Willow gawked at her aunt. She'd known nothing of a garden party before this moment. It was not their practice to mingle socially with clients.

"But what is the occasion for a party?" Willow asked cautiously. "I cannot believe the paint is even dry on the walls."

"They took up residence the very day the last carpenter had gone. The garden party is the first of several events meant to reveal the new house to society. And why not? The tiles in the ballroom alone took more than a year to lay, well before you came to us. Arthur's furniture can be found in nearly every room. She will preen over it, as well she should. But how nice to have some ally among the guests to acknowledge some of the praise. And I'd love to hear what people will say. I'd love to make our services available when they say it."

"But if Cassin and I are unavailable, *you* must go, Aunt," said Willow.

Aunt Mary paused with her teacup halfway to her mouth. "But Willow..." she began.

"No, truly, you should do," Willow pressed. "I was late to the project, after all; you said so yourself."

Aunt Mary smiled and looked to her husband. Uncle Arthur folded his paper and tapped it on his knee. "What your aunt is trying to say, dear, is that *you* and only *you* would be welcome at a party hosted by the baroness. You forget how far from grace Mary fell when she married a common trades-man like me." He winked at Mary. "But a countess and her earl? It should not be difficult for you to wrangle an invitation and pop in, just for a bit. On behalf of the business. Nose about. Fan the flames of adoration, and give credit where credit is due."

"*Oh…*" said Willow, blushing. She was embarrassed to have forgotten the wide gulf between craftsman and society. "Forgive me, but I did not think. You, that is to say, *we* live so comfortably here. And we all sit in meetings with these people for hours; they fawn on you. They take your advice to heart and heed every word."

Mary chuckled. "That may be, but in the end, we are meant to create the backdrop for their lives, *not* appear in them."

"But I hardly feel esteemed enough to garner an invita-tion," countered Willow, looking around the table. "I wouldn't begin to know how to—"

"I'll procure the invitation," Cassin cut in, popping a sau-sage into his mouth. "I've sent an urgent note to Lord Althorp and requested a meeting about Caldera."

"Althorp?" exclaimed Uncle Arthur. "Leader of the Commons?"

Cassin nodded. "Likely, he will be chancellor of the exche-quer after the elections, and his Chancery Court would be the one to hear any case from my uncle's bogus mine. After we discuss Caldera, I will ask Althorp about Lady…who was it?"

"Landfair," provided Aunt Mary, beaming. She reached for Arthur's hand.

"Right. Lady Landfair. Compared to this mess with my uncle, a garden party should be an inconsequential request."

CHAPTER TWENTY-TWO

Cassin's first order of business was his uncle's townhome in Adelphi. He went in person, sending no message ahead. If possible, he would catch the pompous relation off guard.

Sadly, a uniformed butler informed Cassin that Mr. Caulder was "not in." No indication was forthcoming about Archibald's locality, and Cassin hurried away without leaving his card.

Two shillings later, a stable boy informed Cassin that Mr. Archibald Caulder had taken his best carriage to Yorkshire weeks before, with no promise of when he would return. Cassin gritted his teeth and lobbed another coin, asking him not to repeat their discussion.

Next he paid an informal call on Lord Althorp. He'd written ahead but doubled down and called on the politician in person just the same.

Here, too, a restrictive butler refused admittance, but he returned with a summons from Althorp, an appointment for a proper meeting the next day. Cassin was swamped with relief, and he asked the butler to furnish Lord Althorp with a brief report he'd written that detailed the Caldera mining conflict.

With this errand complete, Cassin needed only to procure an invitation to the garden party that had been so adroitly foisted on his wife. He did not fault Mary Boyd for making the request; in fact, he quite liked the idea of squiring his countess around London. But procuring the invitation from Lord Althorp had been an ambitious suggestion indeed, and Cassin mentioned it mostly to show off. Luckily, he had another card to play, and he made his way to quiet, out-of-the-way Moxon Street in Westminster to beg help from a friend of a friend.

"The Earl of Cassin to see Mr. Bryson or Mrs. Elisabeth Courtland," Cassin said hopefully. What were the odds that he'd be denied by the third butler of the day?

"*Brent?*" cried a voice from behind the butler. Cassin leaned in to see Elisabeth Courtland rushing to the door. She elbowed the butler aside and reached for Cassin.

"But we've not heard from Stoker in weeks," Mrs. Courtland said, giving his shoulders a shake. "Tell me now: Is he in London? I swear to heaven, if he is here and has not called on me…"

Elisabeth Courtland had known Jon Stoker since he was a street urchin in Rotten Row, raiding brothels on behalf of her charity. Their friendship had grown, and she began to provide for his education, his daily necessities, and his erstwhile scrapes with the law. When she married her husband, Bryson, the couple became Stoker's surrogate family. Eventually, the wealthy coupled delivered Stoker from the streets and sent him to university in Yorkshire. It was here that the lot of them first encountered Cassin. The Courtlands were Stoker's frequent visitors to school, and Cassin came to know them well. The couple was middle-aged now, with two growing boys. Mrs. Courtland's charity continued to rescue girls from the horror of London's streets, and Bryson Courtland's shipyard was one of the most prosperous in the empire. Stoker's pride had prevented them from asking the Courtlands to sponsor their guano expedition, and Cassin respected his partner's desire to make his own way.

"Stoker remains in Barbadoes, madam," Cassin assured Mrs. Courtland. "I've come alone. Some ugly business with an uncle and my estate in Yorkshire."

"How sorry I am to hear it," said Mrs. Courtland, drawing him inside. She dispatched the butler to fetch her husband. "But how kind of you to look in on us. The boys are in school, or they would be delighted to see you."

"Rudely, I've come to beg a small favor, actually."

"Anything, of course. How can we help?"

"My wife," he began, coughing slightly, "has developed an interest in a certain garden party at the home of a society matron, Lady Landfair. The event, I believe, is set for tomorrow. I was hoping you could assist with an invitation."

"Oh," breathed Mrs. Courtland, wrinkling her brow. "I haven't the slightest notion of *Lady* Landfair or her garden. I avoid parties whenever possible, as you may know, but Bryson will help you, never fear." She glanced to the door. "*However*," she said, turning back, "it cheers me to hear that you and your wife are…enjoying time together while you're in town." She eyed him expectantly. The Courtlands had made no secret of their suspicion of Jon Stoker's hasty marriage to Sabine;

indeed, they found all three rushed marriages very strange indeed.

"Quite so," Cassin said. "Willow's aunt and uncle have been kind enough to allow me to crowd in on them in Belgrave Square. It is my goal to make the most of my time with Willow while I'm in England. When my London business is done, she will travel to Yorkshire with me."

"She will," trilled Mrs. Courtland, clapping her hands together. She smiled and patted his knee. "It's none of my business, I know, but it cheers me to hear that your marriage was not—" She stopped and bit her bottom lip. "I am so hopeful for you and your new bride."

"I feel the same hope," Cassin said, unable to tamp down a foolish grin.

"Cassin!" called a voice from the doorway. "By God, you're a welcome sight." Cassin rose to shake hands with Bryson Courtland. "We had no warning that you'd returned to England."

Cassin nodded and apprised him of the situation with Archibald and the fresh worry with his brother.

Bryson listened carefully, gesturing for them to sit. The older man settled closely to his wife, despite the long couch and collection of plush chairs. He stretched his arm around her shoulder. It was the same comfortable sort of familiarity that Cassin's own parents shared, and he felt a persistent stab of longing. He missed Willow, despite having just left her bed.

"I know Althorp and consider him to be reasonable and fair," mused Bryson. "You should have no trouble convincing him of the machinations of your uncle. His agreement to see you on such short notice is a very good sign, indeed."

"This was my thinking," said Cassin.

"Yes, but what of the party his lovely countess wishes to attend?" prompted Mrs. Courtland.

"Right," said Bryson. "Lady Landfair. I'm in the acquaintance of the baron and his wife—"

"Of course you are, darling," sighed Mrs. Courtland.

"Procuring an invitation should be no effort at all. We've our own summons to a forthcoming ball in their new home. Next month, I believe it is."

Mrs. Courtland made a face. "I won't go."

"You will go, darling," said Mr. Courtland, "if only to compliment Lady Cassin's interiors."

"Oh, I suppose I could be troubled for that." She gave Cassin a wink.

"Thank you so much," said Cassin, rising. "I cannot express my gratitude, honestly."

"Wait just a moment, if you please," said Bryson. "Can we not pry some insight from you, anything at all, into the marriage of our wayward Jon Stoker? Please, Cassin, honestly. What can you tell us? Elisabeth worries so."

Cassin rolled his neck and returned to his seat.

"Anything?" said Mrs. Courtland, scooting to the edge of the sofa. "We have written to Belgrave Square several times to call on his wife, Sabine, but she always sends her regrets. She is perfectly cordial but quite...resolute. We should like to support her in any way we can. It had been our plan to make the acquaintance of all three of the girls. And now to hear that Joseph's young wife is expecting a baby?"

"Yes," said Cassin uncomfortably, locking and unlocking his hands. "I understand your curiosity; truly I do. But there is very little I can say, I'm afraid. You are correct that the marriages were not traditional. But the six of us have made a sort of mutual vow of, er, discretion as we sort things out, each in our own time. For loyalty's sake, all I can say is that your desire to know the brides is no different from my wishes and Joseph's. I cannot speak for Stoker, but I believe it may even be his wish, which is a rare sentiment, indeed, coming from him."

He paused and looked at the floor. "We would know our wives," he said. Looking up again, he told Elisabeth, "In time, I hope we will. I never suspected to be the first to do so, but I will not deny that I feel very grateful. If I had one piece of advice for each of my partners, it would be to facilitate that knowledge as soon as possible. Every day that I did not know Willow was a wasted day, indeed."

Chapter Twenty-Three

Cassin did not fail in his promise to procure an invitation to Lady Landfair's garden party in Eaton Square. The hand-lettered invitation arrived later the same day, while Willow led Cassin on a walking tour of Belgravia.

"*Look what's come*," her aunt sang when they returned.

Willow had been conditioned by these last five months to go very, very still, strumming with breathless hope, when anyone came at her with a letter. She froze in the act of removing her pelisse.

"Landfair's garden party," her aunt nearly whooped, waving the invitation in the air. "When the baroness takes a victory lap, you shall be trotting along beside her."

Willow looked to Cassin. "Thank you," she said softly.

Her husband ducked his head to her ear and whispered, "You may thank me later," before sweeping away her pelisse.

It was a promise that she made good on, although they struggled to keep quiet and resist toppling from Willow's small, soft bed in her basement room.

The next morning was devoted to negotiating with Perry about what she would wear to the party. When luncheon came, they were still at odds. Only when Mr. Fisk was asked to have a say did they settle on a full silk dress in icy turquoise, the soft fabric just a few shades lighter than Willow's eyes.

"You look like a *tropical waterfall*," sighed Perry, fluffing the skirt from the hem.

"Better than a tropical guano mine, I suppose," said Willow, hoping she was not overdone.

Cassin was in meetings all morning and returned to escort her with very little time. Between Perry's secluded efforts on Willow's hair and Mr. Fisk giving Cassin a fresh shave, they did not cross paths until the earl clipped up the stairs to collect her in the parlor.

He froze when he saw her. "I will never grow weary of looking at you," he said gruffly.

Willow smiled, taking her own long look. How was she in possession of a husband so tall, and tanned, and broad chested? Impeccably dressed, a gentleman on sight. The fine wool of his ebony coat stretched tautly over a grey waistcoat and shirt the color of snow.

"How was your meeting with Lord Althorp?" Willow asked.

"Informative," he sighed. "Archibald has been very busy, indeed. Forgery was only half of it. He'd done everything I assumed he'd done—rallied investors, bought equipment, applied to Parliament for a joint-stock company to dig the new mine. There is a chance we will arrive at Caldera and see the thing half dug."

"But can you stop it?"

"Yes. For all practical purposes, it's stopped. The hearing for the joint-stock company has been tossed out. Parliament can hardly proceed with forged documents. And there may be legal ramifications for Archibald. Certainly he will have to repay investors and explain the whole bloody thing." He let out a pained breath. "But I've no wish to discuss the mine or Archibald Caulder now, not when I have a beautiful countess to convey to a glittering party in a home of her own design."

"Well, in a home about which I took dictation while my *aunt and uncle* devised the design."

"That too," he said, extending his arm. "I've borrowed a Phaeton from my friends, the Courtlands," he said. "Despite the chilly afternoon, it pleases me to show you off."

Willow laughed. "We can easily walk. Belgravia is hardly expansive. You saw this yesterday."

"You are thinking like a tradesman, Willow," scolded her aunt, bustling into the room with a fresh rose for Cassin's lapel. "Remember this afternoon, you are a countess."

Lady Landfair knew his mother, Cassin learned. These were the first words from the baroness's mouth.

"But I owe her two shillings," gushed the baroness, "from a ten-year-old game of whist. Oh, how I have missed Louisa in town these many years. And your sisters must be nearly grown. But will they have seasons? You must bring them, Cassin, you must!"

"It is my great hope," Cassin assured her. "We are to Yorkshire tomorrow, in fact. I have been out of the country, and no one looks more forward to our reunion than I do. I shall convey your intention to make good on that bet."

"Oh, please do. I've been so delighted since I learned of your interest in my party—both of you." She beamed at Willow. "Of course the baron knew your late father quite well, Lady Cassin, being a horseman at heart."

"Oh yes, well, he has plenty of company, I should say," said Willow smoothly. "Thank you for receiving us."

"But the honor is mine," said the baroness. "Imagine my shock when I finally made the connection between the Earl and Countess of Cassin and the design service of Arthur and Mary Boyd. Hiring a countess to design my home had not even crossed my mind."

"I am only making the leap myself, my lady," said Willow. "But I am a lifelong student of design, and I feel very fortunate that Aunt Mary and Uncle Arthur have permitted me to contribute to their work. However, I am more of an apprentice than a countess when I step into that role."

The baroness scrunched up her face, unsure how to respond.

Cassin said, "Lady Cassin has the rare opportunity to be both countess *and* artist, but she is careful not to allow one to distract from the other."

"Oh," said the baroness, mentally dissecting this statement, "I see. But how will she—"

By luck, another couple crowded into the vestibule, and Cassin suggested that they not monopolize the hostess.

Willow took two deep breaths and allowed Cassin to shuffle her along. The baroness's half-spoken questions hung between them in the air. *But how will she—?*

How, indeed? Cassin wondered the very same thing. How would his wife carry on with her passion in London when he returned from Barbadoes? And after Barbadoes, he had no option but to take up his rightful place in Yorkshire. The answers eluded him, and he was loath to disrupt his brief time with her to pursue it.

"What can you tell me about the house?" he asked, weaving her through mingling guests to a drinks trolley. "Am I wrong, or is there a predominance of *orange?*" He poured goblets of champagne.

Willow chuckled, glancing around. "You are not wrong. You can't see from this position but"—she took his hand and led him to the drawing room—"*this* is meant to be the centerpiece of the design for this house."

Cassin stared up at larger-than-life oil rendering of the baroness, depicted in a citron-and-lime-colored gown with orange accents. He squinted on reflex.

"Indeed," said Willow. "My aunt believed the best course was to tease out the orange tones, rather than the chartreuse."

"I suppose the suggestion that the portrait hang in the cellar would be unwelcome."

"More like forbidden. And that, I have learned, is the most challenging part of designing interiors."

"Horrible portraits?"

"Preconceived notions of what represents beauty and good taste. I've yet to work on a project that does not come with some preexisting family artifact, treasured souvenir, or ill-advised piece of fine art that must be integrated into the design, generally with great prominence."

"Like the piano and harp in your music room."

Willow toasted him with her drink. "That house comes with rare good fortune, actually. On the scale of strange to ghastly, musical instruments rank very low. But I know of another house that must make room for a meticulously preserved evening gown, reticule, and boots that belonged to the owner's mother. All of it has been stuffed with paper, as if embodied by the woman's ghost, and encased in glass. Candles illuminated it day and night. Still another client insists on the marble statue of a human foot."

"Surely you mean an Athenian sprinter or a cherub with no shoes."

"No, I mean a foot. And we have no choice but to dress the houses around these items."

He laughed, hiding his smile behind the goblet of champagne. She was clever, so very clever. He marveled at the months they'd kept each other at bay when they could have been laughing. Laughing and making love. He smiled down at her, and she grinned back, her turquoise eyes flashing. Desire pinioned through him, a jolt so strong, he almost choked on his drink.

"Laugh if you must," Willow scolded, "but there is no end to the horribleness we are asked to accommodate. Honestly, I don't mind the challenge, but my aunt cannot abide it. Over time, she has honed her ability to hide how incredibly appalled she is at these items, but she rails the moment we are behind closed doors."

Cassin continued to chuckle, swallowing his laugh only when a middle-aged couple approached, asking to make their acquaintance. They were friends of his late father and delighted to see Cassin and be introduced to the new Countess of Cassin. Willow was cordial and polished, making polite conversation before crediting her aunt and uncle with the beauty of their surroundings, while gently inquiring about their home.

Pride mingled with possessiveness and desire, as guest after guest ventured to meet them, and Willow smoothly offered insight on the art or appointments of the house. By the time footmen appeared with trays of food, they'd spoken to nearly every guest in the room.

Cassin took up another drink. "But what of the *garden* in this garden party? So far I've seen only the orange room, the black-and-white room, and the room filled with guns."

"That would be the gun room." Willow sighed, rubbing her neck.

"You're tired," he said. He knew better than anyone that the last two nights had afforded her little sleep.

"Perhaps a little," she said, smiling shyly, "but I do wonder about the garden. Shall we make at least one turn around it? I never called on this job site when the gardeners were not also here. The plants will not be established, but it's meant to be quite an Eden, I believe."

She led him down the main corridor, pointing out the distinctions of each room as they went, and finally stepped through glass-paned doors and down stone steps into an oasis of green.

"Oh, but my mother would adore this." Cassin sighed. "She is an avid gardener."

The garden was not large, but it had been filled with plants, a lush patchwork of leafy textures and tendrils and every known shade of green. The sound of a gurgling fountain rose from behind a yew hedge.

"Yes, it did turn out quite nicely," mused Willow, following a gravel path to a stone bench. "What a shame the party has not moved in this direction."

"In my experience, the party moves only in proximity to where the wine is being poured." He sat down beside her. For a moment, he allowed himself to enjoy the dazed quiet of leaning against her. Her arm was warm against his sleeve, her skirts brushed his leg. He could feel the tickle of her hair on his neck.

After a long moment, he said, "I should bring my mother to London as soon as I am able. My sisters too. They've been very stoic about biding their time in Yorkshire, waiting for me to redeliver us into financial solvency."

Willow chuckled. "Oh, only that small task."

The sound of the fountain drowned out the distant din of the party.

"I remember in your letter," Willow said, "you recounted visits to London when you were a boy and in school. But these people do not seem to know you, not as a grown man. Did you not venture out when you were in London to raise money for the Barbadoes expedition? Before you came to Surrey?"

"Ah, yes, before Surrey." He leaned back on the bench. "I did not venture out, no. When we were not mounting our plan for the guano, I approached financiers about money, but nothing more. And you know what became of that."

"Surrey." She laughed.

He looked at her, trying to memorize the sound of her laughter. "Yes. Surrey." He looked away. "I have not socialized in London since my father died."

"But have you ever enjoyed the city?"

"I enjoy London very much. I simply haven't had the time or the resources to go about as earl, not as we did when my father was alive." He took up her hand. Was there a limit to the number of times he could thank her for the gift of her dowry? "Until today, I suppose."

She smiled, causing the freckles on the apples of her cheek to stretch. He reached out to rub a thumb across the side of her face. No amount of touching her was enough.

"Even if there was money, I have been too preoccupied with the bleak state of Caldera to spare London visits. The responsibility of the earldom…" He let out a harsh breath and released her face. He propped his elbows on his knees, dropping his head. "It is colossal."

"I cannot believe that you were an idle aristocrat's son before you became earl," she said.

He shook his head. "The irony is that I believed myself to be so ready. I wasn't idle, but I had very few proper obligations until this bloody business with the mines. Instead, I occupied myself with the relentless pursuit of one meaningless accomplishment or another. Marksmanship, riding, studies, languages—on and on it went. From boyhood, I was an inexhaustible little bugger, you might say."

"A competitor," she offered.

He shrugged again. "I was the future earl. While some boys might have seen this as license to relax and await the rising tide of privilege, I held the opposite view. I was determined to succeed at every endeavor."

"I've seen this with my own brother," Willow said. "My parents expected so much from Phillip."

"Well, my parents expected me to be a decent person, and they would not tolerate idleness, but they did not compel me to strive the way I did. The diligence came entirely from my own desire to win. At everything. I was to be the eternal champion. I craved deadlines, even before I inherited the responsibility of earl. I held myself to the highest marks, the rank of *first*. It was annoying, actually. Have I ever told you how I met Stoker and Joseph?"

Willow smiled and shook her head.

"We were at university together, as I've said. Norwood, it was called, not far from my home in Yorkshire."

"No Oxford or Cambridge for the fiercely competitive future earl?" she teased.

He made a noise of frustration. "One would assume, but no. I claimed some fealty to the land and schools of Yorkshire and refused to travel farther than Norwood. In truth, I was afraid to take my diligently honed skills so far afield. How would I measure up, going against the sons of other noblemen? I was competitive, but only in a very controlled setting, you see." He winked at her.

"I am impressed that you admit so much about yourself," she said. "Few men can look back and be so critical."

"I need only to look at my uncle to see what becomes of a man who cannot be critical of himself."

"And so Joseph and Stoker were your friends at school?" she prompted.

"Not at first. At first I had very few friends, actually. Norwood, although academically rigorous, is unique in that it welcomes students from all classes and stations. This is why Joseph, a former servant, and Stoker, a former street urchin and petty criminal, made their way to its hallowed halls. Good-hearted sponsors prepared them for university and paid their tuition. Young men from all walks may be accepted, from the sons of wealthy tradesmen, to country squires, to clergymen's sons. And every year or so, a young lordling like myself."

She laughed again. "I cannot and will not regard you as a 'lordling.'"

"Quite so. Please forget immediately that I've said it." He cocked an eyebrow, hoping to look nothing like a lordling. With a cool finger, she reached out and touched his arched brow. Her fingertip was gentle. He captured her hand and held it to his lips.

"Finish, please," she said, curling her hand against his mouth. "I must know."

"Right," he said, kissing her hand again and then resting it on his leg. "As you can imagine, my fierce competitiveness and insistence on winning, not to mention my station as one of the few students of rank, caused me to come off as rather...insufferable.

"It's so clear now, why I refused Oxford," he said. "Why venture into a large pond that teems with other large fish when I could comfortably glide through a very small pond populated by minnows?"

"You were afraid of not measuring up? At Oxford?"

"Afraid? Perhaps, but it was more a matter of why risk it, if I have my own castle and future earldom in Yorkshire, with no plans ever to leave? It was so very safe and guaranteed, don't you see?"

"So ironic," she said, "because the small pond of my girlhood nearly drowned me. I could not wait to escape it. While you reveled in it."

"Yes, and revel I did. I reveled until I was so obnoxious, no other student wished to have me in his room."

"Stop," she said. "You weren't so bad, surely. I adore having you in my room."

Cassin blinked at a fresh wave of desire. She smiled and slid her hand farther up on his leg.

"*Minx*," he whispered, stealing another kiss.

She ducked away and gestured for him to go on.

"In all honesty, I cannot believe I was so terrible. All of us were too smart, and too young, and too fit for our own good; arrogant young men at an expensive school, with our whole lives ahead of us. The two students who dumped me at the feet of Joseph and Stoker were far more terrible than I was."

"You were *dumped* upon Joseph and Jon Stoker?"

Cassin nodded. "What happened is this: I was assigned to a room with two other boys, and they were unhappy about the match. Chronic rule breakers, those two—victimizers of weak first-year boys; thieves of unlocked trunks; debauchers of village girls. In addition to my fiercely competitive champion's heart, I was a natural rule follower. Repeatedly, I foiled their cruelest schemes. And so one night, I suppose they'd had enough. God knows what I had done to irritate them. They vowed to be rid of my sanctimonious, princely behavior, or at least rid of it in their room. So they slipped some kind of poisoned, mind-addling tincture in my food at dinner. When the drug—to this day, I cannot say what it was—took effect, they dragged my addled, staggering, incontinent form into the courtyard."

Willow crinkled nose and shook her head.

"I've no idea why I'm telling you this," he said.

"I've asked you; that's why."

"Should we not return to the party?"

"After." She shook her head. "Tell me the rest."

"Did I mention the louts had shoved my hulking, adolescent limbs into a woman's dress, painted my face, and put ribbons in my hair?"

"Of course they did." She sighed.

"I've only the vaguest, panicked memory of this, because the poison put me entirely out of my head. And so there I was, barely able to stand, dressed like a fool, losing my dinner down my dress, crying out in frustration.

"In the minds of most boys, I suppose it was the perfect comeuppance for the earl's son who was always first to class, the longest report in hand; the boy who practiced the hardest and sang the loudest. And the crescendo of this sad tale"—he sighed—"is that one of my erstwhile roommates gave me a shove as I careened toward the fountain, and I landed, face down, in the water. I was entirely unconscious by this point, and I believe I would have sunk to the bottom and drowned if it had not been for Joseph Chance and Jon Stoker. They happened along, fought their way to the fountain's ledge, yanked me out, and beat on my chest until I spat up half the fountain.

"And then, as I choked and sputtered on all fours, they gave my roommates a beating that they likely remember to this day."

"Because Joseph and Stoker were so outraged on your behalf?" Willow surmised.

Cassin shrugged. "Honestly, I think they were simply glad for the opportunity to fight. They are prodigious scrappers, both of them, and to this day they relish a good row. Certainly they have taught me everything I know about fighting."

"But after that, you became friends?"

"Yes, Willow," he said. "Then we became friends. How could we not? They carried me back to the dormitory, cleaned me up, put me to bed, and regaled me with all the horrid details in the morning. I will be forever grateful to them—for fishing me from the fountain and all the days of friendship that have followed. Even so, they have never viewed it as a debt, God love them."

"And now you are partners."

"Yes. And now, for better or for worse, I have financed our grow-rich-through-bird-shite partnership by marrying us off to women we do not know." He took both of her hands and yanked her to him, tipping her into his chest. She laughed and fell.

"You really don't seem obnoxious to me." She pushed up. "At least, not anymore."

"Well, thank you very much, madam," he said. He gathered her into his arms and rested his face against the cinnamon silk of her hair. "How can I be obnoxious when I have impoverished so many families and made myself the self-styled Guano King of an island nobody's ever heard of?"

"And you acquired a wife from a London advert," she recited against his chest.

For a long moment, he did not answer. He'd never regarded his marriage to Willow as a struggle.

She pushed off his chest. "It's true." She laughed. "This is why you've resisted the marriage for so long. It was another humility?"

He shook his head and bent down to level his gaze with hers, eye to eye. "You were never part of my struggle, Willow. You were the only true win I've had since my father died. And I only resisted marrying you for two days. Two days. Very telling, indeed."

She arched an eyebrow. "What does it tell?"

"It tells that I have wanted you from the start, and two days was the outer limit of my self-control. And I should warn you." He eyed the door and gathered her closer still. "I feel myself pushing up against that same limit, even now. What do you say? Have we given this party its due?"

"I believe we may have done," she said. "Certainly we are the only garden-party guests who availed themselves of the garden."

"Then let us go," he said, sweeping her up, "before I avail us both of this garden in a way that Lady Landfair never, ever intended."

Chapter Twenty-Four

Willow laughed when Cassin asked her if she was able to make the journey to Yorkshire on horseback.

"I may not obsess over horses the way my parents always have," she told him, "but I was raised in the shadow of a great stable, and I was taught to ride properly almost before I could walk. Of course we shall ride. As long as my trunk may follow by coach. I do like to have my pretty things, as you may have noticed."

"'Tis true, my lord," said Mr. Fisk, fastening the locks on her trunk. "You'll be lucky to keep up with her. It's honestly a relief to my nerves that she will be your problem now."

Willow had hugged the old man and assured him she would take care, write often, and return when she could. Behind them, Perry sobbed.

Willow surprised herself by crying a little too, although not until the loyal servants and her friends had gone. Cassin took her into his arms, one of a seemingly endless whirl of embraces and kisses, so many more than she'd ever dreamed that a husband and wife could share. Her parents had always seemed perfectly contented, but she could never remember them actually touching each other. How quickly she could be accustomed to the attention and affection, the intimacy of mornings in bed, of dressing in the same room, of undressing...

And now they would ride together, side by side, traveling together to address a family problem together, like partners in the truest sense of the word.

They swept from London at dawn, riding full-out, and Willow smiled into the cold April air. Their pace was not conducive to talking, but they shouted to each other about this or that landmark as they passed. The manicured parkland surrounding Hardwick Corridor near Chesterfield. The slow-moving River Aire. The ruins of Roche Abbey.

Although they could have easily made Yorkshire in two days, they allowed for three, pacing the horses and enjoying the slow discovery of each other for two nights on the road. There were so many stories of Joseph and Stoker and Cassin, each one more fascinating than the next. Such unlikely friends with such a strong bond.

Their third and final night on the road was spent in the village of Harrogate, just ten miles from Caldera. Cassin had been torn between the desire to press on and the value of appearing relaxed and confident when they arrived to Caldera. If they galloped up, wild-eyed and frantic, the vanquishing effect would be lost on his uncle.

And so they cantered into Harrogate after sundown and took a room at an inn that delighted Willow, a fairy-tale cottage come to life, aglow in candlelight, with an inn keeper and his wife who went almost prostrate with affection when they recognized Cassin as the earl returning home. He was generous and kind, far more lordly than ever she had seen him, and he swore the inn staff to secrecy about his arrival and ordered a private supper sent to their room. To a man or woman, each reverential staff member whispered, "I'm sorry for your loss, my lord"—clearly still mourning his father, the late earl. Cassin accepted the sentiment somberly, despite the five years since his father had died.

Once inside the snug little room, Cassin collapsed into a chair while Willow went through their sole bag of hastily packed clothing, unrolling the wrinkled wad of his best suit and her green riding habit. She sent them down to be washed and pressed, along with Cassin's new boots, which she ordered polished to a high shine.

"And a bath," Cassin called to the maid as she hurried away with the armful of clothes.

"Begging your pardon, my lord?" said the young woman.

"A bath?" he repeated. "Can I trouble the staff to have one brought up?"

"With all due respect, my lord," said the girl, "you might remember that we have a bathing room right here in the inn. Quite popular, actually. Fed by the hot spring, with steaming hot water, if you like. One for the ladies and one for the gentlemen. Just downstairs."

Cassin grimaced and dug in his pocket for a handful of gold coins. Shoving out of the chair, he gestured, and the girl carefully held out her hand. With eyes wide, she watched him drop the coins into her palm with a *clink, clink, clink.*

"The countess and I should like to avoid public bathing, if possible. I know I can rely on you to locate a stray tub and fill it with kettles of steaming water right here in our room."

"Oh," said the girl, still gaping at the pile of coins in her hand, "of course, your lordship." She bowed to Willow, "Your ladyship. Right away, my lord," She closed her fingers around the coins and bustled out.

"I've never had a bath drawn from a hot spring before," Willow mused out loud, glancing at him. "Was it necessary to burden the staff with the trappings of a private bath?"

"I've never had a bath with my wife before," Cassin said, dropping back into the chair. "Hot springs abound in this part of Yorkshire; Caldera has more than one—a bathhouse, too, actually. Ancient Romans left aqueducts and bathhouses in their conquering wake some fifteen hundred years ago. Yorkshire is dotted with mossy mosaics and strange-smelling waters, gurgling to the surface. You may enjoy the hot springs to your heart's content when we reach Caldera, but tonight you shall bathe with me, in the privacy of our very own tub."

"Yes, my lord," she teased, mimicking the reverence shown to him by the maid. There was a mirrored vanity in the corner of the room, and she sat and began to pull the pins from her hair. She glanced at him in the mirror.

"You've picked up on the respect I so rightly deserve, I see," he mused, cocking a brow. His eyes were half-lidded. "I am the bloody earl, or so I've been told, and you'd better be on your best, most deferential behavior, or I shall be forced to lock you in the dungeon of my castle."

"Oh yes, my lord," she teased again. She removed the last of the pins and began to unbraid the long ropes of her hair. "Your castle is so authentic as to have a dungeon, is it?"

"Of course it has a dungeon. This is where I lock up impertinent wives who resist giving me a bath when I order it."

"Oh, and now I'm meant to *bathe* you?" She laughed. Her hair was free now, hanging long down her back, straighter than usual because of the restricting braids. She brushed it in long, even strokes.

"On second thought," he said, watching her as she brushed her hair, "perhaps I will bathe you. And you will call me Brent, instead of Cassin. And I will refer to you only as Countess."

Her brush went still, and she turned to face him.

"Do you really wish me to call you Brent?"

He shrugged, looking away. "You did it once before, and I almost pounced on you at the garden party."

"*Brent*," she tested, smiling, and resumed her brushing. "Brent." She glanced at him. His eyelids had dropped even lower, and he looked at her with an expression that she had come to know in the days since his return. A tremor of excitement thrummed through her.

"Come here," he said.

"I'm brushing my hair."

"Come *here*," he repeated. "And bring the brush, *Countess*."

She rose before she realized it, responding to the underlying command in tone. He made no effort to move from his slouch when she reached him, and without hesitation, she hitched up her skirt and climbed into his lap.

He took the brush and reached for her hair, but she was upon him before he managed it, kissing him, yanking his cravat from his neck, and diving her fingers into his collar. He dropped the brush to the floor and caught her up.

"*Brent*," she sighed, arching her neck to feel the rasp of his whiskers on her skin.

"Countess," he growled, and they clung to each other, indulging in a long, slow, languid kiss until the stable boys knocked on the door with the tub and the first steaming kettles of water.

Cassin awakened the next morning, satiated from the night of lovemaking, a satisfaction to which he could rapidly become accustomed. But now he must focus and prepare himself to evict his uncle; to make the rounds of tenant homes, assuring families; and to look in on his brother. In that order, hopefully. And in a week, if at all possible.

Despite his great love of the green dales and leafy lanes of Yorkshire, he could not linger, not if his ultimate goal was to eventually return from Barbadoes for good and offer a prosperous life to his family and tenants. He'd not embarked on the guano venture only to abandon it before they'd seen it through.

And Willow's time in London had been cut very short, indeed. She would want a speedy return. They had not yet discussed how they might balance her love of London and her design work with rural life in a Yorkshire castle, not really, but she had abandoned projects to make this journey. She would want return to her responsibilities and passions, too, as quickly as possible.

As to their impending separation from each other, Cassin could not think of it without feeling physically ill. How in God's name would he manage to leave her again? It had been a relief and a reward to reveal his true feelings for her. The painful uncertainty and regret would no longer be part of the separation, but they would still be so very far apart. He worried about her in London.

And God, how he would miss her.

But now he had little choice but to push away the impending agony of their separation and press on to what awaited them at Caldera. He shaved and dressed early and waited nearly an hour for her to descend from their rooms. She'd claimed she required more time to dress this morning in order to style herself in the manner of a proper countess. He indulged her and waited. And waited.

When, at last, she descended the stairs into the dining room of the inn, a proud maid hurrying behind her, Cassin blinked in the face of her throat-closing beauty. Even after days of togetherness, he was not accustomed to the shocking radiance of her hair—orange in some light, almost burgundy in others—nor the clear, smooth creaminess of her skin, embellished here and there with tiny outcroppings of freckles. Her blue-green eyes flashed pride and confidence.

"My sisters will believe the Queen Consort Adelaide has arrived," he said, taking her arm.

Willow made a face. "Surely they will not think me that old."

"They haven't the slightest idea of how the queen consort looks, beyond broadsheet sketches. You will fulfill their expectations nicely. And I've hired a carriage so that your beauty will not be wind-whipped. What would Perry think?"

"Oh, lovely," she said, watching a nicely sprung carriage being pulled 'round. "A carriage will allow you to tell me all about the cast of characters in your family. Their letters have been telling, but doubtless you may lend some perspective to what I have gleaned."

He laughed and handed her inside. They passed the short ride discussing what she could expect from his three sisters: Marietta, Violet, and Juliana; and his mother, Louisa, the Dowager Countess of Cassin.

"And your brother?" Willow asked. "There was never a letter from him, but the others spoke frequently of him and his wife. Ruth, is it?"

"Oh yes, Felix and his child bride, Ruth."

"Child bride?" Willow laughed.

Cassin nodded. "Barely seventeen when they married but far better than he deserves. The future earl could not come from a lovelier couple."

Willow contemplated this in silence as the carriage trundled along, and they did not speak until they'd nearly reached the winding path to the castle.

"Not long now," he said. If she heard the anticipation in his voice, she did not remark.

He breathed deeply, filling his lungs with the familiar loamy, acrid scent so distinctive to the place he loved most in the world. He glanced at her, praying God she could develop some manner of affection for the centuries-old castle and land.

"But will I be able to spot the house from some distance, Cassin?" she asked, leaning nearly almost outside the window. "Can you point it out on the horizon, or—"

In that moment, the carriage path curved, and they came upon the familiar gap in roadside vegetation. He held his breath. Instead of answering, he pointed to the view between the trees.

"'Tis not a house," he said, his voice almost breaking. "As I've mentioned before, it's a castle."

CHAPTER TWENTY-FIVE

Cassin held Willow by the waist to prevent her from toppling out the window. She was mindless of her balance, gaping at the grey-and-black edifice that loomed at the end of a long, tree-draped carriage path.

It *was* a castle.

And not a manor house with various fortifications or castle-like flourishes; it was a proper castle, no different from the drawings of castles one might see in a book of children's nursery rhymes.

"But it's…" she began, at a loss for words. The very height of it seemed to reach the clouds, and she could not see the topmost turrets for the trees.

She tried again, her voice in reverent whisper. "But I've never known of anyone who resides in an actual, working castle. I…I thought they'd all gone to dust, or been abandoned, or…I don't know…been grown over by the forest. *A proper castle.* But where did you get it, Cassin? Er, I mean, Brent."

Cassin laughed. "We built it. Or, I should say, our ancestors did. And as for dust or the forest, we keep beating it back,

I suppose. Every swing I take with my bloody pickax, I strike a blow to preserve the old heap."

"Never describe it so," she scolded. "It's *enchanting*."

"It does have one or two charms, for all that."

He rattled off a few basic facts about the castle, how the original structure was built five hundred years ago by the first Earl of Cassin. King Edward had granted the title and considerable lands to the family in gratitude for the first earl's bravery in the Hundred Years War.

No one knew if the first earl purposefully erected the castle amid so many Roman ruins, or if ancestors discovered the ruins in subsequent years, but the grounds were awash in Roman artifacts, and Cassin's brother, Felix, had devoted his life to their excavation and study.

The castle itself had been improved, he told her, shorn up and modernized over the years, but only in fits and starts, when money was available.

Unlike the property of many of the landed noblemen of the day, the tenants on the estate's vast acreage existed in a symbiotic relationship with the Caulder family; they earned their living from Caldera, but at the same time they supported the estate.

"But does it have all the trappings of a real castle?" Willow asked. "Bats and ghosts, moats and dungeons, and fireplaces large enough to stand in?"

"Well, I believe I may have already mentioned the dungeon," he said, winking at her, and Willow felt herself blush. Their lovemaking had taken on a playful naughtiness in the snug little Harrogate inn. Willow's body responded to the memory, already pining for the next night spent in his arms.

He went on, "Moat? No, but we have a lovely stream over which we are just about to cross—see the little bridge? Bats? Probably, as I have not been here to rout them out. Ghosts? Not that I am aware. Large fireplaces? Yes, two of them. Very smoky. A great nuisance. After I save the tenants and teach us all to raise sheep and provide guano fertilizer to the world, I shall learn some new way to ventilate the place. One thing at a time." He gave her another wink.

Willow smiled and watched the castle grow larger and more imposing with each lurch of the carriage. The walls had appeared almost lavender in the distant mist of the morning, but now she could see the stonework was a light, weathered grey. The knobby wall of old stones, deeply pocked and blackened at the edges, reached four or five levels and higher to towers or turrets. Willow counted three or four walks that stretched from one end of the wall to the other, each at different heights. The walkways widened where balconies jutted out, typically beneath a window. She was put immediately in the mind of Rapunzel or Romeo's Juliet. Windows abounded, in fact, scattered in no particular order, and Willow was alarmed to see that many of them were without glass.

"But is the castle open to the weather?" Willow asked.

"Oh, that," Cassin said. "Never fear. The wing of the castle in which the family lives is fully sealed from the elements. Glass in the windows. Doors that open and shut with working locks. Vermin controlled by aggressive cats. But the whole of the structure is too large and open to efficiently heat in the winter. We've been forced to leave non-family areas vacant and open, almost like a folly, while we reside in the family wing. There is plenty of room in the occupied areas of the house, but the entire castle, fifty bedrooms in all, would be too large for our modest brood."

Willow nodded, marveling at this undiscovered part of her husband. Lord and master. Economizer. Router of bats. The need was obvious, certainly, considering the size and age of the castle. But it was yet another reason it must be so difficult for him to leave home to mine fertilizer on the other side of the world.

She glanced at him. He gazed up at Caldera with a critical eye but also with an expression of affection that made her heart flip. Willow looked at the approaching structure, feeling herself fall in love with it because he loved it. And also because—well, it was *a castle*.

When the carriage passed through the outer curtain wall, the wild beauty of the trees along the carriage path gave way to a lush garden, formally manicured. A carpet of bright-green grass stretched on either side of a gravel walk, and smoothly clipped topiaries of different heights lined the distant edge. Low flowerbeds of April bulbs swayed gently with colorful blooms, and mosses and ivy frothed beneath the trunks of stately, intermittent trees.

"*Brent,*" Willow whispered, "it's breathtaking."

He shot her a proud smile, but his attention was on the wall, the garden, the great arched double door in the center of the largest, most central building. *The keep*, Willow assumed.

"It's oddly quiet," he said. "Too quiet." He looked around, his eyes narrowed. "This garden is my mother's pride, and I've never once seen it without at least three gardeners busily at work. And where are the stable boys to mind the carriage? I'm away not even a year and the whole lot goes to—"

Running footsteps interrupted him, and they turned to see a boy dart around the far corner of the keep.

"Lady Cassin!" the boy exclaimed, shouting back in the direction he had come.

Cassin signaled for the coachman to stop. Before the tiger could help them out, Cassin pushed the carriage door open and clipped down. The boy froze, and Cassin smiled at him. He turned and lifted Willow to the ground.

The boy shouted again. "But it *is* him, my lady! His lordship is home! Lord Cassin has come home!"

A moment later, one side of the keep's giant door made a loud clang and then creaked open, revealing a thin, middle-aged woman in a black crepe dress.

She paused, leaning against the door and shading her eyes with her hand, peering out. When she identified the shape of Cassin, she let out a sob and ran to him, her skirts flying behind her.

Cassin took two steps toward her and caught her in his arms.

"Mother," he said, his voice cautious.

"*Brent*," she sobbed, "thank God. You're home. It's Felix…" She dissolved in a fit of sobbing.

"Yes, the cows, I heard, Mother. No, please, no hysterics. We will send for the best—"

"No, no, it's too late, Brent. My son…my poor son Felix. He's dead, Brent. Felix is dead."

CHAPTER TWENTY-SIX

Nothing could have prepared Willow for the agony of meeting Cassin's family in the midst of a devastating family tragedy.

The pleasantries she'd gone over in her mind, the leather gloves she'd carefully packed as gifts for Cassin's sisters—these amounted to nothing. Now she stood mutely in the sunny castle garden and watched her husband try to console his mother while he absorbed his own shock and grief. He staggered a little, and the dowager countess literally hung from his body. Pain was etched on his face as he struggled to draw breath.

Willow was inconsequential to the scene, she knew, but she felt breathless herself. She was overcome with the desire to go to Cassin but restricted by her position as newcomer and outsider. She idled between the door and their embrace, like a new and unknown guest to a terrible, terrible party.

All the while, the selfish truth resounded in her head: Felix was dead, and Caldera's only opportunity for an heir had died with him. The earldom would require offspring, a male if possible, and Willow could provide nothing.

Her knees almost buckled as she thought through the ramifications. Only pride and her love for Cassin bolstered her. There was no time or care for her collapse, mental or physical. A young man was dead. A family was mourning.

Three young women now swarmed the castle door—Cassin's sisters, obviously—and they sprinted to their brother, escalating the scene with a crying, clinging onslaught of tears and sobbing. A fourth woman appeared, Felix's young widow, Ruth, and with considerable effort, she corralled them inside.

It was unexpected to see the grieving widow contain the hysterics and accommodate the surprise guests, but obviously young Ruth Caulder was the most capable woman among the group, widow or not. Gentle nudging and quiet leadership was, clearly, a preexisting role for Ruth, even in non-hysterical times.

"I'm so sorry for your loss," Willow whispered to Ruth when they settled on a threadbare couch before the fire. There was so much to say, but this, Willow knew, must be first.

"Yes, I appreciate it, my lady," Ruth said calmly, pouring tea. "It has been a terrible, terrible shock. We are...overcome. All of us. The dowager countess and Felix's sisters have a more vocal and colorful way of dealing with their grief, obviously. I am not prone to displays of emotion, but my heart has been broken." Here, her voice betrayed the tiniest rasp of a crack.

"I can only imagine," said Willow. She glanced across the room. Cassin leaned closely to his middle sister, Violet, and spoke in low, even tones. His mother clung to his arm, her head against his shoulder. The other sisters, Juliana and

Marietta, clasping tightly to each other, stood behind Louisa, Lady Cassin.

"But I only wish we had known," Willow whispered. "I had no idea that your husband's condition had grown so grave."

Ruth nodded. "Felix was very bad off after the accident; then he rallied these last two weeks. We all felt sure he would recover. Just when we believed him to be better, he lost consciousness. Before we could call for doctors from Leeds, he was gone. It happened very quickly in the end." She passed a cup of tea to Willow and her hand shook.

Willow smiled sadly. "Will you allow me to pour tea for the others?"

Ruth waved her away. "You are kind, but it is my preference to keep busy. My grief is different from the girls' and the dowager countess's. They feel relief in a torrent of tears and carrying on. I feel as if I am on a long, slow walk from hopelessness to... Well, I cannot say where. But I know that I must not stop."

Willow gave another gentle smile and watched the young woman pour tea into five cups. Not only was Felix's wife capable and controlled, but she was articulate and honest. Valued qualities all; qualities Willow would do well to remember.

"I'm not sure why I'm bothering with tea for the girls," Ruth said, staring across the room at the huddle of tears, with Cassin at its center. "They've scarcely taken food or drink since the funeral. Lady Cassin might do, if Brent implores her. She has always been blindly adherent to any word from her boys."

Willow nodded and took another sip and then another. Moments passed. Ruth settled back into the sofa and slowly nursed her tea. Periodically, one of the girls would let out an anguished sob. The longer Willow waited, the more difficult it was to control the doubts and fears welling in her mind.

It's up to Cassin now, she thought.

There is no other way the inheritance of Caldera can be resolved.

He will be compelled to annul our marriage and remarry.

Or he will invoke a surrogate woman to bear him a child.

He will…

Suddenly, she felt physically ill. She shook her head and swallowed hard, gulping the last of her tea. It solved nothing, of course, to indulge in a wild spiral of defeat. Cassin had lost his brother. The household was veritably drowning in grief. She was being selfish and outrageous.

Eventually, in time, she and Cassin would address the deficit left by Felix's death. Perhaps the lack of an heir could be somehow overlooked. Not likely, but perhaps. Perhaps one of his sisters would marry and the law could be manipulated to bequeath Caldera to one of Cassin's nephews. In addition to Willow's substantial dowry, she had inherited significant income from spare properties among her father's far-reaching holdings. It was the money on which she lived in London, and she received it regardless of her brother Phillip's progeny.

The situation was bleak, no doubt. But Willow must not dwell. She must support Cassin until…until the deficiencies of her body forced the issue.

Now she heard the sound of her name and looked up. Cassin was guiding his mother and sisters to her, watching her with sad, tired eyes.

"But I know you will want to properly meet," he was saying, "the woman behind your London correspondence these many months. She was planning to travel here from London without me; did you know it? I caught her in London with just twelve hours to spare."

Willow rose immediately, fixing a look of compassion on her face. She prepared to give a slight curtsy and take the woman by the hand, but Cassin's mother rushed to her with arms outstretched.

"Oh, my darling girl." The dowager countess breathed deeply, squeezing Willow tightly against her. "What a comfort and a joy your letters have been. And to finally make your acquaintance? You are the only bright spot in this horrible time. I'm sorry we are all in such a state."

Lady Louisa's voice broke, and Willow felt her throat grow tight. Her eyes filled with tears. She was unaccustomed to motherly embraces. Willow could not remember ever once being drawn into her mother's arms. She froze at first, holding her breath, but when the dowager did not release her, Willow felt herself slowly relax, to take real comfort from the closeness and the raw, honest affection.

"I'm so sorry for your loss, my lady," Willow whispered against Lady Cassin's shoulder. "So very sorry."

"Yes, well, at least Felix has left us doing the work he loved so. From the earliest age, we could not keep him out of the dales and crags, digging up old relics." She pulled back.

"I am so very sorry, my lady," Willow said, squeezing her hands. "But will you take some tea to refresh yourself?"

"Aren't you *dear*," sighed Lady Cassin, sniffling. "And so beautiful. I knew from your letters that you would be beautiful. Only a very clever, very beautiful girl of good sense would suit my Brent. I am so delighted to finally know you. But you must meet my daughters. Girls?" she called. "But come and meet lovely Willow."

Cassin's sisters crowded around her then, and she found herself staring into the sad-but-curious green eyes of Marietta, Juliana, and Violet. They, too, forewent formalities and leapt at Willow, flinging their arms around her neck and holding fast to her. Cassin stood behind them, his face tight and grim, more agonized than ever she had seen. He looked to have aged ten years since they arrived. He stepped away to speak softly to Ruth, and Willow saw him nod and run a hand through his hair. How she longed to go to him, to hold him and urge him to cry if he wished, to rail or to curse, and to look no further into the future than one hour at a time.

More good advice for herself, Willow knew, but so difficult to accept.

She would tell Cassin this, she thought. She would tell him so many things when, eventually, they were alone. And when this happened, she would not add to his agony by pressing him about his legacy to Caldera or reminding him that he had married a woman who was as barren as a stone—not yet. Not until he could properly consider the new circumstance. Which she prayed God would not be tonight. Or tomorrow night. Or ever.

Just a little more time, she thought. *We've only been married in earnest, a real marriage, for a matter of days. Just a little longer.*

Cassin's sisters had taken a step back, and she could feel them admiring her, whispering about her dress and her hair.

They asked to see her wedding ring. She held out her hand, and they drew her to the couch, sighing over the stone. She was just about to tell them how Cassin had bought it in Barbadoes when they heard the loud creak and scrape of the castle's front door.

All heads turned as Archibald Caulder strode inside, his gloves and riding crop tucked beneath one arm and hat in hand. A butler rushed to relieve him of these items, and he flung them at the servant.

"Inform my valet," he said. "These should look like new before nightfall." He turned to the group near the fire. He squinted the length of the corridor.

"Who's there?" he called, striding to them.

Cassin's sister Violet shot from the couch and raised her chin. "My brother has returned home, Uncle."

"Cassin?" boomed the older man. "Returned from the great wilds of God-knows-where, has he?"

Willow saw Cassin go stiff.

"Yes," Cassin said, stepping to greet the older man. His stiffness gave way to a slow, relaxed stride. He exuded confidence. "I *have* come home. Just as you will now be off to your own home, far away from here. As soon as humanly possible."

Cassin watched his uncle stamp across the great corridor, the familiar manufactured smile on his brandy-pinked face. The older man walked slowly; he would not wish to give the impression that he took orders from his nephew.

He was overdressed for the country, and his bright riding clothes were a marked contrast to the black-clad women's mourning crepe.

Felix, he'd learned, had been buried just two days before. By the time his mother received the letter Cassin had dashed off in Falmouth, his brother was already in the grave.

His sisters had struggled to bear the shock and loss but they were enduring. His mother was on the verge of collapse. The very last thing the household wanted was a shouting match between earl and uncle, but God help them all, they were about to have one. He would mourn the loss of his brother soon enough; at the moment he felt only the desire to beat someone to a bloody pulp. His uncle was not only proximate, but he deserved it. It was all Cassin could do not to take a swing at the man's smug, double-jowled chin.

"How goes your bird-dropping project in paradise?" his uncle asked breezily. "Barbadoes is a might pleasanter, one might guess, than the icy, grey spring of Yorkshire, while one's brother lay dying."

Behind him, he heard his mother muffle a sob. Cassin squeezed his hands into tight fists. "Barbadoes has far exceeded my expectations, in fact," he said calmly. "We intend to clear £300,000 with our first shipment, due in summer."

Archibald missed a step at this pronouncement, his smug expression going a little off. He chortled. "The devil you say. But surely you do not mean to speak of business in front of the ladies. Let us retir—"

"Surely, I do," Cassin cut in slowly. "'Tis for their future this money will provide. Theirs and that of every family at Caldera. I am happy for my mother and sisters to learn how well they will be looked after. And I want them to know that the dangerous legacy of coal mining will not return to Caldera." Cassin paused and then added, "Most of all, they should hear that your opportunistic presence will no longer be a burden or a threat."

Archibald laughed. "Opportunistic? A threat? But what drama you employ. Such a fuss over a visit to my brother's family. You are mistaken, my lord, if you believe this house to have known any unpleasant behavior from me." Another laugh. "Caldera is my boyhood home, as you know. I've begun to feel some nostalgia for the castle, as I age. It does me good to remember days gone by. A simpler life in God's country."

"I'm well aware of what you miss," gritted out Cassin. "I've been three days in London, undoing the mockery of a joint-stock company that you spun out of thin air with my forged signature."

His uncle stood very still, blinking at him, and then some barely contained flow of rage inside him seemed to rupture.

"You've done what?" Archibald hissed.

"Oh yes, you've heard correctly. The joint-stock has been dissolved, Uncle. The Parliamentary hearing will not happen. It is illegal to take up residence on an estate that is not in your possession and begin digging mines and selling shares. I marvel that you even considered such a plot."

"With whom have you spoken?" Archibald bellowed, advancing with his finger raised. "I've every right to return to this castle whenever I please, and I have an obligation to deliver it when you've abandoned it to penury and neglect.

"Why, you weren't even here to bury your own brother. Meanwhile, *my* sons, Simon and Nigel, traveled to Yorkshire in the spitting rain to properly mourn at Felix's sad little service. You might as well know that my boys so admired Caldera that they plan to return with their families."

"*No*," Cassin spat out, "they will not." His voice held loosely controlled fury. He was barely holding on. His uncle's family would *not* colonize his castle.

"But what can you mean, *no?*" Archibald laughed. "And just how do you intend to keep us out? You've no intention of remaining here; if you did, you would have said as much." Archibald rounded on him, still wagging his finger. "It's back to the islands for you, isn't it? Deuced hard to regulate who comes and goes from one's castle when one finds himself an ocean away." More laughter. "Especially a remote castle like this one, populated with little more than unprotected females.

"And," Archibald went on, pointing suddenly at Willow, "you've brought a new one to add to the pile, I see. Someone else to starve on your bloody principles."

To her credit, Willow did not blanch. She crossed her hands over her chest and tilted her head calmly to the side. She looked arrogant and bored.

Nicely done, Cassin thought, feeding off her coolness. Archibald craned and shuffled, trying to better scowl at her, but Cassin stepped between them and crossed his arms over his chest. "My wife may be referred to as the Countess of Cassin, sir, or not at all."

"Better get to breeding on that one," Archibald scoffed, now totally unhinged. "Difficult to get an heir when you reside on a deserted island and your lady wife lives in Yorkshire. And now with Felix gone…"

Cassin glanced at Willow again. Her face had gone white. He would've struck his uncle, but the older man was trying to provoke him, and violence would prove his bloody point.

"*And now with Felix gone,*" Archibald repeated, his pink face brightening, "I feel even less beholden to edicts from you and evictions from my own boyhood home."

"Careful, Uncle," Cassin said tightly. "Do you threaten me?"

"Hardly. Where's the need? You spend most of your time on ships prone to sink, among island savages, and jungles crawling with disease. What need have I to threaten? You'll meet your own demise before long."

Cassin heard his mother's resumed sobbing, and he gritted his teeth. His uncle had it all wrong, but he knew explaining would cause him to sound like he made excuses.

"Let it be known," shouted Archibald, spinning in a half circle, "that all of us are *well aware*"—he pointed to everyone in the room—"of the very simple arithmetic. I am but *one lone man* away from full ownership of Caldera. *Next* in line to inherit. And after me, my boys. You are that lone man, *my lord.* So decree and mandate all you like. Meddle with my affairs in London. Order the magistrate to pass a bloody law that I shall not visit the very castle into which I was born. Ban the tenants from mining the coal that their families have mined for generations. And then take yourself off to the wilds of godforsaken wherever-it-is, and we'll all watch and see if you don't…come…back."

He finished the speech with a dull *tap, tap, tap* on Cassin's chest, and then he turned on his high-heeled boots and stumped away, clomping through the great hall and up a staircase to the guest tower. He did not look back.

Cassin drew a deep, calming breath. He ran a hand over his brow, through his hair, and down his neck.

Think, think, think, he ordered himself. His brain must get around the grief of Felix and the rage at Archibald and control the situation.

Blowing out a puff of air, he turned to face his weeping mother, his wide-eyed sisters, and sad, unflappable Ruth. And then, dear God, Willow, still starkly white, her beautiful face lined with worry.

"No one panic," he said calmly, reaching for the closest sister, Marietta, and pulling her to his side. The other girls fell like blocks against him. "We've informed Archibald of his thwarted plans for any new mines, and no one should be surprised by the result. I'm sorry you had to witness his lunatic rages and threats, but I am too weary to forcibly remove him—yet. That moment will come, never fear. If you'll remember, we have always known this to be his way— Father used to joke about it, in fact. He'll be toppled far more easily if he's puffed himself up, drunk on his own perceived power."

He took another breath. "In the meantime, rest assured that you are quite safe—all of you—and I will not leave Yorkshire until he is gone for good. After that, I'm afraid he is correct. I must go back."

The women raised a collective cry of protest.

"You know me well enough," Cassin said, "to know that I must finish what I have started. But I will put measures in place to keep Archibald and his family *out*.

"Despite that," he went on, "you are all strong and self-sufficient, regardless of how low you may feel at the moment.

And you live in a bloody castle. You are surrounded by tenants who would give their lives to protect you."

They sniffed and wiped their eyes. A few of them nodded. Cassin smiled. "I cannot say the tenants feel the same way about me at the moment, but their devotion and loyalty to you is unceasing. You are safe, and you should be gratified to know that we are all on our way to being very rich, indeed. Richer than small-scale merchants of coal, to be certain. Archibald may paint my business in Barbadoes as a foolhardy lark, but I assure you that my friends and I are accomplishing all we set out to do. Everyone here will be provided for in the manner befitting an earl and his family. The girls shall have seasons in London, if they desire, and this castle shall be our home for as long as we desire."

The end of his speech was met with silence, and he squeezed his sisters more tightly. "We are Caulders, after all. Proud, resourceful, courageous. And takers of great risks. Let us carry on in a manner that would make Father and Felix proud."

This was met with first a snicker, and then a laugh, and then full-on laughter. Felix had been acerbic and cynical, an academic through and through. He would have had little time or care about family pride or enduring spirits. He would have endured Cassin's attempt with a raised brow, a sarcastic comment, and an expeditious retreat.

When their laughter turned, inevitably, to tears, Cassin disentangled himself from his sisters and left them to comfort each other, for better or for worse. He sought out Willow's gaze and gestured to the vestibule.

"Are you alright?" he asked, when she met him near the door.

"Me? Oh. Yes. Your family is lovely, Cassin. I'm so sorry for what we have discovered. Your brother...."

Cassin nodded. He wanted desperately to grab her up and bury his face in her hair, but time was suddenly, urgently, of the essence. If he intended to make good on his promises to his family, to arrange protection for them, to save the whole bloody place from his uncle's crazed threats, he would have to think cunningly and move quickly.

"Can I leave you here with my mother while I see to estate business?"

She nodded immediately, perhaps a little too immediately, and he saw tears shining in her eyes. Her grief touched him, and he reached down to scrape a kiss on her neck. She made a whimpering noise, and he breathed in the scent of her. "Thank you," he whispered against her skin.

And then he kissed her mouth and strode out the door. He whistled for a horse and rode out to pay his respects at his brother's grave.

After that, he would call on the tenants, one by one.

Chapter Twenty-Seven

The master suite of Brent's castle was more opulently turned out than any room on the property. The rugs were not threadbare; the drapes were fresh velvet. The bedclothes were new and expensive.

Ruth had given Willow a tour of the castle's family wing before dinner, and although Willow had been too anxiety-stricken to pay close attention, it was impossible for her designer's eye not to see that the castle, albeit a historical marvel, was in desperate need of new...everything. And *more* of most things. It needed better-crafted pieces of furniture and more thoughtful placement. It needed new window dressings. Fresh paint. The list went on and on.

Despite this, the design of the dwelling was not in the forefront of her mind. Instead, Archibald Caulder's threats followed her from room to room, echoing in her mind. She'd gone miserably along until Ruth led her to Cassin's bedchamber, the only truly beautiful room.

And now, she waited.

She wondered idly if Lady Cassin had arranged for the thoughtful attention to the earl's suite, or whether Cassin himself had arranged them. It was a shame, either way, because the room had sat empty most of this year and the last.

Future years? Willow could not say. She would not be a part of Cassin's future, and it made her physically ill to look at the massive four-poster bed and think of her husband taking another woman…a young, fertile woman…into it, while she—

Well, she had not been able to think her way through what she would do. Hopefully, they would be able to annul the marriage, so she would not be forced to endure the stigma and ostracism of divorce. If the marriage was annulled, she could likely return to Aunt Mary's and Uncle Arthur's, to carry on as their apprentice and perhaps eventually take on design clients of her own. That had been her plan all along, hadn't it? To live with Sabine and Tessa in London and create beautiful places for distinguished people?

Cassin and her love for him had been a new dream, a dream in which she should have never allowed herself to indulge. She had been selfish to even consider it, and now she would pay the price in heartbreak.

And his family, his lovely family, would pay the price in confusion and alarm and, likely, outrage.

Cassin himself?

Well, likely he would be upset for a time (another cause for guilt). But he would recover. He was a wealthy man, an earl with a bloody castle; he would have his pick of women throughout Yorkshire and beyond.

Willow sighed and fell back into the cushioned window seat of Cassin's bedchamber. It was a beautiful spot, perched against a window with gill-shaped panes, both transparent and stained glass. She could see the stars twinkling over Yorkshire, magical and serene. She saw his mother's garden, silver-green in the moonlight. She saw the long, winding road that would take her away from this place, possibly very soon. Possibly tomorrow. The sooner the better, really. The longer she remained, the more painful her heartbreak would become.

Idly, she played with the wedding ring Cassin had given her, turning it on her finger, gazing at the green stone. Would it be too painful to keep it, she wondered. Would the sight of it, or even the knowledge of it locked away in a drawer, prevent the shattered pieces of her heart from eventually fusing awkwardly back together?

She tugged on the gold band, testing its give. She was hit with a wave of misery so complete she nearly toppled from the window seat. She squeezed her hand into a fist.

No, she could not remove it. Not yet. There was too much love and hope and unadulterated joy imbued in the hard, warm metal of the band and the multifaceted twinkle of the stone. And now the tears began to fall, more tears than she ever thought possible, and she held her closed hand to her heart, rested her face on her knees, and sobbed.

The crying, perhaps, prevented her from hearing the heavy chamber door open and close. Or perhaps it was the numb, floating detachment with which she now regarded the world beyond her anguish.

"*Willow,*" sighed a familiar voice.

She looked up.

Cassin stood in the center of the room, his hair wild, his eyes bloodshot, his waistcoat dragging from his hand.

"*Willow*," he repeated, his voice raw. His expression called to her.

Willow's heart squeezed so tightly she thought she would never again draw breath. Fresh tears shot to her eyes, and she bit her lip, willing herself to be strong. She scuttled back into the corner of the window.

"Ruth led me to this room," she said formally. "I didn't know where else to go."

He bent his head, looking at her with tired confusion. He dropped his waistcoat on the floor.

"Willow, please," he said. His voice sounded so very tired.

An unspecified entreaty was not what she expected, and she did not answer. She listened, trying to hear over the pounding of her heart.

He trudged to a chair before the fire. "Will you help me pull my boots?" he asked.

"No," she said, pushing farther back. The blue velvet curtains nearly swallowed her.

"Why not?" He collapsed into the chair and leaned his head back, staring at the beams of the ceiling.

"I think it is better that we not touch."

He looked like a man who had gone ten rounds in a boxing match. She held fast to the cushion of the seat to prevent herself from going to him.

"Now, why, I wonder," he said flatly, speaking to the ceiling, "would it be *better*, on the day I learn of my brother's death, and the day I go toe to toe with an uncle who would like to see me dead, *and* on a day I've been shouted at, and complained to, and challenged by desperate families in my care—why, at the end of that day, would I be better off *not* being touched by my wife? I ask you. Please tell me. Because the prospect of touching you, honestly, Willow, has been the only thing that has seen me through this day."

Tiredly, he raised his head and looked at her.

She shrank back. "Make me out to be cold and heartless if you must, Cassin, but—"

"Call me Brent, for God's sake," he said, dropping his head back.

"I will not call you Brent," she said, coming out from the curtain. She edged to the lip of the window seat. The malaise and self-pity of the day transformed, somehow, into angry energy. "I will not pull your boots. I will not be your source of comfort, Cassin, on this terrible day when you so desperately need it—when I so desperately need it—because it will only make matters worse, more wrenching."

"Forgive me if I cannot see how things could become worse than they are." He sat up and began to work off his boots. "I suppose if Stoker's brig sunk, and we lost our payload. That would be worse. But let us not invent challenges. We have enough actual problems at the moment."

"True," Willow said, carefully stepping from the window. She did not trust herself not to go to him. "Which is why I will not prolong the intimacy that we have shared as husband and wife. The longer we are intimate, the more difficult it will be to separate. At least for me. As I said, I've only remained in your room because I didn't know where else to g—"

Cassin was out of his chair and across the room before she could finish. He took her up by the arm, bringing his face within inches of hers. "Do not even *pretend*," he growled, "that we will end this marriage, madam. Do not."

Willow pulled on her arm, but he would not let her go. "I'm not pretending," she said, unable to stop a rush of tears. "I won't remain married to you when I cannot provide you with an heir."

She jerked her arm again, and he released her. She staggered back and then skittered to the other side of the bed.

He stalked her. "You believe me to care more about an heir than my wife? I don't even care about my uncle, if it comes to this!"

"Comes to what?" she cried. "You have a home and a family that you love. Now that you have shown it to me"—she gestured frantically around her—"I can see why. You have a responsibility to the families on your land, and you take this seriously, as you should.

"Likewise," she went on, "you require a wife who can bear you healthy sons who will keep Caldera from the hands of your uncle. I will not be the reason that you cannot prevent his aggression—not when literally any other woman in the world could bear children for you. In time, you could come to love another woman." Willow's throat burned around the words.

"Explain to me what you intend," he said cruelly. "You would divorce me?"

He rounded the bed and reached for her, but she dove. She landed in the center of the bed and skittered across it.

"No, an annulment," she said, panting with the exertion, "I had hoped you would annul the marriage. If you tell the judge that you've only just learned I am barren, he will grant—"

Cassin caught her by the ankle and pulled, dragging her back across the bed. She closed her eyes and let herself be dragged. His strength exceeded hers. He was so angrily opposed to her suggestion—so much more opposed than she had predicted—and in the pit of her stomach, deep down below the knot of fear and hurt and the thousands of sharp, heavy pieces of her broken heart, a very tiny spark of hope had begun to flicker. And the stronger, and bigger, and angrier he became, the brighter it shined.

"Listen to *me*, madam," he said harshly, flipping her over, "and listen very well, because I'm already bone tired and emotionally spent, and I haven't the power for another battle today. A battle with you, of all people. There will be *no* annulment; there will be *no* divorce. You are my wife, despite the known fact—known within a day of making your acquaintance—that you will never bear children."

"But Cassin," she cried.

"*Brent*," he growled.

"But *your lordship*," she corrected, the flicker growing into an earnest flame, hotter and hotter.

Cassin growled again and reached for her right foot, drawing her leg up. She'd been dressed for dinner, and she'd wore silk slippers beneath a pink gown. He ripped the left slipper from her foot and threw it across the room.

"You will spend your life building Caldera to be the estate and castle that you want it to be." Willow cried. "Safe for your tenants. Home to your mother and sisters for as long as they like, just as you said today. And for what? So that your cousins will take it over and boot them all out when you die? I won't do it," she said, kicking him in the shoulder with her bare foot. "I won't do it."

"And what care have I," he shouted, taking up her other foot and ripping off the slipper, "for what happens after *I'm dead,* if I've been forced to live my life without you? What could I possibly care, Willow?"

He dropped her legs back to the bed and fell over her, holding himself off her with his arms on either side of his head. She stared up and saw that his eyes had filled with tears.

"What life would that be, Willow?" he asked harshly. "Without you? No life at all—that's what. A life I cannot even fathom. I love you, Willow. And my love for you is greater than my love of this castle or my fear about my uncle and his bloody reptilian sons."

She blinked up at him, trying to see him clearly through the tears in her eyes. Quickly, before she lost heart, she allowed herself to swipe out a hand and grab the front of his shirt and to hang on, holding him there.

"We'll sort something out," he said. "My God, I've married a woman I didn't even know for £60,000 and then spent five months pulverizing bird droppings—all in an effort to bloody, *sort something out.* Does this not prove my willingness to be creative and resourceful?"

"But…" Willow began, the hope in her chest now burning like a bonfire, tears streaming down her face and into her ears, "but there is no way around *not* being a father, Brent. It's so very final. Such a sacrifice."

"And what of your sacrifice? I've not even had the time or, honestly, the bloody nerve to ask you how you feel about this moldering castle. But there is little help for whether you like it or not. You've married me, and Caldera *will* be your home, at least some part of every year. Perhaps we can spend some time in London, but your dream of living there? Of designing the new homes in Belgravia? That dream, precisely as you saw it, will not be—not if you are married to me."

He dropped to his knees, laying his body across her, dipping his face just an inch from hers. "And you *are* married to me, Willow Caulder, Countess of Cassin. Irrevocably, you are married to me. Can you sacrifice your dream of living in London?" he whispered.

"It's not the same," she whispered. "My not designing the interiors of homes is not the same as your never becoming a father. No nobleman in England would consider it to be the same. No nobleman in England would knowingly remain wed to a woman who cannot procreate."

Cassin growled with frustration. "You speak of this circumstance with your body as if it is *your* fault, Willow, and it's not. Barrenness is not a…a character flaw for which you must apologize. It simply *is*. Like your beautiful red hair. Or your clever blue-green eyes. I don't care what other noblemen might or might not do. I refuse to hold this circumstance against you—as if it's some deficit we should all feel mournful about. I'm not mournful about it. All I feel is love. For you. Great love. Love that cannot be annulled or divorced away. No matter what you think." He dipped his head and nudged her nose with his, once, twice.

Willow closed her eyes. "I love you, Brent. I love you enough to let you go."

He growled again and swept his arms beneath her, gathering her up. "*Stop* saying that. Please, good lord, have mercy on me. I've dealt with enough agony and wretched news today." He buried his face in her hair. "Of all the times to come at me with this, Willow. bloody hell. I've only survived till this moment because I knew I would eventually get to climb up to this room to you."

Willow released his shirt and wrapped both of her arms around his neck, clinging to him.

"You said every correct thing," she said, kissing the side of face again and again. "You said everything exactly, perfectly correct. Everything about you has always been exactly, perfectly correct."

He laughed at this, laughed through his kisses, and then he rolled over, taking his wife with him, and buried himself in her love and her comfort and her body until he was too exhausted to do anything but sleep and hold her tight.

Chapter Twenty-Eight

The next morning, after Cassin rose and dressed and rode to a meeting of assembled tenants, Willow made her way down the stairs to determine how she could best be of help to Lady Cassin and her sisters-in-law.

The hope instilled by Cassin's very fierce declaration of love still felt very new and tenuous, but it was his very fierceness, somehow, that allowed her to trust what he said. It was not a debate he wished to drag out or return to on occasion, and thank God. Despite everything that she could not do, he had been so emphatic.

Alright, she'd thought when she'd awakened. *Let me determine the best way to contribute what I can.*

She had just finished breakfast when Ruth appeared in the vast, drafty dining room of the family wing. Although pale and red-eyed, the young woman appeared both composed and diligent. After dispatching maids with breakfast trays for Lady Cassin and the girls, she offered to finish Willow's tour of the castle and grounds.

"You cannot feel up to squiring me around the castle," Willow told her. "Won't you tell me some way I may help you so that you may rest?"

"Honestly," sighed Ruth, "I relish the idea of having something diverting to do."

And so they toured. Yesterday they'd canvased the family wing. Despite Willow's mind being miles from beauty and color and design, she had been troubled by what she had seen. The floors were clean and the windows washed, but soot from the fireplaces tarnished every surface, the furniture was forgettable, except when alarmingly damaged by overuse, and the carpets were faded and flat. Despite the many windows, an eye-squinting dimness seemed to hover over the great hall—primarily, Willow knew, because the colors (or rather the lack of any discernible color beyond "drab") swallowed the sunlight.

Although the family wing was large, the various spaces had not been thoughtfully arranged, and the result was an odd mix of emptiness in some spots and crowded overpopulation in others. Beyond the frowning ancestry portraiture, there was very little art. The tapestries on the walls were dusty, moth-eaten, and ages out of fashion. The fixtures for candles and torches appeared to be the tarnished originals from five hundred years ago.

Today, however, she saw the castle with fresh eyes. Yesterday she believed she was literally on her way out; today, conceivably, as countess, she was the mistress of all of it. Not only could she concentrate on it, but she was excited for the tour Ruth would give. She longed for parchment and a pen to scribble down notes. She would die for a measuring tape. Oh, and if she'd only had her sketchbook.

Sensitivity would, of course, require her to manage the dowager countess's sense of ownership and pride in the castle. Lady Cassin seemed to enjoy her gardens more than the interiors, but surely she had some preference. Still, everything in good time. Twelve hours ago, Willow thought she'd never see Caldera again. Today she could resist piling up every available textile and lighting a fire.

"But does the staff not have ladders or scaffolding to dust the ramparts and the ceiling beams?" Willow asked Ruth as they made their way to the open, uninhabited section of the castle.

"I cannot say," said Ruth. "Certainly I've seen ladders in and around the daily upkeep of the castle. I can tell you that Lady Cassin spends the majority of her time in her garden and nowhere else. The housekeeper, Mrs. Grant, is left to her own devices when it comes to the residences, I believe. It would never be my place to criticize. This castle is very grand, to say the least, compared to my very humble beginnings."

Willow smiled at the younger woman's honesty. "How did you become acquainted with Felix? If you don't mind my asking."

Ruth smiled wistfully. "No, I don't mind. I was hired by Felix to transcribe his illegible note-taking and manage other secretarial work related to his research. He was just home from Oxford and was beginning his study of Caldera's Roman ruins. This was six years ago, I suppose."

"Six years ago?" marveled Willow. "But you must have been—"

"Fifteen years old," Ruth chuckled. "Quite young, I know. But the village of Harrogate is largely absent of able-minded, literate applicants who might transcribe academic notes in English and Greek."

"You read Greek at fifteen?"

Ruth smiled, leading Willow from a warm corridor, through a door, and into what appeared to be a cold, vacant ballroom. "Indeed. My father is vicar in Harrogate, and my classical education began very young."

Willow nodded, looking around the ballroom. The dusty floor was parquet, inlaid with geometrical pieces in half a dozen different woods and stains. The peeling, cobweb-strewn walls were paneled, the ceiling a veritable map of intricate raised scroll work. Tarnished chandeliers hung drunkenly at intervals.

"But is this room open to the weather?" Willow said, staring at the windows.

Ruth shrugged. "Glass remains in a few windows, but not many, I'm afraid. This part of the castle has not been in use, I believe, in Felix's or Brent's lifetimes."

Willow nodded, spinning slowly in the vast, forgotten ballroom. "It could be stunning, this room," she said.

"I cannot say what use would come of it," Ruth said. "There are limited families of quality in Harrogate. Lady Cassin and the girls are friendly with the other gentry, but even if every last family turned up on the same night, children included, they would not fill this ballroom, not by half."

Willow nodded, following along as Ruth led her to the next room, a long, thin banquet hall. In this room, the massive oak banquet table remained but only two or three high-backed carved chairs. Willow slowly walked the length of the room, running her hand down the sticky surface of the table. Two birds, nesting in the thick paneling, flushed from the ceiling and startled her. She watched in amazement as they flapped wildly through an open window.

Turning back, she saw that the walls here were paneled too. Willow squinted and leaned in.

But was there…

Yes.

The brushstroke outlines of a faded mural, painted sometime long ago inside each paneled square. She stepped closer. It was a landscape, something pastoral and light. She scraped at the dust and grime with her fingertip and retreated to take it all in.

Faded by age and elements, puckered in spots from water damage, she could *just* make out a sprawling landscape, with blue sky and green hillside, a stand of trees and a pond.

"It's a mural," said Willow, smiling at Ruth, pointing to the wall.

"Is it?" Ruth said, stepping closer. "So it is. Felix never paid this part of the property any mind. About a thousand years too new for our tastes."

Willow nodded, looking to the other walls. How breathtaking a giant mural would be, wrapped around the entirety of the room.

"Felix's sisters have said you are a designer," Ruth said, watching her. "That you select the interiors of great mansions in London."

Willow laughed. "Well, mostly I was an apprentice to my aunt and uncle. You were an apprentice, in a manner, to Felix weren't you?"

"Well, I was his assistant for a time," Ruth said. "In the beginning. Until I was not."

She smiled then and shared how, despite Felix's most noble effort to resist her, they had eventually fallen in love. "We held off a year and a half," Ruth said, smiling. "Until I was seventeen. It was torture."

"I can tell you loved each other very much," Willow said softly.

Ruth nodded. "We loved two things most of all," she said. "Each other, and Roman artifacts. Would you like to see our very own Roman bathhouse?"

Willow nodded, her throat suddenly tight.

Ruth went on, "There are also some twenty-five bedchambers in this part of the castle, but each one is the same as the next, so perhaps we shall tour those another day."

Willow nodded again and followed her through three doors and into the sunny rear garden of the castle. Pecking chickens squawked and flapped from their path, and dogs trotted up to trail behind them.

"That building is the kitchens," Ruth said, pointing to an outbuilding. "The food we eat in the castle is prepared in the original detached kitchen. Staff carries our meals, or tea, or even an apple, if we call for it, across the garden and into the family quarters. Even in the rain."

Willow shaded her eyes and looked at the grey stone outbuilding, its chimneys pumping smoke into the sunny sky.

"And that is the smokehouse; there's the wood store; that's the root cellar; the former arsenal, now used for Felix's and my excavation gear—well, now just mine, I suppose—and that," she finished, her voice rushing on, "is the bathhouse."

"Oh yes. Cassin mentioned that the castle had its own bathhouse. How lovely." They ambled toward it. The building had been built to match the castle, more grey stonework, a flat roof with a walkway lined with a gapped wall.

"Yes, and lovely it shall remain, I suppose. Felix and I were just about to dismantle it, brick by brick. Obviously that will no longer happen."

"Dismantle it? But why?" Willow followed Ruth through the thick double doors into a room that looked so far from what she expected, she stopped and blinked.

"It's so bright," Willow marveled.

Instead of dim sootiness, this room had been tiled, wall-to-wall, with pale yellow ceramic. The yellow was broken at intervals with orange and black tiles, creating a beautiful mosaic that began near the door and zigged and zagged to the far wall. The center of the room dropped into four walled pools, also tiled, with tiled benches lining the sides. It was a room-sized work of art.

"We had a room very similar to this in my parents' estate, Leland Park, in Surrey," Willow said. "It could not have been nearly as old, but it is in far worse repair. I've always wanted to redo it."

"Well, this one is not in what I'd call good repair either, although the family still uses it," said Ruth. "Felix and I promised the moon in the way of improvements to it after we excavated it—this is how we garnered Lady Cassin's support."

"Support for what?"

"Oh, this bathhouse is only about three hundred years old. But it was built *on top* of an eighteen-hundred-year-old Roman structure that was used for the same purpose. An original Roman bathhouse, if you can believe it. The hot spring that feeds the baths today is the very same that the conquering Romans used in 45 AD. We were going to dig down and study the original. We were going to try to recreate the facility as the Romans built it, if we could."

"A hot spring," Willow marveled. "Truly?" She picked at the mortar of a loose orange tile. "Our bathing room at Leland Park was in the cellar, and servants were forced to haul steaming water from the kitchens to fill the bath. The room did not interest my parents, and they would not permit me to remake it. Such a shame, but this is beautiful. I can see room for a few improvements, but by and large, it is a rare and beautiful thing. Truly. The mosaic is a work of art." She turned back to Ruth. "And the water for the baths? Is it nice?"

"Oh yes, lovely," said Ruth. "It's why we put off excavating it for so long. No one was willing to be without the comfort and convenience of the baths. See—here?"

Ruth went to a rectangular spout and turned a lever. After a series of groans and pops, a rush of fizzy, acrid-smelling water poured from the spout into a basin below. "Go on; try it," Ruth said.

Tentatively, Willow held out her hand. The water was hot—almost too hot to tolerate, but not quite—as it bubbled and gurgled against her hand.

"Your neighbors must be jealous," Willow said idly, enjoying the hot water coursing through her fingers. "And the tenants? Are they ever permitted to use it?"

"Oh, hot springs such as this abound in this part of the country. The neighbors and the tenants all have of their own source for a spring. We are fortunate because this very convenient spring was made into a proper bathhouse, but people around Harrogate make due with a wash tub or a trough. Some use the original Roman ruins, if they remain intact."

"I had *no idea*," Willow said, stepping back and wiping her hand on her skirts. "You should see the bathing rooms and pulley systems we are installing in the new mansions in London. The richest families will have hot water at their whim, and upstairs, too, in their bedchambers. If only they could see how it's done in Yorkshire…"

The words were scarcely out of Willow's mouth before an idea struck her.

The idea hit her so powerfully and so fully formed that she fell silent and ceased hearing Ruth's chatter. She blinked and held out a hand to the cool wall for steadiness. Good lord, but if Cassin and his family would consider it, her idea might save Caldera and its people for generations, just as coal mining was meant to have done.

"I must find Cassin," Willow said suddenly, spinning on Ruth. "I must find him straightaway."

Cassin's mood upon returning from his meeting with the tenants was, if not encouraged, then at least not the white-knuckle panic of the day before.

It was clear these men preferred to put their faith in him, the known earl; and they could see his concerns about safety were intended for their own well-being, but they were reluctant to take money from him, even to hold their families over.

He promised a great windfall and explained the work in Barbadoes; he told them he would return with the resources that all of them would require to make a successful go at the noble profession of sheep farming.

The men listened with respect, but it was clear that the prospect of sheep sounded lazy and passive to their generations-old Yorkshire coal mining.

Ironically, Cassin could relate to their skepticism, and he bought a very little bit of legitimacy by explaining to them the mining he had done in the tropics.

Whatever happened, Cassin assured them that he would take their preferences under consideration and study the matter over time. The important thing now was that he was earning the money to invest in the land and the people. And they believed he was making choices in good faith, with their best interest at heart.

Most useful of all, at least in an immediate sense, he had secured the promise of tenant protection for his mother and sisters. He explained the threat of his uncle after he returned to Barbadoes, and he arranged to hire six men in rotation who would provide personal security for the castle while he was away.

Of all of his uncle's threats, the most dangerous had been the prospect of five women living alone in the Yorkshire countryside with no man looking after them. Burly bodyguards could not protect the women from every threat, but Ruth was clever and could provide brains if the hired muscle was not enough.

Not surprisingly, the bodyguards had been Willow's idea. After they'd made love the night before, she'd lain in his arms, listening to him recount his horrible day.

His original idea was to ask the tenants to be vigilant and watchful, reporting his uncle's unwelcome presence to the constable in Harrogate. Willow had considered this and said, "Why not pay the tenants themselves to protect the castle? They could function like castle guards of old."

The grown sons of tenants had fallen over themselves to bodyguard the women in the castle, even without pay. When Cassin had explained that the duty was an actual job with real wages, he saw a pride in their eyes he'd not seen since before he closed the mines.

With guards in place, and most of the tenants trying to be, at the very least, sympathetic to Cassin's reinvention of Caldera, he felt prepared to confront his uncle, to demand that he leave and never return.

"Oh, Brent, there you are," said Willow, spotting Cassin as he stomped mud from his boots at the door. "I need a word."

What a touchstone she was, he thought. Turquoise eyes flashing, auburn hair hanging down her back, that smile she reserved for him and no one else. He'd nearly lost his mind with her efforts to leave him, even the suggestion of an annulment was a slice through his heart. He'd been given no choice but to fight one more battle that day. Everything about the situation had made him angry and petulant and unyielding.

But it was a battle he would fight again, daily, if required. She *would* stay; he could not lose her.

Thankfully, she did not appear to be on the verge of leaving at this moment. She was smiling and engaged, casting her discerning eye on the castle furnishings, which, he already knew, required significant repairs and improvements. He would need an entire shipment of guano simply to satisfy the changes she would make to Caldera. But oh, how spectacular the result.

Cassin was just about to wave her over when his uncle made an indignant appearance on the stair landing, sputtering and berating a footman. He held out a hand to stay Willow. It was time.

"Uncle," Cassin said, clipping up the steps to him. "I have spoken with my mother and sisters, and in this time of mourning for my brother, I respectfully ask you to take your leave of Caldera and return to London. Your presence here has overstepped the bounds of our hospitality."

"You think I have a care for your boundaries?" said Archibald. "I've no plans to depart before Simon and Nigel arrive."

"You mistake me, Uncle," said Cassin coolly. "'Tis not a question. It is an order. Get out. Today. Pack your things. I want you gone before luncheon."

The older man laughed. "Or what?"

"Or I will lift you, bodily, off the ground, strap you to the back of my horse, and pitch you into the road to Harrogate. I've been swinging a pickax twelve hours a day in the hot island sun. Please do not doubt that I can do it."

Archibald's pink face went red, and he screwed up his features. "If your father was alive to see—"

"My father would have done the same thing," Cassin interjected. "Only sooner. Now go. And if ever you make any plans to return to Caldera—alone or in the company of other aspirational relations—you will be met with a full castle guard, under strict orders to eject any of you on sight."

"Castle guard," scoffed Archibald. "What castle guard?"

"The tenants. I would not doubt their devotion to protecting the dowager countess and my sisters, if I were you. Since my closure of the Caldera mines, the castle guard is the only paying job on the property. They will take their jobs very seriously.

"Unless you plan to lay *siege* to this castle," Cassin said, "you may put Caldera and the potential of its coal out of your mind. Go sniff around the death-trap operation of someone else. These lands are not for sale at any price. Caldera belongs to me. I am the earl."

"Not if you cock up your toes on some God-forsaken island—"

"I'm an active man in the prime of my life," Cassin cut in, "and I lift full barrels over my head a hundred times a day. I would put more stock in your own corpulent, brandy-soaked demise than mine, Uncle. This discussion is over. I've made myself perfectly clear. There is nothing more to be said."

Archibald was breathing heavily now, his wheezy gasps whistling through his thick mustache. He looked around, glaring at Willow, who watched from the bottom step. He looked to Cassin's sisters and mother, who had collected in the great hall.

Cassin thought for a moment that he might threaten or refuse him again, but he merely grumbled to himself, threw up his hands, and stomped back up the stairwell, shouting for his valet.

Cassin watched him go. "I should have done that a long time ago," he said, clipping down the steps to Willow.

"He wanted to see how far he could push," she said. "And now he knows."

"I can think of someone else who tested the outer limits of my control. And lost."

"Thank God," she said softly. She reached out one hand and touched him on the chest—a test to see if he was still there. He covered her hand with his own. "What did you wish to speak to me about?"

She beamed at him, her blue-green eyes twinkling. "I've had an idea."

Cassin cocked his head. "This sounds expensive."

"How would you feel about opening up some parts of Caldera to very rich patrons as a beautiful, historic hotel?"

Words escaped him. *Hotel* was the last thing he expected her to say.

"You have ancient ruins and an expert on hand to lecture about them." She pointed to Ruth. "You have an estate full of tenants who want real work of which they can be proud. And you have a castle"—she gestured at ceiling—"in relatively good repair, with plenty of guest rooms, healing waters in an authentic bathhouse, a showplace garden, and a wife with a million ideas about how to make all of it look beautiful and distinctive. But Cassin, this is what wealthy guests from London want."

"How will these wealthy guests discover our lavish, beautiful, and distinctive castle?" he asked, trying to fight back a smile.

"Advertisements," she said.

He laughed. "Bloody hell, not again."

"How lucky for you I am an expert at writing the most persuasive adverts, and they have been known to entice the least distractible and most unyielding of men."

"Allow me to let you in on a little secret, darling; it was not the writing that did it."

Willow laughed. "It brought you to Leland Park, didn't it?"

"Oh, you mean the vagueness and half truths? Perhaps. But these are not the reasons I remained."

She gave him a playful shove. "We'll not need any vagueness when we describe Caldera. The authentic beauty of the castle cannot be overstated. The advertisement will practically write itself. Then we'll print it in the London papers and post it in exclusive districts like Belgravia and Mayfair. We can challenge the city of Bath for its title as England's premier restorative holiday retreat." She paused, smiling at her ambition. "Why not?"

"I can think of a dozen reasons," he said, but the words came out slowly, haltingly. He took her into his arms. "If I know you, there are answers for them all." He kissed her deeply while his mothers and sisters looked on.

In her ear, he whispered, "I've done wilder things and won in the end, haven't I? Why the bloody hell not?"

EPILOGUE

Five years later...

In the summer of 1836, Lord Brent and Lady Willow Cassin welcomed the king and queen of England to Caldera Castle.

His Majesty King William IV and Her Royal Highness Queen Adelaide, along with a retinue of courtiers and five of the king's illegitimate daughters, made the journey to soothe the king's troublesome joint pain in Caldera's Roman baths. After two years of society's enthusiastic talk about the castle, they also came to see what all the fuss was about.

Willow could not have been more pleased. Her goal for the refurbished Caldera Castle had been regal and majestic, with a colorful dash of drama and magic thrown in. The result seemed to please even the most discerning guests. Some came to take the waters, others would come to explore the Roman ruins, but still others, she knew, would thrill to simply spend a few nights in a romantic stone castle, with bright pennants snapping from the turrets and a cavernous great hall. Never

did she dream that the king and queen, both in full possession of their own romantic castles, would be curious about
the stunning but small (if she was honest) Yorkshire estate.
But certainly she did not complain.

The trickle of curious local gentry who patronized the
castle in the early days had eventually turned into a steady
stream of wealthy patrons from all over England; London
especially, with a few guests traveling from the world abroad.
Perhaps it was only a matter of time until they were patronized by the king and queen.

"Willow, Willow, Willow," called Cassin's youngest sister
Marietta, skidding into the castle library in the family wing.
Willow, Ruth, Cassin, and his middle sister, Violet, were
bent over a checklist, going over last-minute protocol for the
royal visit.

Willow smiled at her sister-in-law. "Oh, look at you,
Marietta; how lovely. Your mother and I were right about the
green dress."

"The dress is pretty," conceded Marietta, "but what about
my hair?"

Willow gave her a dismissive wave. "Perry will do everyone's hair."

Marietta looked incredulous and began to tick off Perry's
current burden. "Mama's headdress, Juliana's bun, Violet's
chignon, Ruth's funny hat, and your...your..." She crinkled
her nose. "It's far too much, even for Perry," she exclaimed.

"No amount of hair is too much for Perry, I assure you.
Seek her out upstairs, and ask her to begin."

Marietta began backing away. "But *when* will King William arrive?"

"We won't know until the Royal Guard sends a herald ahead," Cassin sighed, "a condition that has already been explained to you. It's impossible to say, exactly. Go away before we give you a job to do."

Marietta made a face and then darted away.

The role the family played in Caldera's new identity had been strange to navigate. Even Cassin complained that he was the only earl in England who also worked as an innkeeper. In truth, the finances of managing the hotel had appealed to him, and inviting curious outsiders into his beloved Caldera was an unexpected source of pride. It did not hurt that Willow's restoration of the castle took his breath away. The grandeur of the great hall, combined with Willow's signature dash of whimsy and quirk, made a dazzling impression on every guest. He was eager to share the majestic splendor of his home.

And while two of his sisters, Marietta and Juliana, showed no particular interest in the day-to-day running of the hotel, his sister Violet had been almost immediately drawn in. Before they could hire a steward to oversee bookings and guest relations, Violet stepped up to prove her own proficiency at soothing rumpled feathers and making certain every guest received unrivaled service.

This, taken with Ruth's popular guided tours and lectures about Caldera's Roman ruins, meant the title of "innkeeper" was well worth any perceived humility. Meanwhile, Cassin's mother, along with Juliana and Marietta, carried on very much as they always had in the family wing, only they enjoyed a steady stream of London visitors, which now included the king and queen.

"I've prepared a brief and lengthy version of all of my lectures and walks," Ruth said, pulling Cassin's and Willow's attention back to the list. "It's impossible to guess what may interest the king and queen or what their courtiers may want, but I can make changes as needed." She bit her lip. "I do hope they'll wish to sit in on at least one lecture."

"I will encourage them," Violet assured her. "His Majesty was a military man before he became king; surely he will be interested in the conquering Romans."

"One thing is certain," Willow cut in. "They will all wish to take the waters. I've had the bathhouse cleaned ahead of schedule, so the mosaic and pools will appear second to none."

Perhaps the most satisfying part of transforming the castle into a resort was the countless jobs provided for tenants. Mining coal was soon forgotten when Cassin provided steady, well-compensated work for bathhouse attendants and repairmen, farmers to grow food for the lavish resort menu, and kitchen staff to prepare it. The resort required countless footmen, grooms, stable hands, laundresses, maids, porters, and even nursery maids. Instead of risking their lives in the underground danger of damp coal mines, the tenants now worked together to share Caldera with the world.

"I think that just about covers it," Cassin said, remounting his pen. "Violet, Ruth, can you excuse Willow and me for a moment?"

The two women hurried away, invigorated by the task of hosting the monarch. When they were gone, Willow said, "I still can't believe how well Violet has taken to managing the staff and guests."

"I can," said Cassin, dropping into his chair. He held out his hand to her. "She was always bright and bossy. Not unlike someone else I know."

Willow narrowed her eyes playfully and allowed him to tug her into his lap.

"There are worse qualities in a woman than cleverness and leadership." She wrapped her hands around his neck and slid her fingers into the back of his cravat.

"I would not have it any other way," he said. "But may I ask you something?"

"No, you may not seek out your uncle and gloat about receiving the king."

Cassin made a disgusted sound. "Good lord, it was never that. The less said to him, the better."

After the embarrassing work of dismantling the joint-stock company, Archibald had eventually allowed his avarice for Caldera to die away. The tenants were gainfully employed in the castle and no longer listened to his rants, and the success of the hotel could not be denied.

The estate would still go to one of Archibald's sons upon Cassin's death; there was no getting around that fact. But as soon as Cassin saw the potential of Willow's idea, he made it his goal to build Caldera Castle into the most prestigious, highly coveted resort in all of England. Before his eventual death, Cassin hoped to have built Caldera into such a money-making, world-class institution that no cousin would dare shut it down. Considering its success, he was well on his way. In the meantime, Cassin had used surplus income from the guano venture to develop property elsewhere in Yorkshire that would belong to him, free and clear. After his death, that estate could be a home to any remaining dependent who found fault with the subsequent Earls of Cassin.

But now Willow stilled her hands on his neck and frowned. "If it's not Archibald, what do you want to ask?"

"I'm simply wondering what my diligent wife will do after the royal visit," he said.

"Collapse?" Willow laughed. "Take a holiday at someone *else's* hotel? What do you mean?"

"It's merely that you've done everything you set out to do when you redesigned the castle. The property is breathtaking, and the hotel is, obviously, a success. I worry you might grow cagey or bored, now that it's all finished, without new projects to occupy that clever, bossy mind of yours."

"Oh, that…"

"I'll not have you hanging new advertisements because you've grown weary of redecorating the rooms of Caldera, as you did with Leland Park."

Willow chuckled and cinched her arms tightly around his neck, resting her chin on his shoulder. "How could I ever grow bored or weary around this lot?" she whispered into his ear. "Besides, there is always some creative new improvement to be done. You have charged me with maintaining a five-hundred-year-old castle."

"I'm serious, Willow," he said, although his voice broke because she had begun to slowly nibble on his ear.

"Please don't worry about me," she said, snuggling closer. Cassin made a growling noise and scooped her more tightly into his lap. "We are in London often enough that I might find an interesting project to work on here or there. There is one I have been eyeing for quite some time. If only I had a way to introduce myself to the future owners and demonstrate my talents."

"Is that right?" he mumbled, seeking out her mouth. "And what project is that?"

"Just a small residence currently under construction." She kissed him. "Perhaps you've heard of it? It's called Buckingham Palace."

Was guano really a thing in the nineteenth century?

Yes, in fact it was. As I contemplated the great, unfinanced venture on which the heroes of this series would embark, it was important to me that they not buy or sell any goods that were touched by the slave trade, which was still rampant throughout the world in the mid-nineteenth century.

This posed a real challenge, as nearly every top import to England in the 1830s was the result, in part or entirely, of slave labor. However, research consistently pointed to the real-life importation of guano—or, as the story describes it, petrified bird droppings that would be harvested and ground into fertilizer. As it turned out, guano was a wildly profitable venture that utilized *paid* labor.

The more I looked at this practice, the more I learned about the so-called "guano barons" of the day. These were the enterprising sailors and merchants who moved quickly upon the discovery of guano as fertilizer and made millions of pounds importing it to England and around the world. In fact, the richest non-landed-gentry family in England in the mid-nineteenth century made its fortune importing guano from South America.

In the end, the history of guano and other elements of guano mining matched the circumstances of my story so well that I was convinced I could find no better endeavor for Cassin and his partners.

For the purposes of this series, I have put the men's venture at what would have been the very beginning of the guano boom around the world. Guano mining and exportation would not reach its peak until the 1840s and then, alas, would peter out by the 1870s in favor of the next miracle fertilizer, which was chemically manufactured and borne of the Industrial Revolution.

I employed dramatic license when Cassin wrote of the men's hiring practices, which included translators, cooks, and a medic for injuries. As we're all aware, the notion of healthy food for common laborers and workplace safety is a late-twentieth-century notion. And honestly, most of the real-life guano miners were indentured servants from China or the Philippians. Even so, my sympathetic heroes made a point of hiring diligent, honest, free men and compensating them well.

***

Why has Barbadoes *been consistently misspelled?*

The island now known as Barbados, which was a major English stronghold in the British West Indies, was spelled with an extra *e* in 1831, so I have included that spelling in this book. Although most of the guano islands in the actual guano boom were in the Pacific Ocean or on the Pacific side of South America, some Caribbean islands did boast harvestable guano and were mined for it. I placed New Pixham within the easiest possible reach of the Royal Mail and the men sailing back and forth.

***

Was Belgravia really the up-and-coming 'hood of 1830s London?

Belgravia, which is still one of London's most posh addresses today, was constructed as a planned community from a drained marsh on the southwest corner of London, beginning in the 1820s.

***

Roman baths in Yorkshire?

Roman conquerors occupied modern England for almost four hundred years, beginning in AD 43. They left behind lasting influences, such as roads that are still used today, as well as sanitation and sewage systems. Also left behind were relics and ruins, such as the ones dear, departed Felix Caulder and his young wife, Ruth, were excavating in Yorkshire, and where Roman ruins can still be found today. Among these ruins, Felix and Ruth would have recovered tools, pottery, and weapons, certainly, but also homes, amphitheaters, and bathhouses like the one in Caldera's rear garden.

***

Could Caldera really be turned into a hotel?

The real-life village of Harrogate, in Yorkshire, rose to prominence in the mid-nineteenth century as a popular spa town and vacation spot for well-heeled Londoners. Known for its healing waters, natural hot springs, and Roman-style bathhouses, my research showed that, after the invention of the railroad, multiple trains departed London each day to bring wealthy holiday seekers to take the waters in Harrogate. Willow's 1831 idea to open a hotel is consistent with the many real-life hotels that existed (and still exist to this day) in Harrogate. Although there is no record of the monarch traveling to Harrogate, King William did holiday in Brighton on occasion, so here I have invoked dramatic license. King William IV died the year after the date of this book's epilogue, so his health might have compelled him to take the healing waters. His passing, by the way, made way for the crowning of his niece, Queen Victoria, who would move into the newly renovated Buckingham Palace.

Acknowledgments

Much of the research I do as I write commercial romance does not make it to the page—a trade-off I make for pacing. The background information, however, is in my notes and my consciousness, and I hope a dimensional sense of authenticity can be found in the narrative. I am so grateful for the people who help inform this research with their expertise. In this book, the dazzling design talent of my dear friend Sarah helped shape Lady Willow's passion for beauty and her discerning eye. My horticulturist father helped me get a handle on how and why guano swept the world as revolutionary fertilizer of the time, and I have the notes on the nitrogen, phosphate, and potassium content of guano to prove it. My doctor friend Barbara helped assign the correct infection that might render a young girl barren in the nineteenth century.

Thank you also to my writing buddies, Lenora Bell and Christy Carlyle, both of whom helped me brainstorm through rough spots and who read sections of early versions of this book.

I cannot fail to mention how thoroughly and unconditionally my husband and children, my parents, my sister, and my in-laws support me as a writer and a working mom.

Anticipating Tessa and Joseph Chance's story?

ALL DRESSED IN WHITE

Coming Summer 2018!

USA *Today* bestselling author **CHARIS MICHAELS** believes a romance novel is a very long, exciting answer to the question "So, how did you two meet?" It's a question she loves to answer again and again with different characters, each time she writes a book. Prior to writing romance, she studied journalism at Texas A&M and managed PR for a trade association. She also has worked as a tour guide at Disney World, harvested peaches on her family's farm, and entertained children as the "Story Godmother" at birthday parties. She has lived in Texas, Florida, and London, England. She now makes her home in the Washington, DC, metro area.

Discover great authors, exclusive offers, and more at hc.com.

A LETTER FROM THE EDITOR

Dear Reader,

I hope you liked the latest romance from Avon Impulse! If you're looking for another steamy, fun, emotional read, be sure to check out some of our upcoming titles.

We have a delightful, charming debut novel from new author Marie Tremayne! LADY IN WAITING features a runaway bride who takes a position as a maid in a lord's household. He's incredibly tempted by his new servant, but he knows they can never be together due to class differences...or can they? You don't want to miss this fantastic first book in Marie's Reluctant Brides trilogy!

Sports romance fans—get excited! Lia Riley has another sexy new Hellions Angels hockey novel coming. In VIRGIN TERRITORY, Patrick "Patch" Donnelly gives up his plan to become a priest in order to pursue a professional hockey career. When a beautiful yoga instructor crosses his path,

Patch is intrigued. But before he can give into temptation, he'll have to confess his biggest secret...he's a virgin. You know you want to one-click the holy goalie immediately!

You can purchase any of these titles by clicking the links above or by visiting our website, www.AvonRomance.com. Thank you for loving romance as much as we do...enjoy!

Sincerely,

Nicole Fischer
Editorial Director
Avon Impulse